Black Obsidian

Book One

Victoria Quinn

Anytime I was out in the regular world, I
ndered if anyone recognized me for what I really
s—a dark and twisted asshole. The shit I was into
ed most women away. The ones who were
e enough to stick around always changed their
ds. My tastes were specific and they would
er change, which was why I needed to stick to
world and not bother with the real one.

If this really was the real one.

The door to the bar opened, accompanied by
e-cold breeze. I felt it on the back of my neck,
sing the nearly invisible strands of hair that
out underneath my collar. The black suit and
ere my favorites—fit to a T. I had work that
ng, and I always looked the part.

or whatever reason, and for no reason at all,
d my attention to the open door. Two women
inside, one blonde and one brunette. Both
in stature and pretty in their unique ways,
rned heads as they entered.

y eyes went to the brunette.

had a thing for brunettes. Always had and
would.

e wore a black pencil skirt that was snug on
anly hips. Curves that made my throat turn
ght my attention, and I immediately

2

Black Obsidian

Editing Services provided by Final-Edits.com

Calloway

I lifted the glass to my m
cubes slide all the way down u
lips. Like pieces of winter, th
just before the burn of the sc
seared me from the inside ou

I lived for that burn.

Jackson was suppose
fifteen minutes ago, but th
shown his face. A hot little
attention along the way,
sidetracked.

Couldn't blame him.

The black ring on
with commitment. It was
I wore other than my
getting used to. To every
It had no meaning and

But in my world,
clear.

wo
wa
turi
bra
min
neve
my

an ic
cares
poke
tie w
eveni

I turne
walke
petite
they tu
M
I
always
Sh
her wor
dry ca

fantasized about gripping her thighs then slowly raising my hands up her skirt, pulling the fabric along until her panties were exposed to my mercy—or cruelty.

It took a lot to impress me when it came to women, and not because I was picky or superficial, but because I received enough satisfaction every day and every night to dim my desire. My fantasies were a reality, and I had no interest in looking for a woman who couldn't fulfill them.

But she caught my eye anyway.

She had an hourglass figure, perfect for guiding up and down my length with my hands on her hips. Perky tits were pressed tightly against her pink blouse, and she had a slender neck with a pronounced hollow in her throat—perfect for my tongue to explore.

She wore five-inch heels and rocked them as if they were sandals, and thin and toned legs were obvious below the cut of her skirt. They nearly reached her neck because they were so long. Every woman had specific traits that made them sexy. Sometimes they had a nice rack or ass. Sometimes they had a slender waistline that I could wrap my arms around twice. Sometimes they had legs like hers, the kind I pictured around my waist.

But this woman had them all.

My eyes didn't lose their focus as I watched her like a hawk, my mind obsessed and my cock hard. When she passed through the crowd, she parted the way with her natural power. She commanded the room as she held her head high with the elegance of a queen. But her smile was innocent like that of a princess.

My legs wanted to move in her direction and stake a claim before someone else could make a move. I wanted to tell her my name and hear hers in return. She probably had the sexiest voice, classy like the rest of her traits.

But I couldn't.

My hands were tied.

I made a commitment to someone else. Our bond wasn't based on love, friendship, or anything else remotely meaningful. But when I gave someone my word, I kept it. If a man's word didn't count for anything, then he automatically lost his self-worth. That was a lesson my father taught me, and it was the only one I respected.

So I turned away and glanced at my watch.

Where was he?

A woman's voice sounded behind me, and judging by its beauty and power, it could only belong to one person. Without turning around to make sure my assumption was correct, I knew it belonged to the woman who got me harder than steel.

"That guy is such a fucking asshole. I can't believe he did that to you."

I smirked at the way she cursed. She meant every word and said it with a backbone, but her stature made it hard to take her seriously. She was simply too soft on the eyes to have a dirty mouth.

Her friend sighed before she responded. "I know… I went home and cried, and I hated myself for doing it. He isn't worth my tears. He isn't worth anything."

"Damn straight."

I drank my scotch and concentrated on the sound of her voice. Her appearance got me hard, and her no-bullshit attitude got me harder. My attraction usually started with quiet women, the soft ones that were looking for someone to lead them. But her strength was oddly arousing.

A man squeezed into the bar beside me and brushed my shoulder. When it wasn't Jackson, I gave him a terrifying glare. I hated being touched by anyone who didn't receive my explicit permission—no matter how innocent their intention was.

He quickly scooted away, leaving an appropriate foot of space between us. He ordered a beer—a pussy drink. He wore a black suit that was poorly tailored and didn't hide the imperfections of his weak shoulders and laughable build. This guy had done nothing egregious to me, but I despised him for that innocent touch.

The women's conversation continued.

"Oh my god." Her friend gasped quietly but was unable to cover it despite the constant chatter of the crowd.

"What?" She kept her voice strong rather than concerned. Again, she commanded the conversation with just her tone of voice. I'd never known a woman like that.

"That's Dave." Her friend dropped her voice low so no one could overhear them. I had to strain my ears and discreetly turn my head so I could pick up on what they were saying. Their conversation had nothing to do with me, and frankly, it wasn't that interesting. But I loved hearing that woman's voice. "I can't believe he's here. Probably picking up someone else while his wife is at home."

"Are you fucking serious?" She didn't bother keeping her voice down. "That two-timing shithead is here?"

"At the bar."

Their conversation halted for nearly ten seconds.

"Where?" she demanded. "Which one?"

"He's at the front in a black suit."

My eyes discreetly glanced to the man beside me, knowing he must be the man they were discussing. A wedding ring was absent from his finger, and his eyes kept roaming down the bar to the women huddled near the end. He was definitely on the prowl tonight—no doubt about it.

I actually felt bad for his wife.

And I felt bad for whatever my obsession was about to do to him.

"What are you doing?" her friend asked.

"I'm giving that motherfucker a piece of my mind."

I smirked, excited to see her in action. She would probably grab the guy by the shoulder and throw her drink in his face. Maybe I would get a waft of her smell. Maybe her delectable hip would press against mine.

"No, don't—"

The sound of heels clanked behind me, and I knew she was just a foot away from me. This guy was about to get his ass kicked by a woman half his size. And he deserved it. I would stick around for the show. Now, I didn't even care that Jackson was nearly half an hour late.

"Hey, asshole." She grabbed me by the arm and yanked hard enough to get me to face her.

Disturbed by the uninvited touch, I immediately faced her and looked down into her expression. Green eyes, fierce with fire, looked back at me, and her lips pressed so tightly together they were nearly invisible. Her cheeks were flushed with rage, and her long brown hair was pulled over one shoulder, extending past her tits. Her blouse had a V-neck in the front, and I could see the small freckles that I wasn't able to see before. Instead of telling her she had the wrong man, I stared at her in pure fascination. Up close, she was even more beautiful—absolutely fuckable.

She retracted her hand, and with lightning speed, slapped me so hard across the face I actually turned with the force. My neck snapped to the right, and my skin tingled from the collision of her palm against my face. Immediately, my skin burned from the heat of momentum, and the slap of our skin moving together echoed in the bar. My neighbors quieted down, watching the spectacle like a street fight as this woman charged me like a bull.

I turned back to her, and while the rage slowly burned inside my chest, I felt something else. My entire body tensed with the undeniable arousal that coursed through my veins. She hit me—and she hit me hard. That hatred and ferocity got my engine revving like I was about to enter a drag race. My cock was harder than ever before, and I couldn't stop picturing her pinned underneath me as I fucked her until she screamed. She kept slapping me across the face as I pounded her into my mattress, losing the fight we both knew I would win.

Fuck, I was hard up.

Her eyes widened with hostility before that pretty little mouth of hers told me off. "You're absolutely despicable and a sorry excuse for a man. You should be ashamed of yourself for cheating on your wife and for playing games with my friend. There's a special place in hell for assholes like you." She pulled her hand back and slapped me again, putting her entire weight into the collision. Another slap echoed in the bar, ringing loud in my ears. Everyone around us gasped as she laid it on me good.

My spine tingled as the surging desire washed through me like a goddamn tsunami. I wanted to throw her on the bar and fuck her right then and there. I wanted to pop all the buttons off her shirt and rip her panties in half before I shoved her skirt over her tits. In front of everyone in the bar, I would fuck her until I filled her with so much of my seed she wouldn't be able to walk without it dripping all over the floor.

All I had to do was grab her wrist and steady her hand so she couldn't hit me again, but I didn't. All I had to do was tell her she had the wrong man, but I didn't do that either. I'd never felt more alive, more aroused, than I did in that moment.

And I never wanted her to stop hitting me.

"Stop!" Her blonde friend came up behind her and grabbed her by the arm. "Not him!"

She didn't listen to a word her friend said because she shoved me hard in the chest. Like a mountain, I didn't move. In fact, it made her body thrust backward instead. "Not such a tough guy after all, huh? How about I give your wife a call and tell her your dick has been around the block one too many times?"

I stared at her mouth without really listening to her. When she was pissed, she was even sexier.

10

Her cheeks flushed a beautiful hint of rose, and her eyes were greener than the vines on a hot summer day. I wanted her to stay exactly like this, hitting me like a punching bag until my cock couldn't stay in my trousers any longer.

She slapped me again, hitting the exact same cheek for a third time in a row. Now I knew my face was beet red and scorching hot. I knew I would have a mark from her handprint for the next few hours until it faded away. "That's what happens to men who fuck with my best friend." She pointed her finger in my face like it was somehow threatening. "You actually thought you were going to get away with it—"

"It's not him!" Her friend screamed loud over the conversations of the bar, making everyone halt and look at her. "Stop hitting him!"

She finally listened to her friend and looked at her, her face immediately slackening with trepidation. "What?"

The man in the black suit was no longer next to me. The second he saw the commotion, he must have noticed his ex and hit the exit. Smart man. He wouldn't have enjoyed the beating my face had just taken—his loss.

"I told you fifteen times that you had the wrong guy. Dave already left after you slapped this guy the first time."

Her cheeks turned white, the pale rose color fading away immediately. Her green eyes lost their vibrancy, turning a dull gray that I didn't find nearly as attractive. Unable to look at me, she kept eye contact with her friend. Humiliation emitted from her in waves that washed over me like the freezing ocean. Self-loathing and hatred were there as well.

She put her hands on her hips and took a few breaths before she finally turned back to me. Her eyes were on the floor, oddly similar to a submissive, before she took another breath and finally found the courage to meet my eyes. "God...I'm so sorry. I thought you were someone else. I...I'm so humiliated."

I examined her new expression, absorbing all the intricate features I didn't notice before. She had a freckle in the corner of her mouth, so small and slight I hardly noticed it. Like a distant star deep in space, it contrasted against her fair complexion. My tongue shifted in my mouth, desperate to taste that tiny freckle and explore everything else about her body.

She had a petite little nose, slender and nicely shaped. It fit her beautiful face perfectly, like a renowned artist shaped her features until they were just right. Her eyes were large and bright, shaped like almonds. Her cheeks were prominent and curved, giving her a slender appearance that matched her perfect body. From my height, I could see her cleavage line—only I didn't look.

When I didn't say anything, she gave me the same apologetic look, desperate for forgiveness. "I swear, I'm not normally like that. This guy hurt my friend, and I got carried away. I mistook you for him."

The only reason why I hadn't spoken was because I was stretching out the conversation as long as possible, so I could stare at her all I wanted. Her lips were plump and wet. When she was nervous, she sucked on her upper lip. She'd done it twice since our conversation began. I wanted to pull it into my mouth and do all the sucking for her. "Honest mistake. I understand."

Her eyes shifted back and forth as she stared at me. "I really am sorry." Her eyes moved to my red cheek, and her hand moved slightly from her waist like she wanted to touch it. "If there's anything I can do, please let me know." She pulled her hand back to her side, refraining from raising her hand to me again.

Her friend grabbed her by the wrist. "Let's just leave him alone. I think we've put him through enough..." She gently pulled her friend along.

I was losing her, and I had no choice but to let her go. The ring on my right hand felt unnaturally heavy. But then suddenly, I didn't feel it at all. The weight evaporated into thin air like it'd never been there to begin with. "There is something you can do."

She stopped and didn't allow her friend to pull her any farther. "Anything."

"Tell me your name." I took a step toward her, not wanting to miss whatever she was about to say. I lived for that answer, needing to hear it in my ears and taste it on my tongue. When I beat off later that night, I wanted to know exactly who I was beating off to.

"You want my name?" Her voice barely came out as a whisper. "That's all?"

"Yes." My eyes narrowed on her face, needing that answer more than anything else in the world.

She faltered for an instant, unsure if she should give it to me because she didn't understand my motive. Maybe I wanted it so I could report her to the police and press charges. If that was the case, that was my right and she had to cooperate. Her lips were parted before she spoke, and she finally gave her answer. "Rome Moretti."

Chapter Two

Calloway

I walked into Ruin and pushed through the throng of people as I made my way to the bar. Men in black leather held their submissives by leashes and chains. Most of them were on their knees on the floor, looking up at their masters with grotesque fascination. The music was amplified in the sub club, booming loud with the bass and matching the dark tones of the black lights.

One submissive made eyes at me, not having a master to obey. But the second her eyes landed on my black ring, she quickly turned her gaze away and pretended she hadn't seen me in the first place.

I made it to the bar and saw Isabella there. The black ring was on her right hand, and she sipped a drink as she sat on the stool. Dressed in a tight black dress with her hair in a braid, she stood out among the other women in the crowd. Beautiful, dark, and sultry, she was the most remarkable woman in the place. None of the men stared at her because they knew she was off-limits.

Everyone respected that.

When I reached her side, she immediately turned her brown eyes on me. They took me in with fascination, and like the obedient submissive she was, she quickly lowered her gaze and tilted her chin downward, bowing to me without bending her spine. "Master."

"Come with me." I barked out my command and walked away without bothering to look behind me. I knew she was there, following me like the good submissive she was. I didn't need a leash for her because it was unnecessary. This woman had been trained well. With the snap of my finger, she did exactly as I commanded—and she did so without complaint.

She was the best submissive I'd ever had.

We walked to the opposite side of the building on the top floor and entered my office. The furniture was black, and the large window behind my desk was tinted so the outside world couldn't see within. They would never understand people like us. They would never understand our desires and our necessities. To them, we were just freaks.

And I thought the same about them.

My desk was carved from stained cherry wood, and the bookshelves on either wall were the same material. A lone lamp sat on the surface, and once I turned it on, we weren't blanketed in the shadows any longer.

Isabella fell to her knees in front of my desk, taking the position she was expected to maintain whenever she was in my presence. Her braid trailed down the middle of her back, ready to be wrapped around my fist the instant I wanted her.

I leaned against the desk and crossed my arms over my chest. I took a moment to look at her, to appreciate her last moments as my submissive. For the last year, I'd been her exclusive Dom, making us one of the rare monogamous couples within our world. She pleased me exceptionally well, and she required no training. Perfect the way she was, she came into my life and gave me the satisfaction I craved. I never loved her and told her I never would, and she accepted that at face value. "Up."

She rose to her feet, her slender frame uncoiling from the uncomfortable position on the floor. One time, she stayed that way for nearly five hours while I entertained guests over dinner. She didn't move an inch—not even to scratch her nose. Now she watched me with her big and bright brown eyes, waiting for a command she could fulfill. Her universe centered around me, the man she obeyed constantly.

I pulled the black ring off my finger. It was snug before my joint, and I had to twist it until it came loose before I placed it on the desk beside me. A faint tan line marked the skin that had been covered for so long. Now it could finally breathe, finally see the sunshine.

Her eyes widened when she saw my actions, knowing exactly what it meant.

"I'm no longer your Dom, Isabella. And you're no longer my submissive." Our arrangement had an expiration date, and we both knew it from the beginning. Despite how long we lasted, we knew this day would come. Like the sun rising over the horizon, it was inevitable.

In shock, she kept her same expression. To anyone outside of the two of us, they wouldn't have a clue what her thoughts were. Her emotions were hidden deep like buried treasure beneath her permanent mask.

I stepped toward her then grabbed her right hand. I pulled the ring off her finger, feeling the snugness before it finally came off. The band was plain and black, matching mine with the exception of its width. I placed it on top of my ring and made them a pair once more. "You can speak freely." She was no longer mine to control, so she could do and say whatever she wanted. It wasn't the kind of freedom she wanted, but she had to accept it.

Her eyes took in the rings before she returned her gaze to my face. Large like the moon, both were glowing orbs that radiated mystical power. It was one of her features that attracted me to her in the first place. But now, they reflected her disappointment—and her pain. "I don't understand…"

I hoped she would take this separation as emotionlessly as I would. In the beginning, I made it clear what kind of man I was, and I would never change. She claimed she believed me, but perhaps she didn't. "It's nothing you did, Isabella. You're just as perfect as you were when I first looked at you. But I've come to realize I want different things."

Her hands found each other in front of her waist, and slowly, her fingers started to fidget. Her shoulders weren't as straight as they normally were, and the grace she once possessed had disappeared entirely.

I wanted to command her to remain still, but I couldn't. I'd lost my privileges.

"We were fine yesterday. This is just so sudden… I thought you wanted me."

This kind of desperation was pathetic and annoyed me. But she'd been with me for a year, trusted me for an entire year, and I had to be patient with her. I owed her that much. "I'm sorry if it's unexpected. But honestly, my decision is just as unexpected. I still think you're gorgeous, and every man downstairs will fight for you once they realize you're no longer mine. But I'm not going to change my mind."

Her thumbs continued to rub together anxiously, and deep in her eyes, tears started to form. Slowly, they coated the surface until they reflected my cold appearance.

"Don't." I had to stop it before it started.

She took a deep breath to steady her resolve, but the second she left my office, she would sob in the bathroom. I didn't need to be psychic to figure that out. "Cal, is there someone else?"

I knew this question would come up, but I didn't know how to answer it. I wasn't even sure what my answer would be. When Rome gave me her name, my balls tightened back into my body, and I nearly came then and there. No woman had ever conquered my sexual desire the way she did.

Those three slaps were better than any blow job I'd ever received. Instead of being annoyed by her power, I craved it. I wanted to conquer her—and I wanted her to conquer me. "Yes."

She took another deep breath, her eyes watering all over again.

"I didn't touch her. Don't worry about that." Isabella was the only submissive I was monogamous with, and that was because I made a promise to remain faithful to her. I always kept my promises, no matter how much I wanted to break them. With our relationship, there was respect and friendship. I would never betray her, even though my cock was eager to be disloyal.

"When did this happen?"

Just the night before, but it felt like a lifetime ago. I had no understanding of what I was doing or why I was doing it. The second I laid eyes on Rome, my entire world changed. I wouldn't consider myself to be happy, but I was certainly content. But the second she slapped me, I felt distraught over what I didn't have—her. "Last night."

"Oh..." She rubbed her hands together, her fidgeting never stopping. "If you didn't touch her, why are you ending this?"

I wasn't sure. All I knew was I couldn't be with Isabella any longer, not when my cock was this hard and my mind was this obsessive. Now, I only wanted one woman to be underneath me, the creature with the intense green eyes—and it wasn't Isabella. I wanted her to fight me until her back hit the sheets. Then I wanted her legs to wrap around my waist as she begged for more. While love wasn't in the mix, I respected Isabella too much to lie to her. We had a relationship based on trust—and that was something I would never sacrifice. "Because I can't stop thinking about her."

Chapter Three

Calloway

I entered the office on 155th Street. The lobby was pristine, with its granite countertop in the rear, along with the receptionist who guided visitors to the correct floor. A fountain was in the center, emitting the calming sound of running water at every hour of the day—even when the doors were locked. I buttoned the front of my suit, greeted the girls behind the counter, and then took the elevator to my office.

The doors opened, and I walked to my office tucked in the corner. My assistant handed over my itinerary along with my messages before she handed me my morning coffee—black and bitter.

Once I was in my leather chair with my black laptop in front of me, I searched through the messages, hoping to see something from someone in particular—but there wasn't. I opened my computer and worked through the countless emails that required my attention. Sometimes, I wondered if I was the director of Humanitarians United or if I was just a puppet moving through paperwork.

An hour later, Shaylen beeped into my office through the intercom. "Charles is here to see you, sir."

About fucking time. "Please send him in, Shaylen." I shut my laptop and watched the doors open as Charles walked inside. He wore the same brown leather jacket I saw him wear every single day. It was thick and old, holes and stains marked all over the place. He wore dark jeans and heavy boots to fight off the New York chill. "Nice to see you, Charles. Do you have something for me?"

He tossed the folder on the table, his bushy eyebrows giving him an appearance of constant annoyance.

I opened the folder and realized it was empty. I quickly shut it then held it up. "It's obvious you did this on purpose. But it's not obvious why." I tossed it in the recycling bin beside my desk.

"I couldn't get much on your girl." He loomed over the front of my desk, never taking a seat even when I offered him one. At Ruin, he did a lot of digging in to people to make sure they were trustworthy. Not just anyone could enter Ruin and be one of us.

"What little were you able to dig up?"

"She went to Harvard for her bachelor's in social work before she got her master's in sociology. She has a small apartment on the west side, and she runs a small nonprofit called For All."

I recognized that organization. They'd done a lot of work around New York for the homeless and juvenile runaways. They were small but very respectable. "What else?"

"That's it."

"Does she have a boyfriend?" More than anything else, that was the answer I needed. If she was taken, I would be respectful and back off. Nothing irritated me more than when someone chased a person who was unavailable. But even if she was seeing someone, my obsession would still linger—unfortunately.

"I don't know."

I raised an eyebrow. "How do you not know? What am I paying you for?"

"This woman covers her tracks. Other than her credentials, that was all I could find about her past. I don't have a clue where she was born, when she was born, and who her relatives are. Her record is wiped clean. This woman literally has no digital footprint."

Now I was even more intrigued. "How is that possible?"

"She must have changed her name."

She was married? "People get married all the time, but their past isn't erased."

"No, that's not what I mean. She must have acquired a new identity."

I'd seen a lot in my lifetime, but I'd never heard of that.

"She has secrets—secrets she's trying to hide."

What a coincidence—I have secrets too. "Anything else?"

"She's in serious debt. About three hundred grand deep."

"How?"

"Student loans and the nonprofit she owns. She must dump a lot of her own money into it."

Just on paper, this woman fascinated me. Judging by her natural strength as she walked across a room, I would assume she wasn't afraid of anything—that she didn't have skeletons in her closet. The fact that she had a double life, a whole other existence, made me wonder what she was hiding from.

"She's attending the Governor's Charity Ball this Saturday."

That party was such a bore, but I had to attend because I was usually given the Philanthropist Award—but they really should give someone else the spotlight. My company did a lot of amazing things, but it wasn't the only one. It was a great opportunity to get donations from other affluent people in the city. Free advertising. "She is?"

"Yep. And you aren't the recipient of the Philanthropist Award this year."

My eyebrow rose in interest. "Yeah?"

"Rome Moretti is."

***

It was nearly midnight when I walked into Ruin and entered the back office. I had paperwork to deal with, payroll, and a bunch of other bullshit that made me hate being a business owner. When I took over the company, it was with excitement. But lately, I'd only been excited about one thing.

The door opened and shut behind me. "Asshole, I've been trying to get a hold of you all day."

I didn't turn around as I leaned over my desk and searched for the mail. "Congratulations. You finally succeeded."

Jackson walked around the desk then plopped down into the leather chair—my leather chair. He looked up at me, his blue eyes identical to mine. They were piercing and cold, just like the icicles that hung from my roof in January. "I heard you broke it off with Isabella."

I'm sure the whole fucking club knew by now. I opened the first letter, aware of his gaze still burning into my face like hot lava.

"Did you hear me?"

"Yes." I skimmed through the bill and left it off to the side. Then I grabbed the next envelope in line.

"And?"

"And what? Is this gossip hour?"

"Just tell me what the hell happened."

"I don't owe you an explanation, shithead."

He snatched the letter from my hand and slammed it on the desk. "What the hell happened? You were her Dom for nearly a year."

"I'm aware." I was there, after all. I leaned back into the chair and stared him down. "All things come to an end, right? It's not worth talking about. I've had many subs in my lifetime, and she'll have many Doms."

His gaze narrowed on my face, his irritation seeping from his pores. "She said there was someone else."

Why couldn't she keep her mouth shut? I didn't deny it because lying wasn't my strong suit. If a man couldn't be honest, then he wasn't a man at all. "Yes, but I'm not seeing anyone."

Jackson gave me the most quizzical expression I'd ever seen. "What? You aren't seeing her?"

"I met her a few nights ago in a bar. Haven't stopped thinking about her."

"Is she a sub?"

"Unlikely." She had way too much fire in her eyes and too much strength in those sexy hips. There was no way she could follow a command without giving some attitude. Maybe that was why I found her so attractive—even though that was the exact opposite of what I wanted.

"Then what's the deal? You asked for her number or what?"

"No." She slapped me three times like a goddamn pro. "I only got her name. I broke it off with Isabella immediately afterward. It didn't feel right anymore. Isabella trusts me, and I still want to be worthy of that trust."

He rubbed the back of his neck, his eyes shifting back and forth between mine. "What does that mean? Are you going to make her your new sub?"

If I'm lucky. "I'll see where it goes…" She wouldn't be easy to break. I could tell. But I was always up for the challenge.

"Dude, Isabella is the hottest chick in this place. You're going to give her up?"

When I first laid eyes on her, I wanted her. We started fucking, and the sex was explosive. Not long after that, we became an exclusive Dom-sub, which shocked everyone who knew me. Isabella did everything I asked, and she did it well. I was content with her, even happy. But when I set eyes on Rome, it was as if the past year never happened. I saw the world in technicolor, and she was neon green. I had to have her—at any cost. "Yes, she's perfect. It's time for us to both move on."

Jackson pressed the back of his hand to my forehead. "You must be dying of syphilis or something."

I smacked his hand away. "Shut the fuck up, asshole."

"So you don't care if I go for her?"

If he'd asked me that a week ago, I would have turned over my desk with a roar and knocked him out cold. But I didn't feel anything—not a hint of jealousy or an ounce of rage. I didn't feel possessive toward her. Strangely, I didn't feel any type of attention or affection toward her. It was like she'd never meant anything to me—at all. "No."

"Seriously?" Both of his eyebrows rose to the sky.

I hated it when he spoke like a goddamn teenager. "Seriously."

"Because I'll do it. I'll wipe away all trace of you."

"Go ahead."

His eyebrows deflated, and he finally believed me. "Damn, who is this woman?"

Charles wasn't able to dig up much on her, just more mystery, so I didn't have a clue. "Not sure yet. But I'll find out."

Chapter Four

Rome

Christopher and I entered the lobby of the hotel. He wore a black suit with a matching tie, looking like he belonged with the crowd. He actually did his hair, wore a nice watch, and acknowledged the people around us with a smile. When I introduced him, he was polite—which was rare.

We entered the ballroom where the charity event was being held. The chandelier hung from the ceiling, sparkling under the dim lighting of the room. Round tables were spaced across the floor, ivory tablecloths with candles and centerpieces on the surface.

Christopher whistled under his breath. "Fancy, huh?"

"It looks really nice."

His head turned toward the bar in the corner. "Now *that* looks really nice. Full bar, right?"

I tried not to roll my eyes. "Behave yourself, alright?"

"If you wanted someone who would behave themselves, you shouldn't have asked me to come with you."

"If you don't want to be here, just go." I stepped off to the side and looked him in the eye, seeing the brown color that reflected the lights from the chandelier.

"And make you go stag?" he asked with a laugh. "I may be an ass, but I would never do that to you."

"I don't mind going alone." Almost everything I did, I did alone. Not having a man on my arm didn't give me anxiety. I didn't care that I was single and living in a small apartment in solitude. When people asked if I planned on settling down soon, like that's where I should be in life, I usually smiled then excused myself from the ridiculous, mundane conversation and found something better to do.

"Then why did you invite me?" He put his hands in his pockets as he eyed me, his chin covered in stubble and his eyes almost threatening.

"Because..." I was about to answer him when I thought better of it. I struggled with emotional intimacy, and I avoided it at all costs. "I guess I just like spending time with you."

Christopher knew me too well not to notice the apprehension in my eyes. Like a book, he could read every word and every sentence. "That's not the reason, and we both know it. So just be a man and tell me."

"Well, I'm not a man."

"You look like one."

I narrowed my eyes on his face. "You want me to answer you or not?"

He breathed a sigh before he relaxed his shoulders. "Yes. Please."

"I'm getting an award tonight." I didn't wear my heart on my sleeve, so I never confessed my deepest desires. But tonight, it was important for him to be there with me. I wanted him to share this moment with me because, frankly, I wouldn't be here without him.

His eyes immediately softened, one of the rare times I'd seen it happen. "I had no idea. What's it for?"

"Philanthropist Award. It's for the work I did at the homeless shelter this year."

He stared at me with a blank expression, but his eyes held the affection that he tried to hide. He cleared his throat then gave me an awkward pat on the back. "That's awesome. I'm so proud of you."

I smiled when I heard the sincerity in his voice. "Thanks."

"Now I'm glad you invited me. Wouldn't miss it for anything."

"That's the reaction I'd been hoping for."

"Alright. I'll be nice to you for the whole evening."

"Wow." I didn't hide my sarcasm. "Do you think you can go that long?"

"I don't know," he answered. "I've never tried."

A waiter passed with a tray of champagne, and Christopher grabbed two glasses before he handed one to me. "Let's make a toast."

"Yeah?" The corner of my lip rose in a smile.

"Yeah." He clinked his glass against mine. "To the most hardworking and compassionate woman I know." He brought the glass to his lips and downed it.

I smiled before I drank, finishing with a few swallows.

We set our glasses on an empty tray that passed.

"Now what?" he said. "We hit up the bar? Or we take our seats for dinner? There's gonna be steak, right?"

Of course, that's all he cared about—food and booze. "Let's find our seats before we crash the bar and you clean them out."

"Sounds like a good idea."

I looked across the sea of tables for my number. They assigned our seating beforehand, and after we found the correct table number, our names were placed on a card on the china plate. As I glanced around for my seat, I felt a pair of heated eyes sear right through my skin and to my heart. It burned me from the inside out, making the hair on the back of my neck stand up straight. Like prey on the plains, I felt my predator watch me before he struck.

My eyes finally found the culprit. Standing on the other side of the room in a fitted black suit was the man I'd slapped so many times his cheek had turned red. His intense eyes were exactly the same as they were on that night, scorching and ice-blue. He stared me down like he knew exactly who I was—hadn't forgotten the way my palm felt against his face. Humiliation washed over me like the tide and blanketed me with sheer terror. I'd never felt so embarrassed in my life, and I never got out of hand like that. The one time I did, I pretty much assaulted an innocent man. Now I was getting an award for helping people, something he probably thought I didn't deserve. "Motherfucker."

Christopher turned his gaze on me, his eyes the size of melons. "Whoa...where did that come from?"

I quickly turned away from the man I had assaulted just a few days before. "Shit. Is he looking at me?"

"Who?"

"The guy in the black suit. He's near the stage."

"Uh..." Christopher's eyes scanned the opposite side of the room. "I think I see a pretty handsome dude checking you out."

I rolled my eyes. "Believe me, he's *not* checking me out."

"Ro, I'm a guy. I know what we look like when we're picturing a woman naked."

"So he is looking at me?" I asked in horror.

"What's the big deal? I'm totally straight, but this guy makes Clint Eastwood look like a troll."

I quickly told him the story of what happened at the bar a few nights ago, keeping my back to my predator and trying to make it look natural.

"You slapped him? Three times?" His voice rose with his incredulity.

"I thought he was Taylor's ex, okay?"

"And it took three slaps to figure out it wasn't him?"

"I was in the moment. I was pissed and in the zone... I wasn't paying attention."

Christopher kept eyeing him across the room. "Well, he hasn't blinked since he first looked at you. But I still think he's checking you out."

"No. He's picturing how he's going to murder me." I tucked my hair behind my ear, showing weakness for the first time.

Christopher glanced at the ground and lowered his voice. "Incoming."

"Shit." I straightened my shoulders and held myself high, knowing I couldn't back down from a confrontation. I was the one who assaulted the guy, so I should pay the price. The awkwardness fell on me like a weight, and I deserved the pressure. I turned toward him and finally looked at him just as he reached me.

First, he sized up Christopher, giving him a quick glance like he was beneath him. His superiority rang through the air, and if he could have pushed Christopher to the side, he would've. His hostility emerged from nowhere. I wasn't even sure where it came from.

Then he looked at me, his blue eyes bright and crystal clear. Like a remote cove in Fiji, it was virgin and untouched. His soul was a blank canvas underneath, full of so many layers and colors it was undecipherable. Like no one else was in the room, he stared at me. Like a predator seeking out prey, he cornered me and didn't back down. He didn't seem to care that a grown man was standing right beside me, built and toned.

His shoulders looked just as broad as they did the other night. When I first spotted him, I assumed he must be the man Taylor was talking about. Drop-dead gorgeous with subtle stubble around his face, he was so beautiful it was painful. Taylor had gushed about her new boyfriend, and he was definitely someone worth gushing over. The fact that I slapped him three times and he didn't even raise his voice attested to his chivalry. Any other man might have slapped me good and hard. But he found the restraint to do nothing.

I lost my footing as I looked at him, too focused on his corded neck and stern jaw. An image came into my mind of his face between my legs, his stubble brushing against the inside of my thighs before his mouth closed over my throbbing clitoris. I dug my fingers into his hair and screamed because he made me orgasm so hard.

Whoa. Where the hell did that come from?

I knew I should say something, but I couldn't bring myself to do it. Instead, I felt my cheeks flush pink and warm. My mouth suddenly became moist from the kisses we hadn't shared, and my calves yearned to be wrapped around his waist.

He took the reins. "Small world, huh?" Like before, his words came out innately sexy and husky. I wondered if he sounded like that on purpose or if he was just unnaturally blessed with extreme sex appeal.

I took a breath and straightened myself out. I refused to let my words tumble out as incoherent rambling. "Too small, actually." I extended my hand to shake his. "It's nice to see you again. I'm glad it's on better terms."

He eyed my hand for so long I didn't think he would take it. Then he wrapped his fingers around mine and gave me an aggressive squeeze, his thumb brushing along my skin seductively. His fingers migrated to my wrist and gave me another subtle squeeze before he pulled away. "That's debatable."

I wanted to question the odd response but didn't. This guy didn't deserve any presumptions from me—not after the first one I made. "I'm so sorry about the other night—"

"Don't apologize." His voice was exactly the same as before, but it somehow sounded like a command. He turned to Christopher then nodded in my direction. "Your girlfriend has quite the hand on her."

"Girlfriend?" Christopher blurted. "Yuck." He shook his head vigorously then held his palm over my face. "God, no."

I narrowed my eyes at the insult before I turned back to the man I'd aggressively knocked around. His eyes were on me once again, but now the look was different. He stared at me so hard I thought I may melt under the heat of his gaze. Now the mood completely shifted, coming off calm then intense just a second later.

"She's single and ready to mingle." Christopher gave me a rough pat on the back. "Ro, this guy is handsome and pretty damn polite to put up with your bullshit. Go for it. I'm gonna hit the bar." He gave me another pat before he nodded to my visitor. "Nice meeting you."

He didn't watch Christopher walk away. His eyes were on me the entire time. It didn't seem like they would move anytime soon—or ever again.

I was mortified by what Christopher said, but I didn't show it. "Ignore him. He's just quirky."

"Who is he?"

"My brother."

He slid his hands into his pockets and stepped closer to me, closer than any stranger should be. But somehow, he filled the space like he owned it. His powerful jaw was sterner up close, and I wondered how his facial hair would feel against my palm as it slid across his cheek. His eyes were blue, but they sparkled with icy fire. "I don't see the similarities."

Because there aren't any. "We kind of adopted each other." I didn't want to get into my past life. That would take all night, and I doubted a stranger would want to hear about it. I was surprised I'd even told him that much. Normally, I would make some kind of joke when someone made a similar comment.

He must have understood further prying wasn't appreciated because he dropped the subject.

"We both know you know my name. So what's yours?"

His eyes quickly glanced at my lips like he wanted to watch them move as I spoke.

A gentle ripple moved through my spine and up my neck. All the tiny hairs on my body stood on end, and my nipples hardened to the edge of daggers. With a simple look, he made my body hum with life, desperate for physical affection. I couldn't remember the last date I had, and I couldn't remember the last man I was this attracted to. But of course, I fucked that up when I slapped him.

Good job, Rome.

He kept his soft lips firmly pressed together like he didn't want to answer. "Calloway Owens."

My jaw nearly dropped to the floor. I recognized that name because it was prestigious in the charity world. The founder and director of the biggest nonprofit in Manhattan was standing right in front of me—and I slapped him. "Of course you are…" Now I was even more embarrassed than before. Why couldn't he just be a nobody? I was going to receive my first award from the academy, and I was taking it from the man I assaulted. I'd never met him in person and didn't know what he looked like. All I ever heard were rumors about how fine he was. But that name was unmistakable.

The corner of his mouth rose in a small smile. His eyes lit up the same way, amused. He came closer to me, the distance between us so short he could kiss me—if he actually wanted to. "Your secret is safe with me." When he lowered his voice, his sexy tone washed across my skin like a perfect bubble bath. It relaxed me but excited me at the same time. Was he trying to be sexy? Or was he just that good at it?

"You're a lot nicer to me than I was to you." If some guy slapped me in a bar, I'd kick his ass—in front of everyone. I definitely wouldn't have held back and remained patient. This guy had the steadiness of a god.

"Trust me, I'm not a nice guy."

I didn't have a clue what that meant, but it scorched my body all the same. His warm breath fell across my face, and I could smell his cologne— subtle and masculine. Or maybe that was just him. I wouldn't be surprised if it was.

"But I'll be nice to you—for now."

***

After I received my award, I took the seat beside my brother. The metal sculpture was in my hand, my name carved at the bottom. It was in the shape of a tree, the giving source of all life. I set it next to my wine glass and admired it.

Christopher eyed it for a moment before he looked at me. "You did good, Ro."

"Thanks…" It meant the world to me that he was there, even if I didn't show it. He was the only family I had in the world—even though we weren't related. No one understood what I went through better than him—because he was there too.

"You know…" He took the award and put it beside his plate. "I think this would look pretty good on my desk."

"With someone else's name on it?" I asked incredulously.

"I can scratch that right off." He smiled before he handed it back. "Where's this bad boy gonna go?"

"I think in my office at For All."

"There's no other office since you live in a rat hole."

I was used to him making jabs about my tiny apartment, but it still annoyed me. It wasn't much, and I had a few cockroaches for roommates, but it was better than what most people had. So I was grateful. "Your face is a rat hole."

"Good one..." His voice was full of sarcasm.

We finished dinner, and the people at our table began to drift to the bar and the dessert table. There was a silent auction near the back, and people cast their bids on trips to Paris and time on yachts. I wanted to look at Calloway, but I refrained from doing so. I knew he was just two tables over.

"So..." Christopher glanced in the direction Calloway was sitting before he looked at me again. "That guy is hot."

When I looked at Christopher, I narrowed my eyes. "Is there something you need to tell me? Because that's the third time you've said that."

"Hell no. Believe me, I'm all about the tits and the pussy."

I cringed because I wanted to throw up.

"But even I know that guy is good-looking. So are you going to ask him out?"

We didn't talk about my love life often, but sometimes Christopher asked about it out of concern. I hadn't had a relationship in years because I didn't have the time or the energy. Most men were full of bullshit, and I had more important things to do. "Did you already forget I slapped him?"

"He's clearly over it. Just go for it."

"He's the biggest name in this room. That guy has done more for this city than anyone else."

He kept a blank look on his face. "And your point?"

"He's too good for me. I already screwed up my first impression."

Now he just looked annoyed. "Ro, come on. This isn't the woman I know. You go for what you want, and you take it. If you want this guy, make it happen. If he says no, no harm done. You've never taken a hit to your confidence. If anything, asking him out is sexy. He'll respect your ability to make a move after you humiliated yourself. I know I would."

"But we work together. If it doesn't work out, it'll just be awkward."

"Tonight is the first time you've ever met him, so I doubt you'll run into him often."

I didn't argue because he was right.

"Get your ass up and march over there."

"Why do you care so much?"

"Because you need a man in your life."

My eyes narrowed and burned with hostility. "Excuse me?" There was nothing more insulting than someone assuming a woman needed a man to

50

be happy. I was doing just fine on my own and didn't need a man for a goddamn thing.

"Calm down. You know how I meant it."

My brother always meant well, so I let it go.

"Now go get that D." He patted my back with a hard thump.

"I don't want his D."

Now he narrowed his eyes at me. "Is there something you need to tell me? Because every woman in this room wants that D."

"I want more than that."

"Then go get it. Ask him to dinner."

"Stop coaching me. If I want to ask him out, I will."

Christopher's eyes drifted away to a woman passing by. She wore a tight black dress that showed the sexy swell of her breasts and her gorgeous, long legs. She was headed right for Calloway. "You better make your move now. Because that fine lady is going to swoop in."

Jealousy ripped right through me, and I was surprised to feel it when I hardly knew the guy. But I knew this woman was beautiful, and if she got to him first, I would miss my chance. He would go home with her, and they'd spend the night fucking while I went back to my apartment alone. I threw my napkin down and scooted my chair back. "Distract her."

Christopher grinned from ear to ear. "Got it."

I walked to his table with my head held high and my shoulders back. It wasn't like me to chase after a guy, but he was the first guy to give me goose bumps, so I made an exception. His looks weren't the only thing that attracted me. He commanded the room with his silence, he was chivalrous, and he did more charity work than even me. He was a catch and I knew it.

He was sitting at the table near the stage, his eyes on me the entire time I walked toward him. He didn't even glance at the other woman who had just been heading his way. Now she was talking to Christopher, and judging by how long their conversation lasted, she was no longer interested in Calloway.

Just by sitting there he looked sexy. His head was tilted slightly to the left, and his blue eyes reflected the jewels in the chandelier above his head. One hand rested on the table next to his empty wine glass, and a black watch was wrapped around his wrist. Without moving his head, he watched me come closer to him.

My heart was beating fast, but I hid my anxiety. I wore the mask I always wore, appearing indifferent despite the range of emotions deep inside me.

He grabbed the chair beside him and adjusted it so I could sit—right next to him. The chairs were only inches apart, and our legs would brush against each other under the table. "I've been saving this seat for you."

I lowered myself into the seat and kept a stoic expression, not reacting to what he just said. "You knew I was coming?"

"I wore my lucky tie, and that thing works like a charm." He gave me that slight smile, the kind that reached his eyes and gave him a boyish aura. He crossed one leg and rested his ankle on the opposite knee. His chest and shoulders were large, covering the chair that supported his back. Even though he was covered in clothing, the details of his body could be determined by the hug of the fabric. He had a wide and powerful chest, muscled arms, and shoulders that could lift a mountain.

"You should let me borrow it sometime."

"Not if you're going to use it for another guy." His hand rested on his thigh, and the top of it was corded in veins. His forearms were probably the same, masculine with tight muscles. "But I will if you use it on me."

"I don't need a tie." I crossed my legs under the table then poured some wine into his empty glass. I brought it to my lips and took a drink.

He watched me, his eyes growing darker.

I was never this flirtatious with anyone, and I wasn't even sure what was happening. My hormones took charge, and my mind was dulled.

"Congratulations on your award."

"Thank you. I'm sorry I took it from you."

He smiled again, the genuine kind that reached his eyes. "I'm not. You earned it."

"That's nice of you to say."

"And sincere." He took the wine glass from my hand and took a drink. "Where are you going to put it?"

"In my office at work. I think it'll look nice."

"I'm sure it will."

"Where do you keep yours?"

"In my office on the bookshelf."

"Want to know something interesting?"

He leaned closer to me, far too close for a work function. "As long as it's coming from you—always."

I wondered if he laid these moves on everyone. Even if he did, they worked. I was turning into a puddle at the very moment. "I applied to your company twice a few years ago. Never got an interview."

His eyes narrowed in surprise. "That's a shame. We missed out."

"After that, I opened For All, so everything worked out. But I was so disappointed when I didn't get the job. It was the first thing I applied for out of college. I'm such an admirer of your work. You do so much for so many people and never expect anything in return."

"If you're still interested, I could find you something."

I smiled at his generosity. "That's very nice of you, but I'm okay. I love my little company. In fact, I'm glad things worked out the way they did. I love having control in what we do."

"It's a great organization. I've respected your work for years."

He might just be saying that, but I suspected he wasn't. "Thanks. That means a lot."

His eyes scanned across my face, taking in my eyes and my mouth like I was a work of art rather than a person. He didn't hesitate to study me, not caring if I noticed. "I'm going to say something, and I want you to accept it without saying a word."

"Okay…" His intensity was frightening, but it sucked me in. I felt the magnetic pull on my body as I fell deeper into him. This man turned me into a weak deer that could barely stand on its legs.

"Ever since you slapped me, I haven't stopped thinking about you. You're the most beautiful woman I've ever seen—and your palm is even more beautiful."

I breathed through my reaction, keeping my lips immobile even though there were a few things I wanted to say. Instead, I held his gaze, feeling my body elevate in temperature until even my ears burned. My palms suddenly felt sweaty, and my thighs squeezed together under the table.

He hadn't blinked since he said those words. He stared at me with his piercing gaze, seeing right through me and all my defenses. His eyes slowly migrated across my features, taking in my lips, my neck, and then my eyes.

The air suddenly felt heavy, the nearby conversations turned silent, and it felt like we were the only two people in the world. His natural power and masculine strength made me tense in his presence. I'd never met a man who made me feel like such a woman. I wanted his hands on my body, those lips pressed against my mouth, and his cock buried deep inside me. I wanted all of him—tonight. "Can I buy you a drink sometime?"

His eyes narrowed in response, focusing on mine. "No."

I stared at him in confusion, assuming I heard him wrong.

"I'm buying your drinks—for a very long time."

***

He offered to take me home, and I accepted his offer so I could be with him a little longer. We sat in the back seat of the town car while his driver took us to my address. I sat on one side of the car and he sat on the other.

There was no touching—but there was heat.

Just before we pulled up to my building, I remembered Christopher. I didn't tell him I was leaving, and now I felt like a bitch for ditching him. I pulled out my phone and sent him a quick message. *Sorry, I just left. Calloway took me home.*

He responded immediately. *Good. 'Bout time you got some D.*

I rolled my eyes and typed back. *Hooking up with that woman?*

Already did in the bathroom.

I cringed before I tucked my phone into my clutch.

"Your brother seems like a nice guy." His gaze was focused out the window, so he didn't peer at my phone while I was typing. It was simply a good guess.

"He is."

"I like him."

"Everyone does." They found his humor charming and even his insults endearing. "Do you have siblings?"

"One brother. Jackson."

I kept my hands in my lap and stared out the window. My fingers naturally rubbed together, and I forced them to stop so he wouldn't know I was nervous. He kept his calm and indifferent façade, and I wanted to play it cool as well.

When we arrived at my apartment, we walked up to my floor then stopped in front of my door. The hallway was run-down with torn carpet covered in stains. Most of the light fixtures were broken, so it was unnaturally dark. It smelled damp, like a few pipes were busted in the walls and an entire colony of mold was growing. I knew he was extremely wealthy, so this place was definitely a dump in his eyes.

But he never acted like it.

I got my key in the door with my heart racing, prepared to invite him inside. But reason descended on my shoulders, and I knew I was doing this for the wrong reasons. I finally found a man I was excited about, so I wanted to jump the gun. But in reality, I really didn't know anything about him other than his charms and his charity work. I had to slow this down before I did something I regretted.

I turned around and kept my back to the door. "Thank you for taking me home."

He hid his disappointment so well I actually believed it. He must have assumed he would come inside tonight, but he didn't voice that expectation. A guy like him must get action left and right— without lifting a finger. "It was a pleasure. I'm glad I ran into you tonight."

"Me too."

He inched closer to me until I was backed up into the door. My back pressed against the old wood, and I felt his chest move into mine. Both of his hands pressed against the door, on either side of my head. I was caged like an animal with nowhere to run. He eyed my lips before he leaned in and pressed a kiss over my mouth. It was soft, a contradiction to how hard he was, and he didn't use his tongue. He kissed me slowly before he gave my bottom lip extra attention. He pulled it into his mouth before he released me. His eyes leveled with mine, and he stared me down, the veins in his neck protruding harder than they did before. He took a deep breath to restrain himself, feeling that scorching kiss with the same intensity. "I know you aren't the kind of woman to sleep with a guy on the first date. So I'm not gonna push my way through this door until we're rolling around on your sheets." He eyed my lips like he might kiss me again. "But just know I want to."

Chapter Five

Calloway

I jerked off twice when I got home.

Ever since I laid eyes on this woman, I'd jerked off five times. And I never jerked off. I preferred the real thing rather than my imagination and a slick hand. I wanted her tight pussy around my cock— along with her ass and mouth.

I wanted all of her—right this very moment.

Just watching her walk turned me on. She held herself like a queen, her head high and her shoulders back. It didn't matter how tall her heels were. She could still strut across the floor like her feet were bare.

When I first met Christopher, I feared the worst—that she had a man. When I saw them together, I seriously considered killing him. Whoever he was, he didn't deserve her. He wasn't man enough to handle a woman like that—only I was. Fortunately, Christopher was a sibling in her eyes—no threat whatsoever.

I stayed at my table because I wanted to observe her. When we spoke, I detected the arousal in her eyes. Her chest and neck were flushed pink, and her pretty lips were moist from constantly licking them. She hid her desire better than most women, but I could see it if I looked hard enough.

So I left the ball in her court.

And like I hoped, she came to me. Once she saw Patricia making her way toward me, she stepped up and intervened. She sank into the chair I'd been holding for her and claimed a stake.

She wanted me.

Thank fucking god.

Because if she didn't, I was going to make her mine anyway.

I put all my cards on the table and told her what I wanted—her. And when I took her home, I really thought I was going to sink into her and come deep inside her. When she said otherwise, I was surprised I wasn't irritated. I accepted her dismissal when I could have seduced her until I got what I wanted. She was attracted to me and clearly wanted me, but that wasn't a road I wanted to take. I wanted her to want me, to beg me, before I finally had her. I respected her too much to take something that wasn't freely given.

Which wasn't like me at all.

I kept picturing her tied up in my safe room, her wrists chained to her ankles with her ass in the air. I pictured my big cock sinking into that tiny puckered hole and making us both come at the same time. I wanted to gag her pretty mouth so she would have to scream louder to be heard. I wanted to slap her ass as hard as she'd slapped me. I wanted to break her until there was nothing left.

But that would take time.

I wasn't sure if that was a lifestyle she participated in because I couldn't find any information about her. Judging by her ruthless confidence, I had a feeling it was something she'd never experimented with before. But she did have the courage to explore new territory, so there was hope. Maybe she would agree to be my submissive after she got to know me. I wouldn't be the only one getting pleasure out of it. She would get even more.

I waited a few days before I contacted her because some restraint was necessary. If I rushed her too quickly, it would chase her away. It was okay to tell her I wanted her, but if I showed her just how truly obsessed I was, it would turn her off.

It would terrify any woman.

It was a Tuesday afternoon when I walked into her office on 10th. It was a small building with two stories. The top was a psychic palm reader, and on the bottom was her nonprofit organization For All. A small sign was next to the door. Something about the quaint space was innately charming—unlike her apartment. That place was a dump, and it took all my strength not to buy her a condo right then and there.

I walked inside. The place was about five hundred square feet with a small waiting area, a bathroom, and a large white desk against the window. A vase of fresh flowers sat on the corner, a white MacBook was in the center, and a stack of stationery was on the opposite corner.

Her voice sounded from the break room. "Oh my god, Tay. This guy is from another planet. He's so gorgeous I actually want to throw up."

I grinned when I realized she was gossiping about me to her girlfriend. I took a seat in front of her desk and rested my ankle on the opposite knee. I'd stopped by my office at Humanitarians United to do a few things that morning, so I was dressed down in jeans and a long-sleeve shirt. I relaxed and listened to the rest of their conversation.

"He's the director and founder of that nonprofit I told you about. He's a gentleman—"

I wanted to laugh at that part.

"He's funny and sweet. And he's just so...hot. I can't explain it better than that. I haven't felt this way about a guy since...I can't even remember."

Now I was grinning like an idiot.

Her voice turned somber after Taylor said something. "No, he's nothing like that asshole. I can tell."

My smile dropped instantly.

"Tay, I've got to go. I've got so much stuff to do today, it makes me wish I had the money for an assistant." She hung up then walked back into the room, holding a steaming mug. She didn't notice me right away. When she reached her desk, she nearly jumped out of her heels and spilled her beverage all over her body. "Oh god...how long have you been sitting there?"

I grinned in response.

She set her mug down and sighed in humiliation. "Will I ever not embarrass myself in your presence?"

"I hope not." I rose from the chair and came around her desk, entering her personal space quicker than I normally would. After hearing that conversation, I knew she was seriously into me. That gave me some leverage.

Her cheeks started to flush rose pink in embarrassment. She ran her fingers through her hair anxiously, her green eyes no longer possessing their usual fire.

"I'll even the score. After I dropped you off, I went home and beat off twice—thinking about you." That was personal and true, and to most people, probably a little embarrassing. I should have walked out before I invaded her personal conversation, and now I actually felt a little guilty about it. "Does that help?"

She swallowed the lump in her throat, and her cheeks tinted a darker shade. Instead of just being embarrassed, she was aroused. At least the latter was better than the former. "Yeah...I guess."

"And after we met in the bar, I did the same." I put more of my cards on the table, wanting her to know the exact hand I possessed. Her charming personality and her flushed cheeks made me even more fond of her. Unlike most women, she was real. She was upfront and honest, and she wasn't too proud to admit when she was vulnerable. Only a truly confident woman could be that way.

"Getting better."

"And I haven't felt this way about a woman in...forever." That wasn't some lie to get her to open her legs. That was the truth, and I didn't even understand it yet. I saw her in that bar, fell hard, and when she slapped me, I fell even harder. My fascination wasn't just with her appearance and her boldness. It ran deeper than that, but I still couldn't explain it. I wanted her to be my submissive, but since she was nothing like a submissive, I couldn't figure out why I wanted her so much. Maybe because she was a challenge—the biggest one I'd ever faced.

Her eyes softened, and her cheeks finally returned to their naturally fair color. The freckle in the corner of her mouth contrasted against the pale skin, and her bright eyes reminded me of stars. "We're even."

***

I took her to lunch at a Mediterranean place just down the street. To my annoyance, she ordered a side salad instead of anything on the entrée menu. Maybe she had a big breakfast and wasn't that hungry, so I didn't give her shit about it. She was extremely thin but curvy, and I hoped she didn't starve herself to look that way.

Natural light filtered through the window and cast her in a good view. Her eyes reflected the winter sunlight, and her brown hair looked almost red under the bright light. Like an angel with a halo, she glowed.

"What's the next project you're working on?"

She was asking me about work, the biggest thing we had in common. "With the holidays around the corner, we're organizing a gift drive. We're raising money for Christmas gifts for ten thousand working families in Manhattan."

With passion, her eyes lit up. "That's so wonderful. Are you mostly collecting toys?"

"We're collecting gifts for adults too. That way the whole family has something to open on Christmas morning. It comes with a tree, ornaments and lights, and a dinner."

Her eyes glowed even further. "That's such a great idea. That will make their day so wonderful."

"You're more than welcome to participate." I knew her organization had their own projects, but it didn't hurt to team up together. After all, we were all working toward the same cause.

"I would love to."

I knew she would agree, and I was hoping she would for selfish reasons. "What are you working on?"

"Food kitchens for the homeless. They usually receive canned goods from the Salvation Army, but we're trying to get more nutritious foods all year round. Around the holidays, volunteers put the effort in to help, but after January, the homeless are abandoned all over again. I really want to change that." She took a few bites of her tiny salad then sipped her iced tea.

"That sounds great."

"I've got a good team to help me out. I can't be everywhere at once, so they're my eyes, ears, and hands."

"Do you do this full-time?" I already knew the answer from Charles, but I wanted the answer from her.

"Yeah. I founded this company right after college, and I've been doing it ever since. Sometimes, I do family therapy on the side for extra cash, but my schedule is usually so busy I can't do that very often."

I started my company with an inheritance, and after it received critical acclaim, we got regular donors from all over the city. We were a nonprofit organization, but each employee was paid for their work. We were fortunate in that matter, and it wasn't an easy task to accomplish. My personal salary was enough to make anyone envious, but it came from my investments in real estate. After all, I put in a lot of money to get the company off the ground in the first place. "Very noble."

"Where did you go to school?"

I pulled a piece of chicken off the kabob and placed it into my mouth. After a few bites, I swallowed. "I never went to college."

"Oh…" She seemed to realize she put her foot in her mouth because she said, "I shouldn't have assumed. It really doesn't matter if you did or didn't." Remorse was in her eyes because she was concerned she'd offended me, and some people might be offended by that. "I'm sorry."

"No need to apologize. I didn't go to college because I was never interested in school. I taught myself everything I needed to know and went from there."

She stared at me with a mixture of awe and surprise. "That's amazing."

"Thanks."

"And one day you decided to open Humanitarians United?"

"I received a large inheritance from my father and wanted to put it to good use."

Her eyes softened. "That's so sweet…"

It wasn't as sweet as she thought. I made a formidable living running Ruin. My BDSM club was the biggest one in the city, and we usually had to turn new members away because the occupancy limit was maxed. Jackson and I considered expanding, but we never pursued it. No one knew I was the owner. The wealthy and influential people I interacted with on a daily basis would never show their faces in a place like that. "Do you like your salad?"

"It's delicious." She finished it off, eating every single bite and leaving her plate as clean as it was before they put the salad on it. She was either really hungry or didn't like to waste food. "Did you like yours?"

"It was amazing. This is my favorite Mediterranean place."

"Mine too. Why do you think I opened For All just down the street?" She smiled with her eyes, being a little flirtatious.

I liked it when she flirted with me. "Free on Friday night?"

"Depends."

"On?"

"If you're asking me out."

"And what if I am?"

"I'm free as a bird." Her grin widened when she saw the excited look in my eyes.

"Come over, and I'll cook dinner."

Instantly, that smile vanished and she was on edge. You would think I asked her if she wanted to go murder some kids or something. "How about we go to that new Thai place on 3rd? I've been wanting to try it."

I brushed off the rejection like it didn't happen. "Thai is one of my favorites. Sounds good."

"Great. I'll meet you there at seven."

Okay, now something was up. She didn't want to come to my place, and she didn't want me to pick her up either. I didn't want to interrogate her so early in the relationship, so I let her strange comments slide. But once we were acquainted with one another, I wouldn't let anything slide—except my cock between her lips.

***

I just finished a meeting with a special VIP. Famous and recognizable, he wanted assurance that his behavior within Ruin would be kept under wraps. While I couldn't guarantee that, I could say it was very likely. Members kept information to themselves. They never talked about the things they saw or who acted them out.

No one talked about it.

But wearing a mask was always a good way to go. Personally, I never wore them, but I knew people who couldn't fuck without them.

Once the meeting was over and the paperwork was signed, he walked out and enjoyed the scene right outside my door. The bass of the music filtered into my office once the door was open, and I could see the dim lights through the darkness.

It was a beautiful world.

Jackson walked in a moment later, wearing black jeans and a black shirt. "Hook and sinker?"

I nodded.

"Awesome." He sat in the chair across from me, the one my guest had just vacated. "I think we need to have a serious conversation about expansion. We're packed every night, and there aren't enough beds for all the fucking that goes on in this place."

I was preoccupied with other things and didn't want to devote the time to opening a new business. "It's a lot of work and it's risky. When businesses expand, they almost never do well. They split the members between the two sites, and then you're paying more money for the same number of people."

"Not if we have no association with it. What if it's a completely different club? No one needs to know we're involved. It'll attract new members from a different side of town. We can open it under a different name and have a manager take care of the rest."

I was a control freak, and letting someone else run my business was unacceptable. "No. We have to run the show."

"Fine. I'll take care of it."

Like I'd trust him to be an adult. "Both of us."

He rolled his eyes. "When the fuck will you trust me?"

Never. "I don't have the time right now, Jackson. Between this and Humanitarian, I'm running dry."

"And chasing after that little slut."

My eyes narrowed on his face, and I threatened him without saying a single word. Rome was mine in every sense of the word, and no one talked about her like that—not even me.

Jackson noticed my hostility and leaned back. "What's so special about this woman? Isabella is a fine piece of ass."

I didn't care what he said about her. She wasn't mine to defend anymore. "I'll tell you when I figure it out."

"When are you going to bring her in here?"

"I don't know." Probably never. I wouldn't want anyone to look at her and fantasize about fucking her instead of their real partner. I wanted her on my own bed, her wrists tied to my own headboard. Like a bear, I wanted to drag her into my cave and never let her go.

"I'm eager to meet this sexy lady. I get hard just thinking about it."

I gave him the same glare, warning him I would actually kill him this time.

"Shit, calm down. I was just joking."

"You weren't, asshole."

"Alright..." He shrugged. "I wasn't. But you know I would never touch her. That's a line I've never crossed."

But he might try once he saw her.

Out of nowhere, he turned serious, crossing his arms over his chest and giving me the same cold look I gave everyone else. "I'm worried about Isabella. I think you should check on her."

"What do you mean?"

"I haven't seen her around, and when I called her, she didn't answer. Marie told me she's not eating or moving. She's really struggling, man. She took the breakup hard."

Guilt flooded through me, but then rage replaced it. "She was just my sub, and I never made her think otherwise. I made it clear there was an expiration date on the arrangement. I never told her I loved her, and I never slept over. I treated her how I treated all the others. It's not my fault she hoped for more."

Jackson kept staring at me, drilling the guilt deep inside me.

Despite my anger, I did feel bad for hurting Isabella. She got attached when she shouldn't have, but I somehow felt responsible for it. Maybe I shouldn't have let our arrangement last as long as it did. Perhaps I should put a timer down and make sure a relationship never exceeded it—no matter how good it was.

Jackson stood and shoved his hands into his pockets. "Just wanted to give you a heads-up. Do whatever you want." He walked to the door.

"I'm not checking on her. This is her problem, not mine."

He glanced at me over his shoulder before he walked out.

***

After I knocked on the door twice, there was still no answer. "Isabella, it's me."

I finally heard life inside the apartment, and the door unlocked a moment later. Wearing a messy bun and a blanket covering her shoulders, she opened the door. Her cheeks were hollow and her eyes sunken. Heavy bags were under her eyes from exhaustion. She stared at me in surprise, like she couldn't believe I was really there.

"Can I come in?"

She stepped away from the door and allowed me entry before she shut the door behind me.

I turned to her and tried to think of something to say. My lips were immobile and my brain wasn't functioning. We just broke up a few weeks ago, but it felt like a lifetime. My mind and body were in a completely different place—obsessed with a different woman. "Isabella, I—"

She moved into my chest and wrapped her arms around my waist. She squeezed me tightly like

77

she never wanted to let go. A sigh accompanied her actions.

I wanted to let her hold me to make her feel better, but I felt like I was betraying the woman I was working so hard to get. If her ex hugged her, I'd flip the fuck out. So I couldn't let my ex hold me.

I gently pulled her hands away from my waist and returned them to her chest. Then I took a step back. "That's not why I'm here. Jackson told me you were going through a hard time, and I just wanted to see if you were okay."

She dropped her hands to her sides, limp. "I'm not okay, Cal. I don't think I'll ever be okay."

Sympathy and annoyance burned inside me. I could spit back the words she said to me a year ago, but that would make me a dick so I didn't. "Is there anything I can do to make this easier?"

She crossed her arms over her chest, looking unnaturally thin. "No."

I remained in my spot by the door, knowing that wasn't the end of it even though she pretty much just excused me. "I will stay away from Ruin for a while so you don't bump into me."

"I'm not going there anyway."

"I can set you up with someone. With a Dom who can give you what you need."

"Cal, I don't want anyone else. Don't you get it?"

"Well, you can't have me." I wasn't going to baby her because it wouldn't make it easier for her. She had to understand there was no hope for us getting back together. If I didn't squash that tiny possibility, she would keep pushing.

Her eyes widened at my harshness.

"We agreed on what this was going to be from the beginning. It's not my fault you wanted something more. It's not my fault you thought it would turn into something different. I'm sorry I hurt you. Really. But frankly, you need to get over it."

"You wouldn't be here right now unless you cared about me."

"Caring is one thing. Loving someone is another. I don't love you, Isabella. Not you or anyone on this planet." She must have mistaken my kisses and touches for something more. I was never gentle with her except when we were finished. Perhaps I should have broken her more, shattered her more.

"Not even your new whore?" She stressed the last word as hard as she could, insulting someone she didn't even know.

"Don't be ugly, Isabella. You can say and do whatever you want, but nothing is going to change. Acting this way is only pushing me further away. If you were sane, you would understand that."

"This is hard for me, okay? How would you feel if I left because I found another Dom I wanted more?"

"I would let you walk away." If she wanted her freedom, I would have given it to her. I wouldn't have done a single thing to hold her back. I would swallow my pride at her rejection and let it go. "After our year together, I thought you would do the same for me. I never loved you, but I did trust you. You were my friend. I don't understand why you're trying to hurt me like this."

"You broke my trust when you left me for another woman."

"I said I wouldn't cheat on you. And I kept my word."

"So you say," she sneered.

"Why would I lie?" I demanded. "If I fucked someone else, I would tell you. I have nothing to hide and no reason to be untrue. I saw this woman, fell hard, and then came clean about it. I don't know what it is about her that's got me so hard up, but there's something. I'm not going to pretend it's not going on and act like I'm not thinking about her when I'm with you. It happened, alright? I can't change the past, and I can't ignore it. It is what it is. Now be a big girl and get over it."

My speech only heightened her anger. "The bottom line is we would still be together if she hadn't walked into that bar—and we both know it."

"You're right. But it would have only lasted so long, Isabella. One day, I would have grown tired of you and left. That's the cold, hard truth, and you know it. So don't blame her for this. I'm the one who chose to leave—so blame me."

Chapter Six

Calloway

I arrived at the restaurant half an hour early and reserved a quiet table in the back. Candles glowed on the tablecloth, and a small vase of roses sat as the centerpiece. I didn't do dinner, romance, and flowers—but I would do it for her.

It would take some time to open her up and get her to consider my offer. Since I was a renowned figure in the community, I couldn't afford to have her blab the truth of my ways to the public. It would ruin my reputation and shame the organization I'd spent the last seven years building. The people who would suffer the most were those in need—including my employees.

She arrived right on time and found me sitting in the back. I rose to greet her, wearing slacks and a dark blue collared shirt. I skipped the tie and the jacket because that was much too formal for me. I avoided wearing a suit as often as possible—way too stiff and thick.

She wore a short black dress with a deep cut in the front. When she was close enough, I could catch a glimpse of her cleavage. When I first saw her in the bar, I didn't look because I was trying to be polite. But now that she dressed that way a second time, I took her invitation and looked—and didn't bother hiding it. "You look beautiful."

"Thank you." She took off her black coat and placed it on the back of her chair.

I pulled the chair out for her, treating her exactly the way she wanted to be treated. Without knowing much about her, I could tell she was a good girl. She wanted the respect she deserved and expected a man to treat her like a queen.

I could treat her like a goddess.

But I wanted something in return.

I sat across from her and admired the curls in her hair. They were open and long, making the strands frame her face and highlight her naturally flawless features. Her small nose was perfectly centered, and she wore dark makeup around her eyes that made her look sexier than she already was. I pictured that hair wrapped around my fist. Those thick curls would be easy to hook around my palm so I could yank her head back while I fucked her hard in the ass.

My cock sprang to life in record time.

She had rounded shoulders and slender arms. Her neck was one of her best features. It was curved and long, giving her an air of royalty. A gold necklace was around her throat with a circle pendant at the bottom.

I realized I'd been staring for a long time without saying a word. "I love the way you've done your hair."

"Oh, thanks." She tucked a strand behind her ear. "I like the way you've done yours too."

I didn't do anything at all. "Thanks." I returned to picturing my hand wrapped around her hair until I finally forced myself to calm the hell down. "I ordered some wine. Would you like some?" I grabbed the bottle and her glass and began to pour it without waiting for an answer.

She answered when I was nearly finished. "I'd love some." She took a sip before she eyed her menu. Her chest rose and fell at a steady rate, and her cheeks weren't flushed like the last time I saw her. She was calm and in control, just as she was in that bar. Her embarrassment from her phone conversation with her friend was in the past. "Everything looks good."

"Then order everything. I just hope they have enough to-go boxes."

She chuckled before she put the menu to the side. "I could stop by the homeless shelter and give everyone a special treat."

"They'd go crazy for some Pad Thai."

We ordered our food, and the waiter disappeared once more, leaving us to the privacy of our corner. I wished the table wasn't so large and she wasn't so far away. I wanted to wrap my fingers around her wrist and hold her still. But even if I could, that would never happen—because she would see me for what I really was.

She looked so beautiful by candlelight that I wanted to command her to touch herself, to sink her fingers underneath her dress and panties. I wanted her to press her fingers to her clit and watch my face as she got herself off—thinking about me. The words were heavy on my tongue, but I kept them back. I would have to get my dominance under control before I did something I couldn't take back. "How was your day?"

"Good. I had a lot of work at the office. Tomorrow, I'm volunteering at the soup kitchen."

I was all about helping people, but I didn't give up my weekends for anything—except her. "Can I join you?"

"Really?" Her mouth instantly formed a smile.

"Of course. We can get lunch afterward."

"That would be fun. Have you volunteered before?"

"Can't say I have."

"Well, bring some old clothes. You'll probably get dirty."

Her choice of words got me hard in my slacks. My eyes narrowed on her face, and I pictured kissing her hard on the mouth.

She caught on to my reaction but didn't blush. "And I'll get dirty too."

Now she was just toying with me.

The waiter arrived with our food, and I was irritated to see she'd ordered another salad. It wasn't big enough to constitute as a meal, and it hardly looked satisfying. If she were my submissive, she wouldn't be allowed to order a salad ever again. She would get whatever I ordered for her—and she would eat the entire fucking thing. "Were you born in New York?"

"Yeah. In Manhattan."

She just lied to me. If she had been born here, Charles would have known about it. But since I couldn't tell her I was a stalker and did a background check on her, I couldn't call her out on her shit.

"What about you?"

"Born and raised." I studied her face like a scientist looking into a microscope. I wanted to study all of her reactions so I could read her later. For instance, now I knew the face she made when she lied—because she just lied to me. "Christopher too?"

"He was born in Kansas. We met a few years later on."

They weren't related. So that meant one of them was adopted into the foster family. Or there was some other explanation. I wanted to come out and ask her bluntly, but that seemed too harsh. If she asked me personal questions, I wouldn't appreciate it. "Did he have a good time with Patricia?"

"He said they hooked up in the bathroom."

She was easy. Too easy, actually. "Did they meet up again?"

"I doubt it. Christopher isn't really the dating type."

Was he the same as me? I didn't detect any dominance from him, but I could be wrong. There was no reason for him to act that way around his sister. "Good for him. Glad he had some fun at the gala."

"She almost tried to have her fun with you."

I pretended not to know what she was referring to. If we continued down this road, I would have to admit I fucked Patricia once. And I didn't want to talk about other women when I was with Rome. "What does Christopher do?"

"He manages mutual funds."

"Good for him."

"He seems to like it, even though it sounds painfully boring to me."

"Some people are into that—numbers."

"Do you do anything else besides run Humanitarians United?"

I hated lying and avoided it at all costs. It made me feel like less of a man. If you had to hide who you were, then you were weak. But I couldn't tell Rome the truth—not this early on. "I have a few hobbies."

"Like what?"

"Reading, biking, hiking, wine, and classical music."

"We have a few things in common. I love reading and playing the piano."

My fingers tightened around my glass at that response. The idea of her sitting at the piano and hitting the keys with her slender fingertips made my body burn. Knowing she made something beautiful with her body was one of the biggest turn-ons I'd ever experienced. I wanted to throw her on a grand piano and make some music together. "I'd love to hear you play sometime."

"Sure. Sometime."

I detected that distance again. She told Taylor how much she wanted me, but she suddenly hit the brakes and kept space between us. I still hadn't figured out why, but I would know eventually. The mystery surrounding her drew me in. I always dug up information on my partners before I engaged them. Some had a past I couldn't overcome, and some had tendencies that told me they were emotionally unstable. Isabella's file was clean, but she ended up being an emotional wreck anyway. With Rome, I went into it nearly blind, and that only made me more interested in discovering her secrets.

"What's your brother like?"

A shithead. "We look a lot alike. Anyone who sees us together knows we're brothers. I'm the cool, rational one, and he's the immature one. And, of course, I'm simply better looking. That's the biggest difference between us."

She smiled at my cocky comment. "I have a feeling you're right. Can't picture someone better looking than you."

My stomach tightened at the compliment. It was the kind I'd never received before. Women told me to fuck them and make them come, but no one had ever said anything so generous while sitting across from me in a public place. "Then you haven't seen all the underwear models on billboards in this city."

She shrugged. "They all look the same to me— photoshopped."

God, I wanted to fuck her. "Thank you for the compliment."

We ate our dinner while keeping our conversation going. When we stuck to meaningless topics like music and film, my cock behaved itself and remained soft in my trousers. Sometimes I had to go into a Zen mode so I wouldn't grab her by the neck and bend her over the table. It took serious concentration for me to remain in control of my faculties. This woman turned me into a wild animal, a caveman. All I knew how to do was fuck.

"Is there a story behind your generosity?"

I didn't understand the question, so I took a moment to figure it out. "Not sure what you mean."

"Did you know someone who struggled when you were growing up? Or did you have some kind of experience with being in need? I feel like the people who help others the most are those who've suffered through it themselves."

I had my experience with abuse, but that wasn't the underlying reason for my behavior. I was related to the coldest and cruelest man I'd ever met, and it was my responsibility to erase the horrible things he did. Jackson resented me for getting most of the inheritance, and when he realized I gave it away to charity, he wasn't happy. But if he knew why I got that money, he would shut his mouth. "No. The inheritance I received was more than any single person could ever need. I didn't want to keep it all for myself. That's all."

She nodded. "That's very generous of you."

"What about you?" This was an answer I was eager for. I knew nothing about her prior to her years in college. She changed her name at one point, and she was untraceable. It was like she was in the witness protection program—off the map.

"I didn't have a great childhood. My parents were drug addicts, and I grew up in a foster home. That's where I met Christopher." She said the words so simply, like she was talking about the weather when she visited the beach. The expression in her eyes didn't change, and her voice didn't shake.

"I'm so sorry." The words flew out of my mouth before I could restrain them. Pity rose in my heart, and I wanted to fix everything for her. I wanted to go back in time and get her out of there. I wanted to protect her from the horrible things she must have seen.

"Don't do that."

"What?"

"Don't feel bad for me." The same strength I saw in the bar that night came back into her features. She was a fireball that couldn't be doused with water. She burned brighter, making everything else look dark in comparison. "Don't pity me. Christopher and I got out of that situation and made lives for ourselves. We may not have parents, but we have each other—and that's always been good enough for both of us. We have a place to call home, and we have food on the table. I'm the very last person you should feel bad for."

Her resolve only made me want her more. She refused to have a pity party for herself, and when she spoke of her past, she didn't choke. With a spine made of steel, she was powerful and strong. When life pushed her down, she got back on her feet and stood even taller. That resilience was sexier than any submissive I'd ever had—even those with all their daddy issues. This woman was fire and ice mixed together. She was painfully beautiful. "I don't. I admire you."

Her hard expression softened. "Thank you."

Now I wanted to fuck her even more. We just had to get through this dinner, and I would offer to take her home. Once we were outside her door, I would kiss her until she invited me inside. I needed to get naked with this woman and fuck her all through the night. My dick needed to be inside her yesterday.

***

We did the check dance before I finally got my money to the waiter. I suspected she would try to pay for her meal because that was just the kind of woman she was. And I was right. She fought me until she finally lost, but if she were my submissive, the fight wouldn't have taken place at all.

We walked outside, and I headed to my car parked off the street. When I realized she wasn't walking with me, I turned back to her. "Let me give you a ride home. Those heels must be a bitch to walk in." She wore them like sandals, but I knew they must hurt the balls of her feet.

"I'll wave down a cab. Thank you for dinner." She looked up at me with her striking green eyes, hiding something below the surface.

"I don't mind taking you home. It's the least I can do since I didn't pick you up." Actually, she wouldn't let me pick her up.

"Really, it's okay."

My left hand formed a fist, and I had to battle for dominion. I wanted to tell her to shut her mouth and get into the car, but that wouldn't get me anywhere. She wasn't ready to see my dark side even though I was ready to unleash it. "Rome."

She straightened when I said her name, picking up on my tone.

"What's going on?"

"I don't know what you mean."

This time, I couldn't hold back. I snapped. "You know exactly what I mean. Don't waste my time by treating me like an idiot."

She stilled at my command, and instead of being offended, she seemed embarrassed. "I would love it if you took me home. But I don't trust myself around you. I know the second we're in front of my door, I'm going to jump in your arms and wrap my legs around your waist."

"And what's wrong with that?" It sounded like a pretty damn good picture to me.

"I don't want to rush this."

"Why?" Getting straight to the good stuff was how I did things.

"Because I like you, Calloway." She looked into my eyes with her bright ones, looking like a dream come true with her vulnerability. She only lied to me to protect herself, and the moment she was honest again, she was gorgeous. I loved seeing that expression on her face—like she trusted me with the truth.

"I like you too, Rome." Like wasn't an appropriate word to express my feelings. Obsessed was more like it. I'd wanted to get under that skirt the second I laid eyes on her. It was all I'd been thinking about with my hand wrapped around my hard cock. But I wanted the real thing, and I was tired of waiting. She wanted me, I wanted her—end of story.

"I don't want to do something I'll regret." Her voice lowered further, more of her vulnerability coming to the surface. "I've made some bad choices in my life. I'm trying not to repeat them."

She was hinting at her ex, some asshole who did something unforgivable to her. I wanted to pry, but I knew it wasn't my place. If she wanted me to know, she would have told me. "You won't regret me, Rome." When we were rolling around on my sheets, and she was coming all through the night, she would hate herself for waiting so long. She was the ideal woman, and I was the only guy who was man enough to handle her. I was the only man who deserved her. But I couldn't make her see that. She would have to figure that out on her own. "Let me take you home. I'll walk you to your door, kiss you goodnight, and then walk away like a gentleman." Even though I was nothing of the sort.

Her eyes searched mine for assurance. She obviously didn't find it because she said, "Can you promise me something?"

I had no idea what she would ask, but looking into her forest green eyes made me not care about whatever words came out of her mouth. I was hypnotized, as I'd been a thousand times before. This woman brought me to my knees with just an expression—and she did it so many times. "Anything."

"Can we wait a while? Even if I ask, promise we won't sleep together."

Where was the fun in that? How was I supposed to chain her to my headboard when she wouldn't even get on her back? This woman was strong and centered, so why did she need me to make a promise like that? If she were anyone else, I would abandon this hopeless feat and find someone else. "How long?"

She cleared her throat before she answered. "Four weeks."

What. The. Fuck.

Four goddamn weeks?

Is she insane?

A whole month?

Hell no.

Forget that.

No one was worth four weeks. I'd find someone else.

I'd die if I waited that long.

Absolutely not.

Her eyes glanced back and forth between mine, shaking because they moved so quickly. She tried to read my thoughts, but they were tucked away deep inside my chest. She must have expected my refusal because she was looking for it.

Soon, she would find it.

Four weeks was unacceptable. It'd already been two weeks since I last got laid, and I hadn't beaten off so much in my life. Another four on top of that would kill me. My cock would never forgive me, and that resentment would only grow as time passed.

But I couldn't walk away from her. I would regret that even more.

I wanted her to trust me enough to allow me to do some twisted and dark things. I wanted her to trust me to gag her, bind her, and bring her to the highest levels of pleasure. I wanted her to trust me to hurt her, to bend her until she nearly snapped in two. How would I earn that unconditional trust unless I gave her a reason to trust me? This woman wasn't like the others, and I'd accepted that from the beginning. If I really wanted her, I'd have to work for it. And I was always up for a challenge. "Okay."

The strain in her eyes finally dwindled. She obviously expected me to disagree with her request, which any normal man would, and I surprised her when I didn't. But my eyes were on the prize—the best submissive I could ever ask for. "Thank you."

"But what constitutes as sex?" I had a lot of different definitions of the act.

"What do you mean?"

"I won't sleep with you for four weeks—even if you ask me to. But you need to define it better. Can I kiss you? Can I touch you? Can I finger you?"

She didn't hide her surprise at my vulgar questions. "I hadn't thought about it."

"Well, do so now."

"Anything but intercourse."

Thank god. I could work around that. "Alright. I won't sleep with you for four weeks starting today."

"Even if I change my mind in a few weeks." She was obsessed with keeping my cock out of her pussy, but why was it so important to her? Refraining from sex just for the sake of it was stupid as fuck. There shouldn't be a timing threshold for a good lay. When I first met her, I thought she was different than the others. I assumed she thought for herself and lived by her own rules. She lived in the moment and didn't care what anyone thought of her. Maybe I was wrong about all of that. Or maybe I was missing a key factor in the situation.

"Even if you change your mind." If I didn't have my own agenda, I would just break my promise the second she asked me to fuck her. But if I could show that kind of restraint when a naked woman was underneath me, then she could agree to being suspended above the floor while I wrapped her legs around my waist and fucked her.

She got what she wanted. And I got what I wanted. She finally relaxed now that the dumbest conversation in the world had come to an end. "I'd like a ride if you're still offering."

"Baby, I'm always offering."

***

I walked her to her door and pretended not to feel uncomfortable by the place. Just a moment ago, a tattooed gangbanger walked down the hallway with baggy pants and an oversized jacket, probably hiding a delivery of crack. He gave me a threatening look before he kept going—and he only lived a few doors down from her.

I couldn't let her live there.

I wanted to buy her a flat in Manhattan, so she wouldn't have to commute to work. I even considered asking her to move in with me. She could pay her rent by fucking me from the second I got home until the second I fell asleep at night.

I didn't voice my concerns because I knew how she would take them. She was stubborn and wouldn't appreciate my bossiness—just yet. But I could only keep that side of me at bay for so long. It was the bulk of who I was—a Dom who always got what he wanted.

She got the door unlocked and invited me inside. The place was smaller than her office, with a bedroom, kitchen, and living room all condensed into a single room. The only door in the place led to the bathroom. "Would you like something? A glass of wine?"

I just wanted to make out. "No, thank you." I locked the door behind me and tested the door while she was turned away. At least that was secure. The idea of some asshole bothering her pissed me off so much I thought about kidnapping her.

She walked to the wall and grabbed a tiny rope hanging from it. Once she pulled it down, a queen-size bed emerged, with the sheets, blankets, and pillows on top. The only furniture she had was a small armchair, and we both couldn't fit on there—unless she sat in my lap.

And I wouldn't mind that in the least.

"I know it's small, but it's cozy." She pulled out a table from nowhere then rearranged the picture frames on the surface. One was of her and a few girlfriends, and another was of her and Christopher. She sat at the foot of the bed then looked at me expectantly. "Do you want any water?"

"No." There was only one thing I wanted to do. I'd been dancing around her for a while, and now that the ground rules were laid, I wanted to get down to business. Those lips were mine—both pairs.

When I reached the bed, I grabbed her by the waist and tossed her backward until her head hit the pillow. Her eyes widened like she hadn't been expecting me to throw her like a doll. I crawled up her body and immediately separated her thighs with mine. Her dress rose up to her hips, but I didn't look at her panties—even though I wanted to.

I grabbed both of her wrists then pinned them over her head. She didn't fight me but looked at me with the same arousal in her eyes. Her green eyes shined a brighter shade, looking like large leaves in a jungle. They became lidded as she stared at my mouth, her lips desperate for mine.

There were so many things I wanted to do with her, but I didn't know where to begin. So I started with her mouth. I pressed my lips against hers and kissed her so hard her mouth would be swollen the next day. Her soft lips felt amazing against my mouth, and when they moved with mine with the same hunger, my spine stiffened. My cock immediately hardened in my slacks, and I pressed it against her clitoris, wanting her to know how much I wanted her.

I wanted her so fucking bad.

She tried to move her wrists away from my hold, but I kept them firmly planted against the sheets. She was mine, and she didn't even know it. When I wanted her to touch me, I would let go. But for now, I was the one in charge.

Our lips danced together and increased in pace. For the first time, I gave her my tongue, and hers immediately greeted mine. Her mouth tasted sweet, like the wine we had over dinner. Our embrace grew in intensity, and I found my hips rocking into her, dry-humping her like a fucking teenager.

Why did I make that goddamn promise?

Her hips slowly grinded against mine, her desire directing her body. Her legs hooked around my waist, and that didn't help matters.

Now, I just wanted to fuck her even more. "I want you so badly." The definition of my cock continued to rub directly against her panties, and I wished we were skin-to-skin. But I could make her come this way. In fact, I could make her come any way.

She breathed into my mouth when she paused our kiss. "I want you too, Calloway."

My spine shivered when she said my name, and I pictured her screaming it as I fucked her hard into the mattress. I preferred to be called Cal, but I loved hearing my full name on her lips. Her naturally husky voice made it sound so goddamn sexy. No one else could pull that off.

I grinded against her harder, pressing right against the most sensitive part of her nub. I moved her wrists together, so I could grip them with a single hand before I moved my other hand up her thigh, feeling the silky, smooth skin. My fingers dug into her thigh, gripping her harder as I pressed her deeper into the mattress.

This juvenile foreplay was far beneath me in my sexual experience, and the last time I dry-humped like this was in eighth grade. After that, I graduated to fucking hard in the back of my pickup. But somehow, it felt like the sexiest thing I'd ever done. I wasn't inside her, but it felt just as good. I flexed my ass before I thrust my hips against her, trying to feel that friction of her sex against the shaft of my cock. The more we moved together, the better it felt, and the amateur nature of the act turned me on even more. I would never resort to this with other women. I only did it with Rome because that was all I could get. It felt so wrong that it felt right—and I knew I was going to come in my slacks.

Like a fucking teenager.

She tried to free her wrists again, and this time, I allowed it. I wanted to see what she would do with those hands. She cupped my face and kissed me harder, her fingertips digging into my hair. Now she was sweaty and out of breath, clinging to me in desperation. She was on the edge of an orgasm—a gift from me.

Sweat formed on my back underneath my shirt then trickled down. I could strip my clothes away and hers, but this felt so much dirtier. We were so hot for each other that we were making this work, enjoying it as much as we would enjoy actual sex. It only excited me for the real thing—the moment I would finally fuck her. Now I knew she would be a heathen in the sack. Once I had her hands chained behind her back and I fucked her in the ass, she would adore it. I could envision the fun before it even began.

Her hands moved to my shoulders next, and she dug her nails hard enough that I could feel them through my shirt. Slowly, they migrated down to my ass, and she pulled me harder into her, wanting my thick cock to press into her with more force.

Fuck, that was hot.

"You want my cock, sweetheart?"

Her face was beet red, and her lips were parted in preparation for an orgasm. She knew it was coming, and she wanted extra friction to make it combust. "Yes."

Hearing that response made my cock twitch. I deepened the angle on top of her then thrust into her hard, ramming my cock against her throbbing clit. My ass was sore from squeezing so tightly, and my balls were drawing closer to my body as I prepared to come.

I watched her tits shake in her dress as I rocked into her, picturing how gorgeous they would be once her clothes were gone. She had a nice chest, and I planned to tit-fuck her one of these days. Her cheeks flushed further, and her mouth gaped open as the explosion slowly trickled through her body. Her eyes became lidded as she looked at me, and it was the sexiest thing I'd ever seen.

When I was with Isabella, I enjoyed myself immensely. She did everything I asked, even things most submissives wouldn't dare attempt. But even the dirtiest thing with her didn't compare to how I felt now—with Rome. I wasn't even inside her, and I was in heaven. I gave her a final kiss and sucked her bottom lip into my mouth. "Come for me. Now." My Dominant voice slipped out before I could stop it, but I didn't regret it.

Because she came. "Oh god, Calloway."

Now I was going to burst.

She dug her nails into my biceps and grinded against me, her face a beautiful shade of pink and her mouth in the delectable O that I'd wanted to see since I met her. "Yes...fuck." She pulled me closer to her as my cock slid across her folds.

My hand moved under her head, and I fisted her hair like a tyrant. I told myself I wouldn't do that because it was a dead giveaway to who I truly was—a dictator. But I couldn't stop myself. She'd just come and said my name, and now I was prepared to fill my boxers with my come—for her.

She rode the high until it reached its climax then she slowly drifted down. Her nails started to loosen from my arms, but she still moaned quietly to herself. Her eyes were glued to mine, and that look of satisfaction was worth more than a vault of gold.

I grinded against her with a few more strokes until I came with a moan, my eyes glued to her face. I couldn't wait to fill her bare pussy with every drop of my seed. I couldn't wait to claim her as my own. But for now, filling my boxers was good enough. "Rome...fuck." It was the best orgasm I'd had to date—and I almost couldn't believe it.

I was thirty years old, and I just dry-humped someone.

She wrapped her arms around my neck affectionately then kissed the corner of my mouth. It was full of gratitude, thankful for the way I'd just rocked her world through my slacks. The kiss was delicate and soft, but it made my insides burn with longing. "You're such a man."

The unexpected compliment filled me with warmth, and the sincerity in her voice sent chills down my spine. I didn't know exactly what her compliment meant, but I assumed she was impressed I made her come so hard without actually touching her. I made her feel like the sexiest woman in the world.

And I would do that every night.

Chapter Seven

Rome

I got there early and set up the kitchen, a ridiculous smile on my face that wouldn't disappear. Calloway was a phenomenal kisser, and his package was impressive. Once I felt the definition against my clitoris, I was gone.

He gave me the best orgasm I'd ever had.

He didn't sleep over like I thought he might. He went home, and I hadn't heard from him since. He was supposed to help me out today, but he hadn't shown yet. Hopefully, his alarm went off.

The kitchen staff arrived and prepared the meal. We were serving chicken and dumplings, rice, and carrots, along with a piece of French bread. It was warm and filling, and it would give the homeless some respite from the cold.

"Hey, pretty lady." John came behind the counter and looked me up and down. "Do something fun last night?" He wore the same green sweater covered with stains, and his black pants had holes in the knees. He'd been living on the streets for ten years, diagnosed with extreme bipolar depression. Sometimes, like now, he was in a great mood. And other times, I couldn't get him to even speak.

I smiled so I could keep up his good mood as long as possible. "I had a date."

"Ooh...about time. You're always working."

"I know. I need to get out more."

"Well, I'm always available if this chap doesn't work out."

I smiled because I knew he was kidding. "I'll keep that in mind."

"Your services are unnecessary." The threat filled the room and cast a shadow over everyone. Even the guys sitting at the back table could feel it because they all looked at us. Calloway's voice took on a new tone I'd never heard before. Without raising his voice or using explicit words, he managed to terrify everyone. He looked down at John and silently excused him from the conversation.

John didn't stick around after that. He walked into the seating area and joined some of the members of his gang. Their voices fell and they huddled together, obviously talking about Calloway's unwelcome presence.

Calloway walked to me, wearing a gray t-shirt and dark jeans. His clothes didn't look old, and I hoped he was prepared to get them demolished with gravy. The irritated look was still on his face when he looked at me, like I was somehow responsible for what just happened.

My good mood evaporated like steam. "What the hell was that?"

"What?" He kept a straight face like it was a legitimate question.

"You didn't need to be an ass to John. He's a very nice guy."

"Any guy who hits on you is not a nice guy." He grabbed an apron from the pile and tied it around his waist.

"You hit on me."

"Not the same thing, and you know it." He walked away before I could say anything more. He grabbed a stainless steel container full of dumplings and placed it on the food line.

Was the conversation over? I joined him at the counter and put one hand on my hip, giving him a fiery look. "That was unacceptable, and you know it was. He was just joking—"

"No. He wasn't." He dropped the cylinder into the tray then turned back to me. The red apron was tight across his broad and powerful chest. He probably needed one a few sizes bigger—a size we didn't have. "It's one thing to be nice to someone, but it's another to let them walk all over you. He crossed a line, and we both know it. Small talk is fine. But romantic advances are not."

"But it wasn't a romantic advance."

He glanced around us to make sure we weren't being overheard. "I'm all about helping people in need. I've been doing it for seven years. But don't put yourself in a situation where people can take advantage of you. Because I promise you, they will."

"John was just being nice. Now he's going to be depressed for a few days."

"At least he learned his lesson." He walked away to retrieve another tray.

Was this really happening? Last night, we had an amazing night. Now, we were already fighting. He was a different person than I remembered, changing into an evil like I'd flipped a switch. "Whoa, hold on." I caught up to him. "Don't insult the people I look after. Don't boss me around, and don't treat my friends like shit. You aren't my boyfriend, Calloway." Now it was my turn to march off.

He stopped me by the wrist and pulled me into his side with such strength I nearly lost my balance. He looked down into my face, his blue eyes intense with frustration. He practically ripped me apart with just the look. "I am your boyfriend." He squeezed my wrist harder then pulled me further into his chest. "I don't flirt with other women or let them flirt with me. You'll do the same. End of story." He pressed a hard kiss on my lips then released me immediately. He walked off like the conversation hadn't just happened, and he grabbed a tray of food before he returned it to the line. Not once did he look at me, dismissing me like I didn't exist at all.

***

After we started serving the meal, Calloway was in a better mood. He spoke to each person as they moved down the line, asking them how their day was and telling them a few jokes to make them laugh. The good-natured man I knew had returned to the surface, directly opposite of the man I just witnessed a few moments ago.

When John came down the line, he kept his head down and wouldn't even look at me.

"We've got your favorite today, John. Chicken and dumplings."

He only nodded and stuck out his tray.

I served the food on the plate and watched him move down the line, wishing he would talk to me. He skipped Calloway completely and went to the next person in line to get carrots and bread.

I gave Calloway the darkest glare I could muster, hating him for scaring off a man just trying to get by. John refused half of his meal just to avoid him. The guy already had it hard enough before Calloway had to be a jerk. If he really thought John was a threat, he was crazy.

Calloway felt my stare because he glanced at me from the corner of his eyes. Then he moved down the line, cutting in front of the nearby worker, and took John's tray from his hand. He piled the food onto the tray, giving him far more than the others, and then handed it back. "Why was six afraid of seven?"

John stared at him blankly, still cautious.

Calloway continued. "Because seven is a registered six offender."

The corner of John's lip rose in a smile, and finally, a chuckle came out of his mouth. Soon, he laughed. The kind that erupted from deep inside his throat. He moved down the line, chuckling to himself. "Six offender... I'm telling that to the guys."

He grabbed a piece of bread then joined the others at the table.

My anger disappeared, and I finally gave him a smile.

Calloway returned to his place beside me and continued serving the people who came down the line.

I turned to him when there was a break in the line, a smile on my lips. "Thank you."

Calloway said nothing, pretending he hadn't heard me.

***

When the day was over and the soup kitchen closed, we walked out into the freezing cold of the city. Our clothes were dirty, and we needed a warm shower and a change in wardrobe.

I was mad at Calloway initially, but when I saw the goodness within him shine, that resentment disappeared. He didn't apologize for what he did, but he tried to make up for it. And in the end, that's all that mattered.

"Would you like to come over?" Even with gravy stains on his t-shirt, he looked scorching. His brown hair was a little messy, like he woke up that morning looking perfect but a little casual. The stubble on his face was gone because he'd shaved that morning, but by the evening, it would return. "I'll make us some dinner."

A warning blared in my heart the moment he issued the invitation. I still wanted to jump his bones and fall head over heels for this man I hardly knew. My gut and my heart were telling me to go all in without any precaution. But something stronger, my brain, was telling me it was too good to be true, and there was something I was missing. He was just too perfect—his jealous tantrum aside.

But he promised four weeks of abstinence, and I believed he would keep his word. Fooling around was enough for me since he was so good at it. "Sure. I'll go home and shower then I'll be over there."

"Why don't we just go now?"

I understood exactly what he was implying.

"We'll throw your clothes in the wash, and you can wear some of my stuff around the house. I'm sure you'll look better in my clothes than I do." He winked, that childish grin stretching across his face.

Did he get tired of being so irresistible all the time?

"Or you'll look even better wearing nothing at all."

***

I pictured him in a penthouse on the top floor of the highest skyscraper in all of Manhattan. Dark furniture that reeked of sexual conquests with a cabinet full of the hardest liquor known to man. His bed was probably made with black sheets that reflected the dim light of the nighttime buildings across the street.

But he lived in a house.

It was three stories tall with oak trees along the front yard. A black gate kept pedestrians off his property, and rose bushes covered in thorns lined the pathway. A large three-car garage connected to the street behind the house. Since we were on foot, we entered through his front door.

Hardwood made of deep cherry wood was underneath our feet, and the entryway table was just as dark. A long red rug led the way into the center of the house. A wooden staircase was to the right, leading to the other two floors, and an expansive living room was directly before us. The couches were made of gray cotton, and a large flat screen was on the wall. The entryway alone was the size of my tiny apartment.

The kitchen was decked out in granite countertops, black appliances, and a Sub-Zero fridge with a glass door that allowed you to see everything inside. Fruits, vegetables, lean meat, and almond milk were displayed in the forefront. His diet was clearly strict, but I wasn't surprised based on his incredible physique.

The moment I stepped foot inside that kitchen, I was in love. Not with him, but with the room. It was enormous, big enough for him to prep dinner for twenty guests. There was a large kitchen island in the center and lots of counter space on either side. I couldn't stop myself from wearing my heart on my sleeve, and I sighed in longing. "This is the most beautiful kitchen I've ever seen."

He leaned against the counter, his arms over his chest. "You like it?"

"I love it. I've always dreamt of having a kitchen like this."

He watched me admire his home, his blue eyes never leaving my face.

"I don't even have a stove." I laughed because it was funny, but it was also depressing. I had to do all my cooking with a microwave and I ate take out for everything else. It was a lifestyle I chose because it was the lesser of two evils. If I wanted to make a real difference in this world and help people, I had to sacrifice a few things—like having a nice kitchen and being debt-free.

"You're welcome to come over and cook whenever you want."

I smiled when I realized his motive. "You just want someone to cook for you."

"Naked, of course. That's a requirement."

"I'd have to wear an apron at least."

"I'll let you wear panties—but that's it." He didn't smile to show he was joking. He looked dead serious.

My ears started to feel warm, so I changed the subject. "This isn't where I pictured you living."

"And where did you think I would live?"

"In a penthouse."

"I did for a while. But I like the feel of a house. No neighbors and no elevators. And I like having a yard."

"Do you have a dog?"

"No. But maybe someday."

I could picture him with a black Lab or a golden retriever. He seemed like an outdoor pet owner. But perhaps I misread him.

He pushed off the counter with his hips. "So, I could make dinner while you're in the shower. Or we can both shower and make dinner together." He closed in on me until my body was pressed against the counter. His hands gripped the edge on either side of me, and he looked down into my face with a hungry expression. He eyed my lips like he was restraining himself from sucking my bottom lip into his mouth.

I was already wet.

I wanted to see him buck naked. I wanted to see those chiseled lines of muscle I knew were under his shirt. My fingers wanted to travel down, feeling every bump and groove, until I found his happy trail between the V of his hips. And I wanted to see that enormous cock that dry-humped the fuck out of me last night. No other man in my life had gotten me this hot and bothered. Calloway brought the desire out of me, pulling it from every pore until I was a dog in heat. Sometimes, I couldn't tell if it was his beauty or his charisma that brought me to my knees. I hated giving head, but all I wanted to do was put that big cock in my mouth and bring him to his knees the way he did to me last night.

His eyes scanned my face, searching for the slight hints I couldn't stop myself from giving. He scanned my lips then my eyes. His gaze turned to my chest, watching it rise and fall at a quickened pace. "I want to see every inch of you." With his eyes glued to mine, his hand moved to the front of my jeans and unbuttoned them before he yanked down the zipper. Then his hand slithered down my front until he found the cotton fabric of my panties. His fingers gently explored, feeling my lips as well as my clitoris. He took a deep breath as he explored me, and once he secured his fingers over my clit, he rubbed it in a circular motion.

My knees wobbled because his fingers felt so good. With immense experience, he rubbed me off just the way I did to myself when I was alone. Like he was a woman himself, he understood exactly how I wanted to be touched. I gripped his arm and held on as he set me on fire.

His fingers moved farther back until he felt the soaked fabric just below my pussy. He moaned quietly from deep in his throat, recognizing the moisture that pooled just for him. His jaw became stern and his neck corded with arousal. His breathing picked up just the way mine did, both of us deep in mutual arousal.

I wanted him to fuck me.

I almost asked him to.

His long fingers pulled my panties over before they pressed directly against my clitoris. The pads of his fingers were rough, but they felt good against my slick nub. He rubbed it with more pressure than before, and he nearly brought me to an orgasm right there. "You're so beautiful when I touch you." His fingers slid farther back until he reached my entrance. He slowly slid them inside, feeling the resistance of my small channel before he finally squeezed through. He clenched his jaw in pleasure, loving how soaked I was deep inside. "Fuck, you're tight." He slowly moved his fingers in and out, lubing them with my own arousal.

"It's going to be hard to get your fat cock in there."

He took a deep breath and practically winced in pain, his fingers buried farther inside me. He pressed his face against mine, his lips right next to my ear. "Be careful, baby. Keep it up, and I might not keep my promise."

I wasn't one for dirty talk, but this sexy man turned me into a horny woman. "Maybe I don't want you to."

He winced again, burying his face into my skin and gently nicking my flesh with his teeth.

What was wrong with me?

He picked me up and pulled my legs around his waist as he carried me upstairs. We went to the third floor then entered his dark bedroom. A gray comforter was on his king-size bed, and he laid me down on the surface before he stepped back and undressed himself. He pulled his gray t-shirt over his head and threw it across the room.

His chest was exactly as I imagined it would be. His pecs were toned and strong, and his shoulders bulged with intricate muscles that were chiseled by the hand of god. His hips were thin and narrow, and his happy trail was cleanly shaven into a single line down into his jeans.

He unbuttoned them and took them off, standing in his boxers. His thighs were thick and powerful, looking like tree trunks that were strong enough to combat a hurricane. A spot of moisture was at the front of his underwear, where he'd been leaking while he fingered me. He grabbed his waistband as he stared me down, and then he pulled them down slowly, practically giving me a stripper show.

Inch by inch, his length appeared. The head of his cock was thick and swollen, a shade of red and blue from the blood that rushed down there. He kept going, showing more and more of his steel shaft until he reached his trimmed balls. Nine inches of pure man with an impressive girth. He belonged in a porno.

My mouth went dry, and I couldn't think straight. All I could think about was getting that cock inside me and wondering if it would even fit. He would stretch me until I tore, and while it would hurt, it would feel so damn good.

He wrapped his fingers around his shaft and cradled his cock. "On your knees."

I didn't let anyone boss me around, but the second he gave the command, I obeyed. I moved to the rug and folded my knees underneath me, knowing that thick cock was about to fuck my mouth so hard my throat would be sore tomorrow.

"Take off your shirt."

I pulled it over my head, sitting in just my bra.

He positioned himself in front of me. "Suck me off. Lots of tongue and lots of hand." His hand wrapped around my hair until he had it locked in a tight fist. He pointed his cock against my face and unleashed another command. "Get to work, sweetheart."

I opened my mouth wide and took his length deep into my throat. It was the biggest one I've ever taken, and it was so salty and sweet. I loved the way it stretched my mouth, practically unhinging my jaw. The saliva pooled from my cheeks and seeped out of my mouth because I couldn't contain it all. It poured down my chin and to my neck. The harder he pushed in, the more spit spilled out.

He thrust into my mouth, his eyes on me the entire time. "Just like that." His other hand moved behind my head, and he continued to thrust into me hard, not an ounce of gentleness within him.

I wrapped my hand around his shaft and pumped him as I moved him into my mouth, growing more turned on the longer I tasted him. His pre-cum leaked into my mouth, and I could feel it across the back of my tongue.

"Touch my balls."

My fingers moved to his sack, and I massaged the tender area as I sucked his cock into my mouth. I breathed whenever the opportunity presented itself, but he didn't give me a lot of time. His cock was rammed deep inside me most of the time, and no matter how hard he tried, he couldn't get it all in my throat. He was simply too long, and I was too small. But that didn't stop him from thrusting and gripping me at the same time.

His harshness should have bothered me, but it was just the opposite. I loved how aggressively he wanted me, how much he needed to relieve the sexual frustration I caused. After the dirty things I said to him, I couldn't blame him for needing to fuck my mouth like this.

He stared into my eyes the entire time, his thigh tightening with every thrust he made. "Swallow."

He was about to come. My pussy clenched at that knowledge, and I wanted his seed in my throat and my belly. I'd never been so eager for a man's cum, but I desperately wanted it now. When there was a quick moment to breathe, I spoke. "Give it to me."

His hand dug into my scalp, and he released a loud moan he couldn't contain. "Fuck." He shoved his cock far inside me, forcing my head into his crotch so he could insert as much of his length as possible. Then he came, squirting his hot seed into the back of my throat and practically making me choke. He gave me so much, dumping ounces as it slid down my throat and into my stomach.

When he was satisfied, he finally pulled his softening cock out of my mouth. He looked at me like he'd never seen me before. Awe and desire were heavy in his stare, and it seemed like he wanted me even more.

He threw me onto the bed and yanked my jeans and panties off until I was bare underneath him. He didn't waste time examining me or studying my naked pussy for the first time. He shoved his face between my legs and sucked my clit so hard I almost came. The slight stubble from his face rubbed against my inner thighs, and just like I imagined, it felt so goddamn good. My hands dug into his hair, and I pulled his face farther into me, loving the amazing things his mouth was doing. "Calloway…"

He sucked my clit harder into his mouth then drove his tongue deep inside my pussy, tasting all my arousal. It came in a flood, and I was so slick I couldn't have taken his cock if he tried to shove it inside me.

"I'm gonna come."

His hands reached up and squeezed my tits through my bra, his mouth still sucking and licking my pussy like he was starving. He ate me out, lapping and enjoying the area like a feast. He circled my clit harder, and with a burst, he pushed me over the edge.

I arched my back across the mattress and pulled his face farther into me. "Yes…yes." My fingers nearly cut his scalp, and my nipples were sharper than the edge of a knife. I saw the cosmos and the heavens as I fell into the euphoria. It was so good I could barely breathe. I gasped for air, but it was never enough. I was in a moment of pure bliss, not thinking—only feeling.

Calloway pulled his mouth away when I was finished, his lips covered in a film of my arousal. He moved over my body, kissing my stomach and my chest until he rested on top of me, his lips hovering near mine. "You're a beast." He kissed me softly on the lips, in direct contrast to the hardness he'd just shown me. "Just like me."

Chapter Eight

Calloway

She had work in the morning, so she didn't try to sleep over.

Which was a relief.

I could hold off on sex for four weeks, as impossible as it seemed, but I couldn't share my bed with someone. That was a hard limit, and there was no way around it. If she really wanted to spend the night, I had a spare bedroom for her to use. But since our relationship was different than the usual ones I had, it would be a difficult conversation.

I hoped I could avoid it as long as possible.

I went to Ruin late that night to check on a few things. I couldn't walk in during the day because I was needed at Humanitarians United, so the late evenings were the best time. And if I kept seeing Rome, the only time I could run my business would be when she was at home and asleep.

I felt dishonest not telling her about my other business, but at the same time, I didn't think it was any of her business. She'd only shared a small amount of her past with me, so I didn't feel obligated to expose more of myself to her. Besides, she would never understand.

When we fooled around last night, she surprised me with her aggression. She said the dirtiest things I'd ever heard, words that made me so hard my dick actually hurt, and she sucked dick like an Olympic contender. Maybe she would understand Ruin if I gave her a chance.

But now wasn't the time.

When we started fucking, I would have a better idea of whether she would be a good fit or not. She seemed open-minded, intelligent, and she had a distinct talent when it came to foreplay, so it could work out the way I wanted.

She would be such an incredible submissive.

I let myself get carried away a few times. One instance with John, which I knew was a fuck-up. Rome was pissed at me until I played nice with the guy. And the second instance was when I treated her like a submissive and commanded her to suck my dick.

Thankfully, she went with it.

But I had to be more careful from now on. If I came on too strong, I could push her away entirely. And I couldn't afford to lose this woman. She did incredible things to me. Just a simple look was enough to get me hard. No woman ever had this hold on me. No woman had ever made me abstinent for four weeks.

It was a record.

I moved through the crowd of dancers on the floor and passed the bar before I headed to my office in the back. On the way, I saw Jackson grinding up against some woman in a gas mask. I hoped he wouldn't see me.

Of course, he did. "I was wondering when you would show your face in here again."

I walked inside and ignored him, unbuttoning the front of my suit coat before I sat down in my leather chair. "I was wondering when you would come up for air from that friend of yours out there."

He fell onto the couch facing my desk, wearing a navy blue suit with a vest underneath. Black and blue. They were the two colors we usually wore. We looked so much alike people couldn't tell us apart sometimes. But I always wore black, and he always wore blue. That usually helped people. "How's she doing?"

I assumed he was talking about Isabella. "We had words. She pissed me off. End of story."

"What about the beginning? And the middle?"

"Nothing substantial." Isabella pissed me off. She became emotionally attached, and now she was haunting me with her baggage. I never deviated from our agreement. She did. But somehow, I was to blame for it. "She's upset with me, and she'll be upset for a long time."

"It's because of Rome, isn't it?"

I didn't like it when he said her name. Far too possessive. I wanted to be the only man to ever say her name, but of course, that was ridiculous until she became my sub. Then, I could give her a whole new name altogether. "Isabella blames her for ending our relationship. I explained that wasn't the case. I would have left anyway. She doesn't see it that way."

"Women are jealous. No way around it."

"If she expects me to feel bad for her, I won't." She could threaten to jump off a building, and I still wouldn't do a goddamn thing. I'd been a prisoner once before, and I wouldn't go down that road again. It was one of the reasons I lived a life of dominance. No one could cage a beast like me.

"What now?"

I shrugged. "I tried to find her a new Dom, but she didn't want one. She's on her own now."

"I wonder if she'll come back in here."

"Hope not." I hoped I never saw her again. If Isabella had been mature about our breakup, we could have remained good friends. I still would have respected her and cared for her. But this childish behavior made me question the entirety of our relationship. Like a smoke screen, it made me wonder what we truly had.

"So, how's it going with Rome?" He leaned back and crossed his legs.

I didn't discuss personal shit with my brother, but I knew he wouldn't stop questioning me until he got his answers. "It's alright. She doesn't want to have sex for four weeks."

"What?" His jaw dropped. "Is this a cruel joke?"

I wish. "No."

"And you agreed?"

Because I was a madman. "Yeah."

He continued to stare at me with a shocked expression. "Is this woman ever going to be your submissive? Or is she just a regular woman?"

"She will. I just need some time with her. If she wants to take it slow, I will."

"But why? Why wait? Find someone else."

I didn't want anyone else. "We fool around, so that's fine."

"But why does she want to wait? What's that about?"

I still didn't have the answer to that. "Not sure. She didn't elaborate."

He crossed his arms over his chest, his blue eyes focused as he tried to find the answer on his own.

He should leave the thinking to me.

He snapped his fingers like he found the answer. "She's a virgin. She's gotta be."

I nearly laughed because it was ridiculous. "Trust me, she's not."

"How would you know unless you've fucked her?"

"Believe me, she's very experienced. She gave me the best head I've ever had. And she talks dirty like no one else."

"But what if she is."

I didn't mess with virgins. I popped a few cherries when I was a teenager, but never since. There was always emotional attachment, and the women expected it to be some grand adventure they would look back on with fondness. She'd think it was the beginning of a long relationship, possibly with her husband. No way in hell I would mess with that. "She's not."

With that declaration, Jackson backed off. "Hmm…then, why?"

"She said she wants to take it slow. That's all I know."

"Sounds like she wants love and flowers. And we both know that will never work."

I got that impression as well. She wanted a knight in shining armor, a prince charming. Maybe that was the case. But once she trusted me, I could show her a new life she never considered before. She would love it and become immersed in the darkness. Together, we could be a Dom and a sub who fulfilled every fantasy that crossed our minds. But I had to be patient and wait for the right time. "She'll change her mind if I give her enough time."

"And what if she doesn't?"

The answer was simple. "I'll walk away."

"You would really walk away from this woman?" He raised an eyebrow incredulously. "Because you broke off your relationship with a beautiful woman and stalked her like a madman. I don't think you can give her up that easily."

I felt something special for this woman—there was no doubt about that. But if we couldn't come to an agreement about this, I would have to walk away. There was no way around it. "I can. And I will."

***

I stopped by her office on my lunch hour. I'd thought about her all morning and couldn't get her out of my mind. While I was hungry for food, what I was really hungry for was her.

I stepped inside and spotted her sitting at her white desk. A mug was on the surface with the string from a tea bag hanging over the side. Her hair was done in nice curls, and her green eyes were glued to her laptop. She wore a white dress and dark pantyhose on her legs to keep them warm.

She looked up like she expected to see a customer. "I'll be right with you—" She faltered when she realized it was me. "Oh, hey. I wasn't expecting you."

I wanted to keep her on her toes, to never know when I might drop by and take what I wanted. I walked to her desk then leaned over the wood, giving her a soft kiss on the lips. "Hey." Last time I kissed her, I could taste my cum on her lips. Now they just tasted like raspberry lip balm.

She visibly melted underneath me, affected by my touch just the way I was affected by hers. Her eyes grew heavy and lidded, like she wanted to be alone with me in a cold and dark bedroom. "What a nice surprise."

"I wanted to see if you were in the mood for lunch." I gave her a dark look, telling her what kind of lunch was on my mind. It wasn't Mediterranean or Italian. It was the sweet and salty entrée right between her legs. I didn't mind eating pussy, but for some reason, I loved eating hers. It was so fucking sweet, like pineapple.

She caught my drift immediately because her cheeks blushed. "As appetizing as that sounds—"

The door opened, and Christopher walked inside wearing a designer suit and tie. He looked as if he belonged on Wall Street with his perfectly styled hair and clean-shaven face. He wore a thick jacket to fight the cold, his black dress shoes still shiny despite the sludge of the city. "Wow. I never thought I'd be so excited to see another dude." He extended his hand and shook mine. "So, you're seeing each other?"

Rome looked mortified by her brother's intrusion.

"Yeah." I returned my hand to my pocket. "It's been a few weeks."

"That's so goddamn awesome." He fist-bumped the air. "My sister is finally not a loser."

Not that I should care, but it pleased me she hadn't been hot on the dating scene. The fact that she made an exception for me told me I had a serious chance of getting what I wanted. And I wanted to be her one and only Dom.

"Shut up, Christopher." Rome packed her laptop in her bag and stood up. "Otherwise, we aren't going to lunch."

Christopher turned to me. "You want to come, man?" The exuberance in his eyes told me he wouldn't take no for an answer. Since he wasn't related to Rome, I could've been a little threatened by him, but it was bluntly obvious he had no attraction toward her. Somehow, he really did see her as a little sister—which was why I liked him immensely.

"He can't," Rome interrupted. "He's got plans."

"Plans with you." I turned to her, the corner of my mouth raised with a smile. I knew exactly what she was doing. She didn't want her brother to embarrass her more than he already had, but I wanted every piece of information about her I could get. Maybe he would spill some secrets during lunch. I couldn't miss the opportunity.

Now she glared at me.

"It's settled, then." Christopher clapped his hands once and turned to the door. "Let's go to that deli just down the road." He walked out and waited for us outside.

I looked at Rome, loving the irritated look in her eyes. "After you." I gestured toward the door, waiting for her to walk out.

"I apologize in advance." She walked past me.

"For what?"

"For making you witness my brother's murder."

***

I was beginning to notice a pattern.

Just like Rome, Christopher ordered a salad. A tiny-ass salad with some chicken on top. Rome did the same, and they split a single bag of chips. They both ate every single morsel off their plates, wiping it clean.

What the fuck?

I ordered a large chicken sandwich with avocado and all the produce, and it was so delicious that I felt bad the other two were eating rabbit food. Christopher worked on Wall Street, so I knew his eating choices weren't based on money. Then what were they based on?

"So…getting pretty serious, huh?" Christopher eyed us back and forth from his seat on the other side of the booth.

"Christopher, don't." Rome had a distinct warning in her voice but not enough to stop him.

"What?" he asked in mock offense. "I'm just curious. If the guy has been around this long, he must be really into you. Why else would he put up with you?"

I really liked this guy.

I thought brothers were supposed to be protective and caring, but he was nothing like that. He pushed Rome to do things she wouldn't normally do, and not once did he give me an interrogation about my intentions, my income, or my relationship history. He just accepted me—for exactly who I was.

"Just mind your own business, alright?" Rome threw the empty chip bag at him. It barely flew through the air before it came drifting down, harmlessly.

Christopher eyed it with a smug look on his face. "Ouch."

She rolled her eyes. "Just be cool, alright?"

"I am," he argued. "This is the first guy I've seen since—"

"Is that Scarlett Johansson?" She pointed over his shoulder toward the door.

"Oh my god." He snapped his neck toward the door and jumped up in his seat. "Where? I need to ask her to marry me. I've been meaning to get around to it."

I chuckled under my breath.

Rome sighed when she'd accomplished what she set out to do.

When Christopher realized the actress wasn't there, he turned back around. "What the hell? Was she really there?"

"Yes," Rome lied. "She must have walked by already. You know New Yorkers are fast."

"Damn." He slammed his hand on the table. "My future wife slips out of my grasp…"

"You said the same thing about Blake Lively and Kate Beckinsale."

"I'm Mormon," he said. "I can have three wives."

Now I actually laughed.

"Like you're man enough," Rome said under her breath.

"Oh, I'm man enough." Christopher pointed his thumb into his chest. "Just take my word for it.

Patricia has been calling since our date in the bathroom. The ladies always want more."

Well, Patricia was a whore, so that wasn't surprising.

"Let's change the subject before I throw up," Rome said.

"Good idea." Christopher faced me again. "So, am I going to be seeing you around for the near future?"

"Christopher!" Rome was about to smack him. She grabbed my arm. "Just ignore him. I swear, he's just trying to embarrass—"

"Yes." I looked him in the eye as I spoke. "I'll be around as long as Rome wants me."

Her hand immediately loosened around my arm, taken aback by what I said.

Christopher nodded with a smile on his face. "Awesome. So, like, should we do something together? Get to know one another?"

I'd never met family members before. But Christopher was there the night we met, and I actually liked the guy. There was no way around it, and I didn't mind getting to know him. Actually, we were a lot alike. "Sure."

"Cool," Christopher said. "You want to go to a strip club tonight?"

Rome narrowed her eyes at him. "You aren't taking Calloway to a strip club."

"Not my cup of tea anyway." It wasn't a line to get Christopher to like me. I really did prefer clubs like Ruin. Women didn't dance around for you to see. Instead, you went and grabbed what you wanted and dominated. That was the kind of pleasure I enjoyed.

"Lame," Christopher said. "Just when I thought I liked you."

I chuckled.

"You want to go to the Yankee game with me and some friends tomorrow night?" he asked. "I've got an extra ticket."

I didn't follow sports religiously, but I enjoyed them. "Sounds cool."

"You really don't have to hang out with him," Rome said. "It's not a big deal—"

"I want to." Rome clearly wanted to keep us apart, but I wanted to get closer. The best way to dig up dirt on her was from someone who knew her better than anyone else.

Christopher nodded in agreement. "Rome, I really like this guy. Keep him around, and give him a real chance."

A real chance, huh? That was interesting. "She doesn't have a choice. She's stuck with me." I wrapped my arm around her shoulders in the booth, keeping her tucked under my arm like I owned her.

Rome's cheeks tinted, and she tried to hide her smile.

She should take my words literally—because that was exactly how I meant them.

Chapter Nine

Rome

"You need to chill out." I brought the bottle of wine to the tiny table in front of the couch in my apartment. I popped the cork and poured two glasses, sitting on the floor while Christopher sat in the chair.

"Me? No." He swirled the wine before he took a drink.

"I'm serious. I like this guy."

"I know." He waggled his eyebrows. "He's a stud."

"Stop checking him out."

"I'm not. I just have a healthy respect for good-looking people. If he wasn't seeing you, I'd ask him to pick up girls with me. Dude, we would dominate every bar in Manhattan. Women with their best friends would be lining up to take a ride on the pony express."

Vomit filled my mouth like lava from a volcano. "Don't be gross. I'm your sister."

"I'm not being gross. Just being myself."

Christopher meant well, and I knew he had a heart of gold, so it was impossible to be mad at him. His talkative nature and constant need to make a joke made him endearing, despite how annoying he could be. In spite of everything he'd been through, he still saw the world in a positive light. People were innately good, and he chose to believe people would do the right thing when faced with a difficult decision. "Just don't talk about me when you go out with him tonight."

"How am I going to do that?" he asked incredulously. "The whole reason we're hanging out is because of you."

"I just mean, don't tell him anything too personal. We're still pretty new, and there's a lot he doesn't know about me." I didn't want to talk about the past because it was bleak for both of us, but I had to get my point across.

"He doesn't know?" His eyebrow arched toward the ceiling, and he held his glass in his hand. It was half-empty, and he would need a refill in about a minute.

"No."

"Why?"

"We've only been seeing each other for a few weeks. I don't want to dump my emotional bullshit on him."

He stared into his wine then swirled it without taking a drink. When he sighed and put the glass down, I knew a serious conversation was coming. "Alright, you know me. I don't like to get all serious and crap. But there're a few things I gotta say to you. First of all, this guy is seriously into you. How do I know that? Believe me, I just do. I'm a guy, and I understand guys."

I hoped Calloway was into me, because I was really into him. My thighs wanted to squeeze his waist while his cock rammed into me. My body hummed to life anytime he was near, and he made me come so hard that I felt like the sexiest woman alive. On top of that, he was sweet and kind, and his heart was in the right place. There was nothing sexier than a generous man who committed his life to helping other people. He was so perfect I questioned if he was real. There must be something missing, some skeletons in his closet.

"Second of all, you can't have a relationship unless you're totally honest with him. So don't hide your past like you're ashamed of it. Shit went down, but you got out. Look at you now. You're the strongest chick I've ever met. If anything, it'll just make him admire you more. And if it doesn't...he's not man enough for you."

"He's definitely man enough." There was no doubt about that. He was the strongest and most confident man I'd ever come across. It was no wonder why my knees grew weak for him. I'd been searching for someone like him my entire life, and the idea of finding him scared me deep inside.

Because what if I was wrong?

"That's sweet of you to say, Christopher." He picked on me like every brother in the world, but once in a while, he complimented me in a way no one else ever did. He never lied to me, so when he did say something sweet, it was from the heart. "But it's really early in our relationship, and he's not even my boyfriend."

"He didn't make it seem that way."

He gave us the label when we worked at the food drive last weekend. At the time, I thought he was just jealous and possessive. We hadn't talked about it since, and I thought it was too soon for either of us to assume we were exclusive. I really liked him, but I didn't walk into any situation blind. "He's just..." I searched for an explanation, but I couldn't find one. "Just don't tell him anything. When I'm ready, I'll say something."

Christopher would obey my wishes even if he gave me shit about it. That was certain. "Whatever, Ro. You've got a Prince Charming at your feet, and you're too scared to look at him."

I changed the subject because this conversation was running too deep—and becoming repetitive. "You want to watch *Die Hard*?"

"Thank god." He turned his body toward the TV. "I'm terrible at these gossip girl nights."

***

Toward the end of the movie, a knock sounded on my door.

"Who stops by at ten?" Christopher asked from his place on the couch. "It better be Prince Charming."

"Don't call him that." Calloway was so manly he made Prince Charming look like a girl. He wasn't bendable and breakable. He was authoritative and powerful. He understood I could take care of myself and respected it. He was much better than Prince Charming.

"You're right," Christopher said. "That would make you a princess. And you're way too ugly to be a princess."

I looked through the peephole and saw Michael on the other side. I suspected it was him. He was the only person who came to my apartment at this hour. He wore a baggy sweater with holes in the sleeves, and his backpack was over his shoulder.

I opened the door. "Hey, honey." He only came by when his dad was drinking and trashing the small apartment they had in Brooklyn. There weren't many places for Michael to hide, so I told him he could always come here. I smiled and tried to get his mind off his hardship. "I missed you." I pulled him against my chest and gave him a hug, the kind he never got from his mother.

"Hey, Ro," he said quietly. "Do you mind if I—"

"I was just about to order a pizza. Are you hungry?"

"Yeah, sure."

"Great." I guided him inside and set up the table for him. "We were just watching a movie."

Christopher waved. "Hey, Michael. How's it going?"

Michael nodded back. "Good. You?"

"Just watching *Die Hard* and drinking wine," Christopher answered. "So can't complain."

Michael smiled slightly then took his seat at the table.

"Want to watch the movie with us?" I asked. "We've seen it a million times, but it's Christopher's favorite."

Christopher threw his fist into the air. "Die Hard!"

Michael chuckled. "Nah, it's okay. I have to do some homework."

"Alright. We'll try to keep it down." I squeezed his shoulder and gave him another smile, feeling my chest ache for this amazing kid. He worked so hard and he was so sweet, but his father didn't know how to appreciate him. It broke my heart so many times there was nothing left to break. I wanted to contact the police and social services, but Michael begged me not to. He said he would never forgive me if I did. "The pizza will be here soon."

"Thanks, Ro." He opened his textbook and binder and began to work.

I returned to the couch beside Christopher.

My brother gave me a grim smile then wrapped his arm around my shoulder. He pulled me into his side for a quick hug, telling me everything he couldn't say with words. He was proud of me for helping someone who couldn't help themselves, knowing we weren't so lucky when we were that age.

Chapter Ten

Calloway

Christopher introduced me to the guys before we entered the park. Young and affluent, they reeked of Wall Street experience and money. In jeans and polo shirts, they looked like they grew up in the Hamptons and moved to the city for work. Christopher shared some similarities, but overall, he was nothing like the other two.

We went to the concession stand, and not surprisingly, Christopher only ordered a bag of chips and a beer for lunch. I loved ballpark food, so I got the chili dog and fries without feeling any shame for it. We took our seats near the dugout and watched the game, heckling the players from the other team and having a good time of it.

Sometimes, I forgot Christopher was Rome's brother altogether. He was laid-back and easy going, and it wasn't hard for us to form a genuine friendship. He had the natural charisma that made everyone want to be his friend. I was a little cold on the outside, an exterior so hard it was impossible to break through. Christopher clearly didn't notice.

In the fifth inning, I mentioned Rome for the first time. "What does Rome say about me?"

Christopher smirked before he took a drink of his beer. "You want the scoop?"

"Yeah. Is she really into me? Or do I need to step up my game?"

"Nah, your game is fine. She's smitten."

Yes. "Cool." Rome kept a noticeable wall between us, keeping me a safe distance away at all times. But when we fooled around, she couldn't get enough of me. She pulled me harder into her, either my hips or my face. "Sometimes, I can't read her."

"You and every guy in America." He chuckled at his own comment then reached into his chip bag. "Even I can't read her sometimes. She puts on a brave front for the world, but she's just scared like the rest of us."

"Scared of what?"

"You know, getting hurt. Making mistakes. Shit like that."

I wanted to know more, and I knew I'd have to push for answers. A gentleman would wait for the lady to spill her secrets, but I wasn't a gentleman. I was after her for one reason only—to be her Dom. "Bad breakup?"

"You could say that." He kept his eyes on the game and didn't give me any more information. He brushed off the questions like an experienced lawyer deflecting an incriminating interrogation from the judge. "Rome's had a hard life. She acts tough, because she is, but underneath that armor, she's just as vulnerable as anyone else."

I drank my beer and tried to think of my best move. This guy was loyal to his sister, and he wouldn't tell me a damn thing unless he thought it was necessary. "Sometimes it seems like she's trying to push me away. I told her I was her boyfriend, and she seemed uncomfortable by the thought. When I wanted to move our relationship forward, she hit the brakes. I haven't dated in a long time, but I know that's not how it's supposed to go."

"Why not?" He winked. "You're a hit-it-and-quit-it kind of guy?"

"Something like that." I wouldn't count my time with Isabella as a relationship, just an arrangement. I hadn't asked a woman on a date in so long I couldn't remember the last time. It was something I had no interest in until that fireball walked into my life and turned my world upside down.

"I always thought when I met the right one, I'd keep my dick in my pants." He chewed on a chip loudly, crunching it to pieces between his teeth. "But that hasn't happened to me yet. I want kids and a house outside the city someday. But she's gotta be hot, you know? Like, so hot that the sex never gets old."

"I understand."

"Is that what Rome is to you?"

The question unnerved me because it was so personal. I didn't want to lie through my teeth and pretend I was looking for a woman to settle down with. Monogamy was doable with the right partner but romance and marriage...never gonna happen. Christopher basically asked me if Rome was the one I'd been searching for. "I'm not sure. All I know is, I've never met anyone like her, and I want more than what she's giving me."

"Well, I hope you have a lot of time on your hands because it's gonna be a while. But if it makes you feel any better, she's been easy on you. Other guys get maybe a date or two before she pulls the plug. And the guys are usually pretty nice too."

What was different about me?

"So it's safe to say you've got the best shot of any guy in this city. Whatever you're doing, keep doing it."

All I was doing was making her mine.

And she would be mine—eventually.

***

When I was sitting at my desk at work the following morning, I couldn't stop thinking about Rome. I pictured her underneath me, her wrists secured to my headboard with her legs wrapped around my waist. I was thrusting inside her, dominating that pussy and making it mine. The thought was so arousing I was hard in my slacks and seriously tempted to jerk off.

Fooling around was satisfying, but it would never compare to fucking. I couldn't wait for that moment when she finally spread her legs and allowed me to take her—to take all of her until there was nothing left.

It'd only been two weeks.

Two more to go.

It felt like a goddamn eternity.

I straightened my tie before I pulled out my phone and texted her. *Sweetheart.* I commanded her attention before I elaborated, wanting all her focus like the Dom I was.

159

The three dots appeared. *Sexy.*

My eyebrow immediately arched at the nickname. I was expecting a question in response, not a tease. *You're coming over for dinner tonight. Be there at 7.*

Bossy, aren't we?

Baby, you have no idea. *I suppose.*

What are we having?

For an appetizer, you. And for the main course, me. She didn't know the half of what I wanted to do with her. If she did, she would run away screaming.

Sounds delicious.

I'll see you at 7. No panties.

Pardon? I could hear her attitude through the phone. I could even picture her hand on her hip, her eyes burning in molten fire.

You heard me. No panties.

The three dots disappeared. Instead of being concerned I chased her off, I was confident it pulled her closer. Her thighs had to be pressed together, and her pussy would be slick thinking about what my mouth was going to do with her. The second she walked over the threshold, I would yank up her dress and inspect her obedience.

I hoped she disobeyed me.

Because I would love to punish her.

***

A little after seven, she arrived. She wore a black dress with a thick jacket on top. Knee-high boots were on her feet, and a red scarf was wrapped around her slender throat. She held a bottle of wine, trying to be polite.

I didn't care about the wine.

I put it off to the side then inspected her further. Her long hair was straight and full, framing her beautiful face and highlighting the gorgeous color of her eyes. She didn't wear tights under her dress, making for easy access.

I didn't say a word to her.

She didn't say anything to me.

I wrapped my arms around her waist and pulled her close, feeling her tits press against my chest. I wanted her nipples to grind against me, hard and pointed. I wanted her to come to my doorstep wrapped only in a jacket and shoes— nothing on underneath. But this turned me on just as much.

I brushed my lips past hers without giving her a kiss. A quiet sigh escaped her lips, so muted I barely heard it at all. She smelled like roses and Christmas, mixed together in a beautiful package.

My hand automatically fisted her hair so I had the right grip on her, and I yanked her head back so she was exposed to me. The fact that she allowed me to do it turned me on more. She could easily fight me, but she didn't.

I kissed the corner of her mouth, covering her freckle with kisses. I loved that thing and that it contrasted against her pale skin. Naturally, it turned me on—the only flaw to her perfection. "I missed you." My fingers tightened around her hair, securing her like a boat to shore. She hadn't given herself to me yet, but I was taking her—bit by bit. I kissed the other corner of her mouth before I finally pressed my mouth against hers—right in the center.

God, it was good.

Her plump lips felt heavenly against mine, so soft and smooth. I remembered how that scorching mouth felt around my cock. So tight and wet. Just a simple kiss from her was erotic. My tongue slipped in when I tried to restrain it, and that made my cock press tightly against the zipper in the front of my jeans.

I wanted to push her up against my door and fuck her.

My hands glided down her back, feeling the curve until I reached the dip just above her ass. My fingers kept moving down, feeling her perky cheeks before I reached her thighs. I grabbed the fabric of her dress and pulled it to her stomach, revealing the lower half of her body.

My fingers returned to her ass, and that's when I felt the fabric of her thong.

She disobeyed me.

I kissed her harder, bruising her lips. "What did I say?"

"I don't care what you said."

I guided her against the door until her back was pressed into the wood. My mouth was still pressed to hers, and her hair was securely wrapped in my fingers. "When I tell you to do something, you do it. Do you understand me?" I kissed her freckle again before I finally pulled away. I looked into her eyes, dominating her with my scolding look. I wanted her to obey, but having her not obey me was hotter.

"I don't do what you tell me. I don't do what anyone tells me." She matched my fire, her dominance trying to overshadow mine.

Like that would ever happen.

My fingers slipped down the front of her panties and found her clitoris immediately. It was already throbbing, telling me she liked this game more than she let on. I rubbed it vigorously, moving in a circular motion that made her gasp immediately. "I'm the exception." I pressed my mouth to her ear, my hand still fisted in her hair. "I'm your man, and you'll do exactly what I say."

She breathed hard as I lit her body on fire. "You aren't my man."

Now that just pissed me off. I rubbed her harder, rubbing the juice from her wet pussy over her clit. "I'm yours. You are mine. Period." My cock ached from pressing so hard against my zipper. It wanted release—inside her tight little cunt. "Take off your panties." My fingers slid across her soaked clitoris, using her own arousal as lubrication. I knew she enjoyed this and was about to come against my fingers. "Now." I growled in her ear then stopped my fingers altogether.

Her hips automatically bucked against me, wanting me to keep going. Her cheeks were flushed, and her eyes were watery from desperation.

I bit her earlobe. "Now."

She struggled against me, not wanting to obey my command but wanting to come. The only way around her headstrong temper was her sexual appetite. I'd been down this road before, and I always knew which way would win.

After a moment of hesitation, she pulled her black thong down her legs to her ankles.

The sweet taste of victory flooded my mouth.

I always won. Every single time. But winning against a worthy opponent made the triumph sweeter. "Good girl."

I hooked her legs around my waist then carried her to the top floor where my bedroom was waiting. It was dark inside, and I removed the comforter so only the sheets remained. I knew we were going to get dirty, so I was prepared.

I threw her on the bed before I yanked her dress off then her boots. She was in just her bra, a sexy black push up. I left it on then undressed in front of her, letting my cock come free. He leaked from the tip because he was ready for that cunt. Like he had eyes of his own, he pointed directly at it.

I got my shirt off then moved on top of her, her head on a pillow. Dinner was ready downstairs, and it was going to get cold, but the second I saw her, I needed to get off. And I could tell she did too.

I moved between her thighs then shoved two fingers inside her. Like last time, I felt her tight channel. She was seriously narrow, the soft flesh of her pussy wet and tight. I felt the lubrication drench my fingers before I pulled them out and ran them across my cock. I coated myself in her pussy juice, lubing myself from my tip to my balls.

She watched me, her green eyes darkening in desire.

I pumped myself a few times, testing the friction. "That's all you, sweetheart." I moved on top of her and pressed my hard shaft right against her throbbing clitoris. Both slick, we moved together.

She moaned the second our skin came into contact. Her hands moved to my arms and dug into my biceps, squeezing me like an anchor. She cried louder than when we dry-humped on her bed. Now she was delirious with pleasure, feeling our bodies mold together like they were made to become one.

My cock loved the feel of her wet clitoris. Her lips opened for me every time I moved, and the moisture made a distinct sound as we grinded over one another. It was nothing like sex, but it was still so fucking hot I wanted to come. This woman made the amateur stuff feel like the greatest sex I'd ever had.

"Calloway..." Her hands immediately went to my chest, her fingers spread out to feel the expansive muscle. "So good..."

"I can't wait to fuck you, sweetheart." She had the wettest and tightest pussy I'd ever felt. My cock would be in heaven when it finally happened.

She moved her hands up the back of my neck and into my hair, her palm cupping my cheeks as our bodies coiled around each other. "Fuck me now, Calloway. Please."

Holy fucking shit.

I kept grinding against her, my cock twitching in anticipation. He wanted to be deep inside her, buried in that little pussy and claiming it as his own. He wanted to fill her with so much cum it leaked down her ass crack.

"Please." She looked into my eyes, the green flickering like a forest fire. Her lips were parted and desperate for mine. She was already on the verge of an orgasm. She dug her nails deeper into me, begging me with her touch.

There was nothing hotter than a woman begging.

Oh, fuck.

I wanted to fuck her—so hard.

But she made me promise I wouldn't. If I broke my word, she wouldn't hold it against me. Any man would do it after listening to her beg twice. I was only human, and my cock only had one goal.

But I wanted her to trust me.

If she didn't, I would never get what I wanted.

And that was more important than fucking her for the first time.

Because I wanted to fuck her a lot more.

I pressed my mouth against hers and gave her a hard kiss, crushing my mouth against those soft lips. My tongue danced with hers, playing a sexy game of hockey. I grinded against her forcefully, moving over her soft, wet folds until I reached my breaking point.

I needed her to come.

"Baby, come for me." I gripped the back of her neck and rubbed my cock against her forcefully, making sex noises that amplified in my bedroom. It felt so good, and the burn blew up my shaft from my balls. I couldn't hold on much longer, not after listening to her pleas, but I needed her to get off first.

She obeyed my command unconsciously, and she came with a scream. Her nails dragged down my back slowly, moving all the way to the top of my ass. Her hips rocked with mine, wanting as much friction as she could get.

My bedroom reeked of sex.

"Calloway." She looked into my eyes with a wide-open mouth, her eyes holding the satisfaction I loved to see on a woman.

She finished, and now it was my turn. I exploded onto her stomach and chest, hitting her right below the chin and in the valley of her breasts. I kept squirting like a geyser, trailing all the way down to her belly button. My tip pointed into her navel, and I deposited the rest there.

My handiwork was a turn-on in itself. She was covered in my cum, her bra stained with my semen. I wanted her to stay like that forever just so I could look at her. I didn't go inside her, but I felt like I claimed her in an even more sexual way.

And I wanted to claim her like that again.

***

Instead of wearing the clothes she arrived in, she borrowed a pair of my boxers and a t-shirt. She looked sexy in my stuff, sexier than I ever did. She sat across from me at the kitchen table and sipped her wine.

I put the plates in front of both of us and began to eat. It was chicken caprese with ravioli and a side salad. It was more food than I would normally make for myself, but since she always ordered a salad, I wanted her to load up on some calories. She probably didn't want to eat what I made her, but I knew she was too polite to let it go to waste.

She cut into her chicken and ate slowly, taking her time as she enjoyed the two different sides. She sipped her wine intermittently and stayed quiet. After sex, I was usually tired and in a quiet repose. She seemed to be the same.

"Do you like your dinner?"

"It's amazing," she said. "You're a great cook."

"I'm glad to see you like other things besides salad."

She held my gaze but stopped eating. Her gaze was unreadable, but my words clearly meant something to her. She turned back to her plate and kept eating, not making eye contact with me again.

Did I hit a nerve?

She took a few bites of her ravioli, eating so slowly she reminded me of a sloth. Slow and steady, she continued the race and eventually ate everything on her plate, not leaving a single crumb behind. When one of the tomatoes fell off the chicken, she stabbed it with a fork and placed it in her mouth.

I was impressed. "You must have been hungry."

"I don't like to waste food."

"So you weren't hungry?"

"I was. I just don't normally eat that much."

Tension hung in the air, and instead of letting it continue to grow, I decided to cut through it. "Is there a reason why I hardly see you eat?"

She directed her callous eyes on me, her defenses coming up. I could tell when she was provoked. There was a metallic gleam in her eyes. Methodically, her brain worked to find a suitable answer. The question was simple and nearly harmless, but she absorbed it like it was a question under oath. "I feel guilty."

I hadn't finished my dinner, but now I lost my appetite. Without knowing exactly what she meant, I knew she was opening up to me, revealing an aspect of herself she'd never showed me before. The careful choice of her words and the strength of her voice told me it was a serious matter. "Why?" I set my fork down and gave her my full attention.

"I feel guilty eating when there are millions of people who are starving." She held my expression like a ruthless queen, absorbing every single reaction I made with my features. My house was unnaturally quiet. The sounds of traffic couldn't even be heard from outside. It felt like just the two of us in the known world.

"Starving yourself isn't going to change anything."

"I don't starve myself. I just consume as little as possible so nothing goes to waste. There's a difference."

This was a tense subject. I could tell by the tightness of her shoulders and her jaw. Instead of speaking my mind, I had to tread carefully. "You grew up hungry." I didn't phrase it as a question because that would feel like an interrogation. I would put my curiosity on the table and leave the door open, inviting her to elaborate or end the discussion altogether. Her mystery and majesty intrigued me, obsessed me, but I wanted her to confide in me because she wanted to, not because she was pressured to.

"Sometimes, I was locked in a basement without food or water for days. The longest I've ever gone is five."

I held her gaze but immediately felt my spine prickle with destruction. A kind of pain I'd never experienced washed through me, burning me with satanic fire. My sympathy only extended so far, but with her, she took all of it. She told me not to pity her, but I did. I felt terrible for her, so bad that I wanted to do everything I could to fix it. I wanted to buy her a new apartment, a car so she wouldn't have to take the subway, and anything else she could possibly want.

"When you're hungry for so long, you stop feeling hunger. It's a relief, but it's also the moment when your body starts to feed on itself, cannibalizing your muscles for energy. You barely have enough strength to move, let alone think. It's the most terrifying and humbling experience anyone can ever know. It makes you understand just how fragile you are, that you're susceptible to something everyone else takes for granted."

I hadn't blinked once. The pain in my chest was impossible to understand. I didn't feel sympathy for other people, not after what I'd experienced. People always thought they understood true suffering, but their problems were always petty. But with Rome, I'd met my match.

"You're doing it again."

I didn't look away. "Doing what?" My voice came out weak, and I didn't clear my throat. The weakness escaped, and I couldn't hide it.

"You feel bad for me."

"How can I not?" I would have to be dead to feel nothing.

"Because I'm one of the lucky ones." Her voice grew strong once again, full of life and vibrancy. "I got out of that situation, and now I'm free. I have access to food and water whenever I need it, and there's not a single person in the world who can deprive me of it. Most people don't get out. Most people don't survive. But I did. So don't look at me like that anymore. Please."

I rested my hand on the table but couldn't break my gaze. And I certainly couldn't change the way I felt. "You're asking me to do something that I can't do. I'm sorry."

"Just don't think about it." She pushed her empty plate off to the side then sipped her wine. She finally broke eye contact with me, staring at the surface of the table.

"Was Christopher in that basement with you?"

"No. He was in a different basement in a different place. We met once we were placed in the same foster care. I was fifteen, and he was sixteen.

We understood each other from the moment we met. Everyone has their own unique hardship, but ours were strangely similar. We decided we were family, brother and sister. And when families came to adopt us, we said we were a pair. If you wanted one of us, you had to have both."

The story was fascinating, but I wished it wasn't true. "I noticed he doesn't eat much either."

"He had it worse than I did. He was locked in his basement for a whole week."

How Christopher was so warm and fun was beyond me. Both of them were unnaturally strong and kind. Without knowing about their pasts, I wouldn't have guessed it. It was a miracle they got through it, let alone escaped with their minds intact. "After that, everything was okay?"

"No." She shook her head. "The man who adopted us seemed normal in the beginning. But once the social workers stopped checking on us because they assumed we were in a good home, his true colors came out. When we were both eighteen, we ran away and started our new lives."

I couldn't bear to hear any more of this story. Knowing she starved alone inside a dark basement was enough to make me snap. I couldn't handle any more of it. I'd assumed I was devoid of all emotion, unsympathetic to anyone and anything, but she proved how wrong I was. "I'm sorry for my behavior at the food drive." Now I understood why she was so upset. I understood I crossed a line I shouldn't have crossed.

"It's okay," she whispered. "You didn't know."

Now I wish I did.

"I didn't tell you this so you could treat me differently. I didn't explain my past so you would be delicate with me. I assure you, I'm a happy person who feels lucky to be alive. Give your sympathy to someone who truly deserves it."

No matter what she said, I couldn't give her what she wanted. I didn't look at her as weak. Quite the contrary. But the inexplicable need to protect her came forth. I wanted to buy her the world so she wouldn't have to worry about anything ever again. "And there was some asshole boyfriend in the picture too?" I probably shouldn't have said that, but now my rage was doing all the talking.

She eyed me suspiciously until she figured out how I knew that information. She was on the phone at her office when I walked inside and heard her entire conversation. Instead of showing her anger, she kept it back. "You don't want to hear about him."

"As your boyfriend, I need to know."

"When did we decide you were my boyfriend?" The fierce opponent I met in the bar was staring back at me. She wasn't easily provoked, but she became very defensive when she was cornered.

I didn't do the boyfriend thing, but I needed to be that for her so we could move on to something better—something greater. "The moment I laid eyes on you." When I spotted her in that bar, I knew I had to have her. Maybe she didn't feel the same way at the time, but within our first meeting, those feelings were there. The only reason why she hadn't let me in was because she was scared. If she hadn't been tormented in the past, we'd be in a much different place. "Take down your walls and let me in."

For the first time during the conversation, her eyes softened.

"Baby, let me in."

Chapter Eleven

Calloway

"How is she today?"

Theresa walked with me down the hallway and into the room. The furniture was white with hardwood floors, and vases full of fresh flowers were placed everywhere. That was something I recognized from my youth.

And it reminded me that some things never change.

"She's good." Theresa opened the door to the balcony. The patio looked over the garden outside. Roses, lilies, and dandelions soaked up the sun and moved in the slight breeze. It was an unnaturally warm day for winter, even in Connecticut. I felt like I walked into a different time.

She was sitting in her rocking chair, knitting a scarf. It was covered in kittens with different colored bows. Slowly, she rocked back and forth, the creak of the wood audible under her light weight.

"Laura, you have a visitor." Theresa kept her voice cheery, like this meeting was the most exciting one she would have for the day. "He's from Humanitarians United, and he's come to read to you today."

She turned to me with her dark, curly hair, her blue eyes no longer clear, but covered in a heavy fog. She stared at me with indifference, not recognizing a single feature on my face. Like I was a stranger and nothing more, she turned away.

No matter how many times I saw the look, it hurt.

I took the seat beside her and opened her favorite book, *Harry Potter*. "I'm Calloway. It's a pleasure to meet you."

She stared across the fields, her hands still knitting. "Calloway... I like that name."

Theresa eyed us both before she walked away and gave us some privacy.

"Thank you." I opened the book and turned to the first page. "I've got a book I think you might like."

"What is it?"

"*Harry Potter*."

She arched an eyebrow and turned her gaze back to her knitting. "Never heard of it."

I knew that would be her answer but it surprised me all the same. The hopeful side of me expected something different every time I came to visit. By some miracle, I hoped she would suddenly remember more than just her name. "I think you'll like it."

She finally stopped knitting and turned to me, her cheekbones high and her lips pursed in displeasure. "You're a good-looking young man. Are you married?"

"Thanks. And no, I'm not."

"No kids?"

"No." Even without remembering me, she was disappointed.

"What a shame." She started to knit again. "What do you do at Humanitarians United?"

"I'm the director."

"Wow. That's impressive."

"Thanks..." It was all the pride I was ever going to get from her.

"So why are you reading to an old woman like me?"

"You aren't old." In fact, she was way too young to be in here.

She smiled. "That's sweet of you to say, Cal." Naturally, she called me by my nickname, how everyone referred to me. She picked it up just the way she used to, not breaking her stride.

"I guess I'm a sweet guy."

"And you really aren't married?"

I smiled. "No." And I never would be.

"One day you will be, and you'll make some woman very happy."

"Yeah...I'm sure I will. So, shall I begin?"

"No. Can we just sit and talk? I feel like I don't talk to anyone around here."

My lips dropped into a frown, but I tried to hide it. "Of course."

"Tell me about yourself. Do you have any siblings?"

Jackson never came with me to the assisted living home. He said our mother died a long time ago. Visiting her ghost just made it more hurtful. "I have a younger brother named Jackson. We're only a year apart."

"That's wonderful. Are you close?"

Not really. "Yeah."

"Delightful. What about your parents? Is your father handsome like you?"

Jackson and I both looked like our father—it was frightening. "My father passed away eight years ago."

"Oh, I'm sorry," she whispered. "Your mother?"

I stared at her hair, seeing the gray strands creep into her dark hair. There were faint lines underneath her eyes, and the corners of her lips had tiny wrinkles that were hardly noticeable. In her youth, she was beautiful, but I still thought she was a pretty lady. "She passed away too."

"Dear, I'm so sorry." She reached for my hand and grabbed it, her cold fingers somehow feeling warm against my skin.

I squeezed her hand back, enjoying the limited affection I shared with her. I was just a man who came to visit her. She pitied me for everything that I lost, but I pitied her because she didn't remember anyone she lost. It wasn't a contest, but if it were, neither one of us won.

***

I'd just walked out of the office when she called me.

"Hey, sweetheart." My mood immediately picked up once I saw her name on the screen. After dinner the other night, it seemed like things were different between us, more intense in a good way. Some of her walls had come down, and she actually made an effort to let me in.

"Hey, sexy."

"I like that nickname."

"I think it's suitable."

"So what does my lady want?"

She paused when she listened to the way I referred to her. "To see if you wanted to do something tonight."

I wanted to do a lot of things tonight. "Come over for some popcorn and a movie. And a little bit of Frenching."

"Just a little?" she teased.

"Alright. Maybe a lot." And there would be a lot of pussy licking too.

"Sure. Want me to pick up some food on the way?"

"Nah, I'll make something." She never asked me to do something this casually before. It was like we were longtime partners who preferred to hide away from the rest of the world. All of this was new to me, but I caught on pretty quickly. I'd had a girlfriend once in high school but never since. "You just get that fine ass over here." And lubed up.

"Okay, I will. See you soon."

"Bye, baby." I hung up then walked down the sidewalk until I reached my car. I was glad she didn't invite me to her place because I hated that goddamn apartment. It was run-down with bad people around. The idea of her sleeping there without any protection put me on edge. I would buy her an apartment if she'd let me. But I knew how that conversation would go.

***

We sat on the couch with our wine and popcorn. The movie played on the TV, but neither one of us watched it. She crawled into my lap then straddled my hips, her pussy sitting right on the definition of my hard-on.

She ran her hands up my chest, her long hair pulled over one shoulder. "How was your day?"

I cherished the feel of her nails against my t-shirt. I loved the pressure and the memory of her gripping me the last time I made her come. "Good. Yours?"

"It was slow at the office. I've had a hard time getting donors."

"Want my advice?"

"Always." She tilted her head slightly, showing her slender neck.

"Go to the donors."

"I'm not a salesperson."

"Then don't act like a salesperson. Show them how their donation can get them some spotlight.

Maybe some of these people are genuine and want to help others. But most of them just want the credit. Play to their egos, and you'll always get what you want."

"You're clever, aren't you?" Her hands moved to my shoulders, and she massaged them gently.

"Very." I gripped her lean thighs then slowly slid my hands up to her ass. I loved that perky backside of hers. I couldn't wait to rub my cock between her cheeks before I shoved my thick cock in her puckered little asshole.

She adjusted her hips slightly, feeling my hard dick through my jeans. Anytime she was near me, I was hard because my mind was so obsessed with this woman—and no one else. "Can I ask you something?"

I didn't hesitate to reply. "Yes."

"It's personal."

She told me something personal about herself, so I could tell her something personal about me. "That's fine."

"When you said you were my boyfriend, did you mean we're exclusive?"

"You bet your ass I did." If she even hugged another man, I'd be livid about it. I hadn't fucked her, but she was mine. I wished I could give her a black ring to put on her right hand so people would stay the fuck away from her.

"So...you aren't seeing anyone else?" The hope picked up in her voice.

I swallowed the insult deep down into my gut. "No. You're the only woman I've touched, kissed, or pretty much looked at since I saw you in that bar."

Her eyes softened, and a small smile formed on her face. "You're such a catch. I guess I'm surprised you aren't playing the field more. You know, sowing your seeds."

"There's only one field I want to sow my seeds in." My cock twitched at the thought of her pussy overflowing with my cum. "I'm a one-woman kind of guy when I meet the right person." Isabella and I were exclusive because she was the perfect submissive. Prior to that, I had short-term flings with strangers. It was never about playing the field. I'd always been seeking the perfect sub to fulfill my fantasies like no one else ever could.

"And you think I'm the right woman?"

"Yes." I gripped her thighs and pulled her closer to me.

"Why?" She tilted her head to the side again, interested in my response.

I couldn't tell her the truth, that she looked like the ultimate woman I could break. She was strong as steel, and I didn't want to bend her, but snap her in two. One day, I would come clean about my intentions. But, for now, I couldn't. "It's one of those situations where you can't explain what you see and what you feel. Like a rock deep in the pit of your stomach, you just know it's there. All I know is, when I saw you walk into that bar, I was a goner. And when you slapped me, with that fire in your eyes, I knew I'd met a woman powerful, strong, and resilient as fuck. And that turned me on like nothing ever has."

She hung on to every word, trying to understand what I meant. "You liked it when I slapped you?"

She put me on the spot, so I answered. "Yeah. You've got spunk. I like that."

"Even though I didn't bother to make sure I had the right man?"

I searched her face, concentrating on those beautiful green eyes that always took me to a peaceful place. "You did have the right man." I pulled her ass closer to me until her chest was right in my face. I leaned my head on the back of the couch and looked up at her, her dark hair forming a curtain around my face. My hand fisted the back of her head, gripping her strands. I looked up at her and listened to her breathing, noticing how uneven it was. It was the most romantic thing I'd ever said to a woman, and being romantic was never my intention.

She pressed her face into mine and kissed me softly, her lips desperate for mine in a restrained way. Her hands cupped my face, and she deepened the kiss, her bottom grinding over my cock.

It was the first time I didn't want sex. I was hard as hell and eager for her, but this was enough for me. Just feeling her lips was enough to satisfy me. I pulled her closer and continued the tender embrace. When I was with her, I was a different man. I wasn't so callused and hard. Somehow, I had a heart that I had assumed stopped beating a long time ago.

And I had a soul.

***

It was nearly midnight, and we both had work in the morning. On top of that, I had to go to Ruin and check on a few things. Jackson wasn't trustworthy when it came to the business side of things. He tried to be responsible but always got sidetracked by the company inside the club—not

189

that I blamed him. But that meant Rome needed to go home.

She was on top of my chest on the couch, her hair a mess across my shirt. A red blanket covered her torso and kept her warm, and my body was a natural heater to fight the cold. I didn't want to move her, but I didn't want to have a sleepover.

It practically gave me anxiety.

I sat up and moved her with me, my hands circling her petite waist. I adjusted her against my chest so she wouldn't tip over and fall back on the couch. A waft of vanilla and lavender hit my nose, her scent mingled with the light perfume she wore. Every time I smelled her, it was a little different. She was always changing it up like her outfits. "It's getting late. Let's get you home."

She moaned against my chest. "I'm too tired."

The soft side of me wanted to let her stay. She would be harmless in the bed beside me, fast asleep through the entire night. The following morning, I would wake up to the peaceful expression on her face. But the hard side of me always prevailed, and I knew letting her stay wasn't an option. "That's okay. I've got you." I lifted her from the couch and carried her toward the garage.

Lighter than air, she nearly had no weight. But when she struggled in my arms, I could feel the strength of her frame. "What are you doing?" She was slowly stirring, coming back to reality.

"I'm taking you home."

"What time is it?" She squinted at the clock on the microwave as we passed. "Oh, it's midnight. I'll just stay here, then. Not much point in going home right now."

I kept going because she wasn't staying here. "I don't mind, sweetheart." I grabbed my keys off the counter and walked into the garage.

She wiggled in my arms until she moved down to her feet. The look she gave me was like a laser beam. With high voltage and magnitude, she peered at me like a woman who could read my mind. "Do you not want me to sleep here?"

This was dangerous territory, and I would've rather avoided this conversation if possible. Things were going well between us, and I didn't want to move backward. "No. I just have to up early tomorrow—earlier than usual. I'd have to take you home around five, and no one should be awake that early." I relied on my charming grin to persuade her, using all my ammunition to get out of this war zone.

She must have seen something reassuring in my gaze because she bought my story. "Alright. I'm not a morning person, so I wouldn't appreciate that very much."

Crisis averted.

***

When I walked her to her door, I heard the loud bass coming down the hallway from one of the neighbors. At midnight on a Tuesday, it was obscene. The music amplified against the walls and must have disturbed the entire building.

Rome acted like she didn't notice anything. She got her key in the door and unlocked it. "Thanks for giving me a lift."

My eyes moved down the hallway and landed on the nearest door. I was pretty certain it was coming from that apartment. "Is this normal?"

"The music?" she asked. "Yeah, I just try to ignore it." She walked inside and set her purse on the entryway table. "I have a white noise machine, and it covers most of the sound."

I wanted to write her a check then and there so she could get the fuck out of that place. It was full of drug dealers and assholes. I didn't want her sleeping there alone, not when I didn't know if she was safe. I could tell her to move, but I knew she wouldn't take the suggestion well. And I couldn't have her stay over with me, or I'd have a meltdown. So there was no solution.

"Well, goodnight." She stood on her tiptoes and gave me a soft kiss on the lips.

The embrace didn't dim my anger. Usually, the touch of that full and wet mouth took me to a new place. But now, I was too annoyed to appreciate anything about her beauty. "Goodnight."

When she pulled away, she searched my gaze. Her eyes darted back and forth as she focused on mine. She picked up on my mood, feeling it through her skin like heat waves. "What is it?"

My eyes broke contact, and I stared across her tiny apartment. The veins in my forearms bulged, and my temple started to pound with a migraine. I was a man who always got my way, and the fact that I had to hold my tongue made me sick. "Have you considered moving?" I phrased it as politely as possible.

"Because of the music?" she asked. "He usually turns it off by one, so it's not a big deal."

It was a big fucking deal. She practically lived in the projects, and a beautiful girl like her shouldn't sleep in a place like this unprotected. If she lasted this long, she obviously knew how to look after herself, but that wouldn't stop the nightmares from killing me. "Because of everything."

She crossed her arms over her chest, the fire slowly coming into her eyes. "What are you saying?"

She already knew, so what was the point in me hiding it? "I don't think this is a place for a single woman—that's all."

"It's fine." Her voice was cold like chipped ice. "It's in my budget, and there aren't many bugs, so I'm grateful. A lot better than where I came from."

Just because she was used to shit didn't mean she should keep living in it.

"Don't worry about me. I've been living here for a while, and I like it."

Well, I fucking hated it.

She ignored the frustrated look on my face. "Goodnight, Calloway." She kissed my cheek then grabbed the door so she could close it.

I had no choice but to retreat. She was too headstrong to take a check from me. Even if I arranged some kind of stunt, she wouldn't buy it.

"Goodnight, Rome." I walked over the threshold and faced her.

"Don't worry about me. I'm a tough chick."

That didn't matter. No matter how fierce she was, she deserved to be taken care of. She deserved to walk into a palace of jewels. She deserved a crown made of all the stars in the universe.

She gave me a slight smile before she finally closed the door.

I stared at the black wood for nearly a minute before I decided what to do next. I walked to the apartment where the music was coming from and banged my fist against the door so loudly it rivaled the sound of the bass.

A man answered the door, looking like someone who just got out of jail for a double homicide. "What?" he yelled over the music, and I could still barely hear him.

I pulled out my checkbook. "How much will it take for you to pack and move?"

"Say what, asshole?"

"I want you out of this building tomorrow. And I'll give you ten grand if you do it. What do you say?" I wrote out the check and held it up. "I'm good for it."

He eyed the money in my hand, his eyes narrowing. Without hesitation, he snatched it and shoved it into his pocket.

"We've got a deal?"

He nodded then slammed the door in my face.

Chapter Twelve

Rome

I sat at my desk and ate my yogurt. I didn't get paid until Friday, so I had to make whatever was left in my fridge stretch for a few more days. At this time of the month, I always lost a little extra weight—but not on purpose.

I arranged a food drive that morning that would take place the following Saturday. It was a breakfast drive for the homeless in Brooklyn. From police reports, a lot of them were Vietnam vets who never found their footing when they returned home. Government constantly moved homeless people from one place to the next to get them off the street, but that didn't solve anything. What we needed was a new system to rehabilitate these people—not put them on a different sidewalk.

The door opened, and the sexiest man in New York walked inside. Wearing a black suit that made the black ink of my printer seem white, he walked inside and owned the room I paid rent to keep. He wore a silver tie and an ivory collared shirt, looking like he was running for president of the United States.

Every time I saw him, I got a little shaky.

He walked to my desk without saying hello, his eyes glued to my face like a predator searching for prey. When he looked at me like that, he didn't just make me feel desirable—he owned me down to the bone.

"What a nice surprise." I'd been seeing him for weeks, but he still made me nervous in that butterflies in the stomach kind of way. Stubble was thick on his cheek because he didn't shave that morning, and I kept picturing how it would feel against my thighs. I'd already felt that sensation a few times—and it never got old.

"I like to keep my lady on her toes." He leaned over the desk and kissed me, his stubble feeling good against my mouth. It was more than just a hello kiss. He let it linger longer than necessary because our lips felt so right together.

My lady. I liked being his lady. "You're turning me into a ballerina."

He pulled his lips away, but his face still hovered near mine. He looked at me with those beautiful, icy eyes and somehow made me melt.

"I'm taking you out to lunch." He glanced at my half-eaten yogurt. "For some real food."

Now that I'd started the yogurt, I had to finish. No way in hell was I throwing it away. "Sure. Just let me put this away." I slipped it into a zippered bag then placed it in the fridge in the breakroom. When I returned, Calloway didn't tease me about it like other people would. He respected my beliefs and didn't try to change them—one of the things I liked most about him.

He wrapped his arm around my waist as we walked down the street. His large hand fit comfortably wrapped around my frame. His fingers were warm as they gripped me tightly, and he kept me tucked into his side like I might fly away if I ventured off too far. "Anything particular come to mind?"

"No. I'll eat anything."

"How about pizza?"

I nodded. "I could go for some pizza."

We went to a small pizzeria and ordered. I got a single slice because I couldn't eat anything more than that. Just having someone buy me lunch made me feel guilty. Calloway never let me pay for anything when we went out together, and while it was sweet, sometimes I didn't know how to handle his generosity. I'd never forget the night I slept on the sidewalk, and some nice man gave me a hundred bucks for food. I burst into tears when I realized there were so many good people despite the evil ones. Calloway was one of those people, giving and selfless. That was probably why I was so smitten with him, nearly head over heels.

Calloway ate across from me, eating two slices and a salad. He didn't comment on my lunch or even look at my plate.

"Thank you for lunch."

His expression softened for an instant, but he tried to cover it up. "No problem, sweetheart."

"I hope you let me pay sometime."

He released a sarcastic laugh. "Don't count on it."

"Well, one of these days, it's gonna happen. Be prepared."

"Call me old-fashioned, but my lady doesn't pay for things."

"Call me progressive, but women are equal members of society."

He eyed me, the corner of his mouth still lifted in a grin. "I hope this isn't going to turn into a debate about feminism."

"Me neither."

"Because I do believe in feminism. But you bet your ass I'm gonna open every door for you and pay for all your things."

It was a direct contradiction to everything I believed in, but his words somehow made me feel warm. I didn't let anyone take care of me because I'd never been taken care of before. All I knew was how to survive and rely on myself to get what I needed. But that didn't mean the fantasy wasn't still alive deep in my heart. Calloway was man enough to be what I'd been missing my entire life. I knew it deep in my gut, and that was why I was still seeing him. Most guys didn't get a date in the first place. "I'll make a deal with you."

"I'm listening."

"I'll let you do all of those things if you let me do something."

"Such as?" He raised an eyebrow, unsure what to expect.

"If you let me take you out to dinner one time."

He shook his head. "I don't want to be taken out anywhere."

"Come on, Calloway. I think that's fair."

"No."

"I didn't realize you were so stubborn." I knew I was getting a rise out of him by pushing him. But he would only bend so far before he finally broke.

"I'm not stubborn."

"Then let me take you out one time."

He mumbled under his breath. "I can't believe I'm having this conversation…"

"Think about it. If you do this for me, we never have to do the check dance ever again. It sounds like a good deal to me."

His eyes narrowed with interest.

I knew he was taking the bait.

"Alright, I'll do it. If you never try to pay for anything ever again."

"Deal." I extended my hand to shake his.

He snatched my wrist quicker than a viper, and then turned it outward, exposing my wrist to the ceiling. He pressed a wet kiss to the soft skin, his tongue moving along the sensitive nerves of the area. His eyes were glued to mine the entire time.

My mouth went dry.

He returned my hand to the table because I'd lost all feeling. I couldn't even move. "Deal."

***

We sat across from each other at his dinner table and finished the pasta he made. He was a

202

pretty good cook, better than most guys I knew. Christopher considered a bag of Doritos a good dinner, and he hardly had food at his apartment. He claimed it stopped the women from sticking around, but I knew he was just lazy.

"Where did you learn to cook?"

He finished his plate entirely, only leaving a few streaks of sauce behind. "My mom taught me a few things. But mostly YouTube." He gave me that charming smile across the table, his eyes intense and playful at the same time.

He didn't talk about his personal life much, and I really didn't know much about him. "When did she pass away?"

"About seven years ago." His voice suddenly grew melancholy, like the subject was bringing him down.

I decided to change it. "Last week, when we were fooling around…"

His eyes picked up in interest when he stared at me. The blue color of his eyes was more vibrant than the deepest sea. He hung on to my every word without giving his thoughts away, his mind still wrapped in mystery.

"I'm kinda embarrassed to talk about it." I broke eye contact because I spotted the heat on his face. He knew exactly what I was referring to. It was obvious by the look in his eyes. "But I pretty much begged you to sleep with me, and you didn't. You have a lot more strength than I do." As soon as things got hot and heavy, I didn't care about my principles anymore. I just wanted this gorgeous man to fuck me into his mattress and give me the most profound high.

"It wasn't easy."

"I'm surprised you didn't do it."

He leaned back into the wooden chair, his wide shoulders looking menacing. "I made a promise to you, and I always keep my word. I want you to trust me, and I know I need to earn it. Hopefully, you're beginning to."

I was beyond beginning to. "I think you're a great guy, Calloway. Honestly, I'm not sure what you see in me. You can have the most beautiful woman in this city at the snap of a finger."

His gaze darkened. "I already do."

Instantly, my heart tightened in my chest, and the butterflies soared all over again. "That's sweet…"

"I mean it." It wasn't a cheesy line, and I knew he didn't mean it that way. He was a natural with words, saying the most beautiful things and making them absolutely sexy. Having a rugged and compassionate man like him chase me was a dream come true. I still didn't understand what I did to deserve it. "Want any dessert?"

My hand moved across my belly under the table. "No, thanks. I'm pretty full."

His eyes narrowed. "Not that kind of dessert."

***

I went down on him, taking his big cock deep into my throat. It was so thick and long it made tears pour out of my eyes. Even though my jaw nearly snapped trying to accommodate him, I loved every second of it.

He threw me back on his sheets then separated my thighs. His mouth trailed up my body to the valley between my breasts. He cherished the area with delicate kisses before he sucked each of my nipples into his mouth. Sometimes, he did it so hard I winced. But inexplicably, the pain felt incredible.

His mouth moved to my neck, slowly making its way up to my earlobe. He nibbled on the soft flesh before his tongue darted into my canal. His heavy breathing fell on my ear before he spoke. "I can't wait to fuck you, sweetheart."

My hands groped his biceps, feeling the power and strength underneath his skin. He was the definition of the ideal man, tall, rugged, muscular, and authoritative. I'd been searching for a man like this my entire life and assumed he didn't exist.

He held his face above mine and kissed me hard on the mouth. Our tongues danced together in desperation, wanting more of each other because we simply couldn't get enough. He went down on me and did a remarkable job making me come. I did the same to him, but we both needed more.

"I can't wait for you to be inside me either." It would be a tight fit, but I was sure he would make me wet enough that it wouldn't be a problem.

His eyes darkened in their typical way, clearly pleased by what I just confessed. "Are you on the pill?"

"No."

"Then you need to start. I'm not wearing a condom." He bossed me around like I was his employee, but when we were fooling around, I didn't mind it. In fact, I liked it. Sometimes, he grabbed me harshly, pinning my wrists above my head or yanking me into his side when another man came too close. They were all things I would normally despise. But with him, he could do no wrong.

"Okay."

Pleased by my lack of argument, he kissed me again. "You give amazing head, by the way."

"You do too." I could only assume he'd had years of practice.

"Your pussy is so sweet that I can't get enough." He sucked my bottom lip into his mouth. "Tastes like watermelon."

I wrapped my arms around his neck and my legs around his waist. His cock was hard against me even though he just came in my mouth less than ten minutes ago. Our sexual relationship was scorching hot, and I'd felt myself get burned a few times. "Maybe we should forget about the four weeks..." Two weeks was long enough. I didn't think I would rush into something so serious, but I didn't think I would meet someone like Calloway. I wanted to give him everything—every piece of me.

He growled against my mouth. "As appetizing as that sounds, we have to wait."

"Even if I beg?" I ran my hands up his chest and over the grooves of his abs.

He growled again. "Don't test me, sweetheart." He rolled off my body and lay beside me on his massive bed. The sheets were soft as rose petals, and the mattress was way more comfortable than the rock-hard bed in my apartment. If I fell asleep, I would never wake up. His house was so quiet. The traffic outside didn't permeate through his thick windows, and the blinding rays off nearby streetlights didn't flood into the bedroom. It constantly smelled like him—mint mixed with masculinity. It was starting to become my favorite place in the world.

He pulled me into his side and placed my leg around his waist, pulling us close together. His cock was still hard, but it always seemed that way. He placed one arm in the crook of my neck and the other around my waist.

I stared into his handsome face and thought he was the most perfect man in the world. Without even realizing it, I knew I'd started to fall for him. I wasn't sure when it began, perhaps the night at the charity gala, but I'd been falling fast and for a long time. "You're perfect, you know that?"

"Me?" The corner of his mouth rose in a smile.

"Yes." I rested my hand against his chest. "You."

"How so?"

"For one, you're sexy as hell."

He grinned from ear to ear. "I really like this conversation. What else?"

"You're compassionate. You help people for a living, and that's the sexiest thing I've ever seen."

He didn't say anything to that, hardly acknowledging it.

"You're a really good kisser."

He smiled again. "It takes two to tango, sweetheart. But, thanks."

"When I asked you not to feel bad for me, you listened."

His smile disappeared instantly.

"I've been looking for a someone man enough for me my whole life. I didn't think there were any real men out there."

"I'm definitely man enough for you." He gripped my hip then slid his hand to my lower back. His fingers dug into my skin with authority, claiming my body as his to enjoy. "I'll make every other man you've been with look pathetic."

My track record was pretty low, so that wouldn't be hard for him to accomplish. I had trust issues, so it was impossible for me to let anyone in. But Calloway was different, and I knew it. He carried the same kind of scars I did even if he didn't show it. I knew he understood me, respected me, and would never hurt me. "You already have."

He kissed the corner of my mouth and tightened his grip around my waist. "Did you ever slap the man you originally meant to slap?"

"Taylor's ex?"

"Yeah."

"Actually, no. After I made an idiot out of myself with you, I kinda forgot about it. She did too."

"He cheated on her."

"He was married with two kids and never told her—despicable."

He nodded in agreement. "If you can't be faithful, don't be in a relationship. It's that simple." He eyed my lips like he wanted to kiss me again. "I'm sorry for your friend."

"She bounced back. I just feel bad for his wife. She's married to an asshole, and she doesn't even know it."

"Taylor never told her?"

"No." She didn't want to break up a family and have that guilt on her shoulders for the rest of her life.

"Hopefully that was a one-time thing," he said. "And maybe now he appreciates his family."

I highly doubted it. "But I'm glad I slapped you instead of him. We wouldn't be here now if I hadn't…"

"That makes two of us." His hand moved up my spine until it dug into my hair at the back of my neck. He fisted it like always, grabbing the strands like reins. "And you can slap me again whenever you want."

I chuckled. "Maybe if you're bad."

His eyes darkened in intensity. "I'll be bad if you slap me."

My chuckles died away as the confusion took over. I thought he was kidding about the slaps, but now I couldn't tell. "What?"

He kissed me slowly on the mouth and changed the subject, making me focus on the way his soft lips felt against mine. He gave me some of his tongue, his breaths coming out hot and fiery. He suddenly pulled away and settled next to me again like nothing happened. "You asked me if there was a reason why I help people. You asked if I suffered something myself."

I remembered that conversation. When he told me his childhood was normal and he didn't suffer, I wasn't sure if I believed him. He seemed so dark at the time. "I remember."

"Well, there is a reason. I just don't like to talk about it."

"You don't have to talk about it now if you don't want to." He never pressured me to open up about my past. He only took what I gave and appreciated it. I didn't want to push him when he didn't want to be pushed.

He ignored my last statement. "My dad was a substance abuser. Mainly coke and alcohol. When he took too much, he became a different person. He did things to my brother and me that we'll never forget. And he did things to other people...people who didn't deserve it. I was grateful when my mother passed away, so she didn't have to know about the shit that happened."

My chest ached in response, feeling the exact same kind of pain he felt. Whatever he felt, I felt it twice as hard. I'd suffered a lot in my young lifetime, but knowing someone else went through it didn't make me feel better. In fact, it made me feel worse. "I'm so sorry."

"It's okay. It was a long time ago."

"It doesn't matter how long ago it was," I whispered. "You never forget."

His fingers gently glided through my hair and down the back of my neck. "No. But it gets easier."

It was the first time he told me something private about himself, and I was grateful he shared it. "Thanks for telling me."

"You can trust me. And I can trust you."

"Yeah…it seems so."

He kissed my neck before he sat up and eyed the time on the clock. "It's getting late…" It was his somewhat polite way of excusing me.

My neck practically snapped at the whiplash I just received. One moment, he was sweet and open, sharing a secret he never told anyone else. And the next, he was kicking me out of his bed again.

What was his deal?

"I have to work in the morning, and I know you do too." He pulled the covers back and sat up. "Come on, I'll take you home."

"Uh, seriously?"

"Seriously, what?" He turned his body and looked at me, his chiseled physique unable to save him this time.

"Don't couples sleep together?"

"Yeah. But what does that have to do with this?"

"Why don't you want me to sleep over?" I sat up and pulled the sheets over my chest, hiding my nakedness now that the sweet and tender moment was over.

"It's not that I don't want you to sleep over. It has nothing to do with you."

"Then why are you kicking me out?"

"I'm not kicking you out," he argued. "It's just getting late, and we should get some rest."

"And we can't do that here?" This guy was perfect in every way except for this. It seemed like he was hiding something, but what? "Are you seeing someone else?" I said the words but couldn't force myself to believe them. I said them because I was mad more than anything.

Now his eyes turned hostile. He glared at me like I'd just crossed a line drawn in the center of the bed. "Don't insult me like that ever again."

"I'm just asking—"

"Then don't ask. I told you I'm yours and you're mine. Don't doubt me like that ever again."

"Then explain to me—"

"I don't owe you an explanation. I don't owe you a goddamn thing." He got out of bed, his body thick and threatening. "All I asked was to take you home, and you turned it into something else. Maybe I'm not ready to sleep with you yet. You won't fuck me, and I respected that, so you need to respect this." He grabbed my clothes and threw them at me. "Get your ass dressed, and let's go."

My jaw dropped to the floor because I was shocked by what he said. With the snap of a finger, his anger exploded, and he told me off like I did something terrible to him. Just a second ago, my heart was aching for him. Now, I just wanted to slap him upside the head. "Don't talk to me like that."

He pulled his shirt over his head and got his jeans on. "I'll say whatever I damn well please. Get over it."

Now my anger reached an all-time high. He turned into a different person right before my eyes, and I didn't like it one bit. My rage took control over my body, and I marched to him then slapped him hard across the face. I put my entire body into it and hit him as hard as I could, making my palm slap audibly against his hard cheek.

He turned with the hit, his face snapping to the right as the momentum of my palm collided with his skin. The rest of his body remained stationary, his wide and powerful shoulders not shifting a single inch. His chest rose and fell with heavy breaths, his body tense to the breaking point.

He slowly turned his gaze back to me, his blue eyes suddenly looking gray. His heavy breathing continued, and his powerful chest rose with every breath. His nostrils flared as he looked down at me, and like a rhino free from his cage, he was about to charge.

I held my ground and dared him to make a move.

He suddenly reached for me, grabbing me by the neck and pulling me into him.

I threw my elbow down and severed the touch before I slapped him again.

His eyes widened, and his body tensed even further. "Fuck."

I didn't know what was happening between us, but I couldn't tell if it was good or bad. I should've felt threatened, even in danger, but I didn't. Scorching heat flowed between us, and I felt it burn me all the way through. Inexplicably, I wanted to slap him again—and again.

He snatched me again, this time, getting both of my wrists behind my back before he threw me onto the bed. He pinned me down with his size and kept me pressed into the mattress without any hope of escape.

He squeezed my wrists so hard they started to ache.

"Slap me again and see what happens." He pressed his cock into my thigh, the definition obvious through his jeans. He was harder than ever before, solid as steel. "Slap me if you want to get fucked so hard you can't walk. Slap me if you want to get fucked in your mouth, your pussy, and your ass. Do it."

My nipples hardened so much they actually hurt. They were sore as they rubbed against the padding inside my bra. They ached like someone just sucked them raw. My thighs tightened together as a pool of moisture flooded between my legs. Instead of being scared and appalled, I was insanely aroused.

He continued to stare into my eyes with the same threatening expression, promising to make good on his word if I didn't take him seriously. He finally released my wrists and stepped away, his shoulders still tense with imminent threat.

I didn't say another word.

I didn't know what was happening. I didn't know what just happened between us. It was borderline violent and inexcusable, but at the same time, I'd never felt so alive. The blood in my veins sang because it felt so wrong, it felt right.

"I'll take a cab." I just wanted to get away from him as quickly as possible. Despite how aroused I was, I needed to run. I needed to think about what just happened here and make some sense of it.

"No. I'm taking you home." The quiet threat in his voice told me not to disobey him. If I did, there would be serious consequences.

And I believed him.

Chapter Thirteen

Calloway

I stormed into the office and grabbed the nearest table before I picked it up and smashed it into the ground. Two of the legs popped off, and the wood cracked right down the center. "Motherfucker!" The lamp fell on the ground but didn't break, so I grabbed it and threw it against the wall. Like glass, it shattered.

Jackson closed my office door and stared at me in shock, his lips pressed tightly together like he was preventing himself from saying something that would set me off. He locked the door from the inside and continued to watch me, his eyes following my movement. "Bad day, huh?"

"Fuck off, Jackson. I'm not in the mood." I walked around my desk and dropped into the large leather chair. Not a single picture frame was on my desk because I didn't have anyone waiting for me at home—not even a dog.

I rested my elbow on the desk then rubbed my temple, trying to rid my head of the migraine that appeared from nowhere thirty minutes ago. Blood pounded in my head and ignited my temper even more. I could've killed someone—with my bare hands.

Jackson slowly trailed farther into my office, his hands in his pockets. "I'm guessing this has something to do with that vanilla girl?"

Vanilla girl.

How ingenious.

He lowered himself into the chair facing my desk. "What happened?"

"Stop asking me shit like we're friends."

"We aren't friends. We're brothers. So talk to me."

I didn't tell anyone anything. I'd been that way my entire life. The more someone knew about you, the easier it was for them to tear you down. But Jackson was right. He was my last family member in the world, and I shouldn't take him for granted. One day, I could lose my mind just the way my mother did, and my life would have absolutely no meaning—because I wouldn't remember it. "I fucked it up."

"What happened?"

"We were lying in bed and everything was fine. Then I told her I would take her home."

Jackson remained quiet because he knew there was more to the story.

"She wanted to stay, and I said no."

"Why did you say no?"

"I don't do sleepovers. Never have and never will." Isabella understood this because she was my submissive. I told her it was a hard limit for me, and she never broke it. She listened to my word like it was rule of law. Why couldn't Rome do the same?

"You told her that?"

"No. I didn't really give her an explanation. I lost my temper and said a lot of stupid shit. Then she slapped me...and that fucked things up even more."

"She slapped you?" He grinned. "She's got balls."

She absolutely does. "She slapped me a few more times, and I almost raped her on my bed. Somehow, I found the strength not to. Immediately, I switched into my dominant side. I told her to obey me or I would make her obey me. I completely lost control. And I'm pretty sure I lost her too." She wasn't ready to see that side of me. I didn't ease her into it or even explain what kind of man I was. She just saw the beast come out without any warning.

"Shit..."

"Yeah." I kept rubbing my temple, wishing the night was just a nightmare.

"Again, why didn't you just let her sleep there?"

"How am I supposed to come down here when she's sleeping in my bed? She'll know I go somewhere at night, and I'll have to explain Ruin...and she won't understand right now. We aren't there yet."

"Honestly, I don't think you're ever going to get there."

My blood went cold. "What's that supposed to mean?"

"Open your eyes, man. She's never going to be a sub. She's vanilla, and we both know it. Do you really want to hide who you are? Why do we run this place? It's so we can be ourselves with people just like us. With this chick, you're going to have to be someone you aren't. Is that what you really want?"

It didn't take me long to find my answer. "No."

"Then cut her loose, and go back to Isabella. She'll take you back in a heartbeat."

That was where I met my obstacle. "But I don't want to go back to Isabella. I want Rome." I couldn't deny it because the feeling was deep in my gut. Despite her plainness, I craved her. I wanted to drag her into the dark with me, becoming swallowed in the shadows until we were one with the darkness. I didn't want to do it with anyone else—only Rome.

"Well, you can't have vanilla girl. You tried and failed."

"I didn't fail. We just...hit a rough patch."

"After what happened, she's not going to want anything to do with you, man." He shook his head, his hard jaw stern just like mine. He had the same predatory look I had—the same look our father had. "She's going to think you're a freak. A monster."

Unfortunately, he was probably right about that.

Chapter Fourteen

Rome

"Yo, what's up?" Christopher walked inside my apartment and grabbed a beer from the fridge. "What's the big emergency?" He fell on the moth-eaten couch and put his feet on the coffee table. He turned his ear toward the door like he was listening for something. "It's awfully quiet around here. Did someone move out?"

"The guy across the hall did."

"The one that plays music all night long?"

"Yeah."

He nodded. "Good riddance."

I sat beside him with a glass of wine and the full bottle in hand. "I don't know what to do about Calloway. It might not work out."

Christopher almost spit out his beer as he swallowed. "Whoa, hold on." He wiped his mouth on his collared shirt and set the beer on the coffee table. "What did you say?"

"We got into a fight last night, and weird stuff happened..."

With both eyebrows arched, he stared me down. "You're going to need to be more specific than that."

Christopher and I weren't related by blood, but it was still weird to talk about my love life with him. It was something neither one of us ever mentioned. "We were in bed and…" I felt awkward just saying that much. "And I wanted to sleep over, but he wanted me to leave."

His eyes narrowed as his gaze darkened. "He slept with you then kicked you out? Now that's a dick move."

"We didn't sleep together. We just…yeah." God, this was weird.

"Oh…gotcha." Christopher would normally make a joke or two, but he kept his maturity unnaturally high. "Did he say why?"

"No. And then I got kinda mad and said some things I didn't mean…that he was going to go out and hook up with someone. Then he yelled at me and told me to mind my own business. So I slapped him." I cringed at that last part.

"Shit. That sounds like a real fight."

"It got out of hand." To say the least.

"Why are you thinking about stepping away? Couples fight all the time."

"But don't you think it's weird he won't let me sleep over? It's the second time he's done that."

Christopher grabbed his beer from the table and took a drink. "Honestly, I'm on his side for this one."

"What?" Seriously?

"You haven't been seeing each other long, and you haven't slept together. If the guy doesn't want you to sleep over, I think he's entitled to that. Frankly, if a woman said that to a man, no one would blink an eye over it. He would have to respect that and back off. This is a double standard."

My jaw dropped. "It's so not a double standard."

"Sorry, sis. It is."

"But you don't think it's strange he won't tell me why?"

He shrugged. "Have you told him everything about you?"

"Most of it."

"I don't know... I think everyone is entitled to a little privacy. If you guys had been dating six months, I would say otherwise. But right now, I think he's right. And I think you need to apologize to him for slapping him."

"He was an ass to me."

"Yeah, he probably was. But he never raised a hand to you, right?"

I knew he had me.

"Double standard—again."

I covered my face with my hands because I knew he was right.

"I don't think you should break up with him. But I think he's probably going to break up with you."

My heart fell into the pit of my stomach when the truth seared my blood. Christopher was right, and I knew he was. The situation was bad all around, but I was the one who lost my temper first. We were lying together so peacefully when he suddenly pushed me away. Deep down inside, I knew that was the real reason I was upset. I simply didn't go about it in the right way.

"At least I'll have a stud to pick up girls with. The guys from the office are too nerdy."

"Christopher." I wasn't in the mood for his jokes.

"What? If you break up, I can't be friends with him anymore?"

"You can't pick up chicks with him."

"Why?" He finished the rest of his beer and set the empty bottle on the table. "I won't bring it up to you or anything."

I rolled my eyes because he didn't get it.

A knock sounded on the door. It was loud and slow, telling me a man was on the other side.

Christopher's eyes darted to the doorway. "Wonder who that could be?"

Shit. Calloway must have stopped by on his way home, and he was going to kick me to the curb before he moved on with his life. The end was here, and now I couldn't swallow it. My body came alive for him in a way it never did for anyone else. Did I ruin the best thing that ever happened to me?

Christopher turned his gaze back to me. "Grow some balls and answer the door."

I would normally tell him off, but in this case, he was right. I took a deep breath before I turned the knob and opened the door.

Calloway stood on the other side, wearing a black suit with a black tie. Looking like a million bucks, he made the hallway look like a narrow tunnel. His dark hair was messy from running his fingers through it, and his intense eyes held their typical frozen gaze. His thoughts were unreadable, buried under layers of armor.

I knew what was coming. "Hi."

He didn't reciprocate the greeting. All he did was make a slight nod of his head.

Christopher cleared his throat then walked past me to get to the door. He moved past Calloway awkwardly and gave him a quick wave before disappearing into the hallway.

Calloway kept his eyes on me like he hadn't noticed him.

"You wanna come in?"

Calloway walked inside, bringing a shadow with him. He straightened his sleeves out of habit and stood in the middle of my tiny apartment. The place looked even smaller with him in it, like a cage too small for an enormous animal. He glanced around the apartment in a quick scan before he turned back to me.

I shut the door and stood a few feet away from him, suddenly feeling anxious and nervous. His cheek wasn't red from my palm, but his exterior still held signs of obvious irritation. When he dropped me off last night, he didn't say goodbye to me. He waited for me to get inside my door before he walked away.

He slid his hands inside his pockets and shifted his weight to one leg, looking like every woman's fantasy.

I forgot how hot he was.

Now getting dumped would be even worse.

He still didn't say anything, like he expected me to speak first.

"I know why you're here. And I think we should just get through this as quickly and painlessly as possible."

"Painlessly?" His eyebrows arched in a sexy way. No one else could pull that off. "There's no pleasure without pain."

"What?" I didn't understand his meaning, and it seemed like I was supposed to.

He didn't elaborate.

I wasn't getting anything more out of him, so I moved forward. "I know you're here to break things off with me, and that's fine. I understand you're upset, and I think you have every right to walk away. But I want you to know that I'm sorry. I'm sorry for slapping you—"

"Don't ever apologize for that." Aggression seeped from his throat unexpectedly, hitting me like a bolt of lightning. The look he flashed me was a little terrifying—and a little sexy.

"But it was wrong of me. I don't even know why I did it..."

"Because you liked it. And you knew I liked it." He closed the gap between us, getting so close we could kiss. "I'm not here to break up with you. In fact, I'm here to beg you to stay with me."

"You don't need to beg."

"Then I'll just ask." His hands moved to my hips where his fingers dug into my sides gently. "I'm sorry I snapped at you. I just have...issues."

"What kind of issues?"

"Anger issues."

He hid it so well up until that point.

"Control issues."

I picked up on that one.

"And I'm never going to change. It's who I am, and I'll dull it down whenever we're together. But sometimes, I'll slip up. If you're okay with that, then I'd like to make this work."

"In your defense, I feel like I provoked you."

"No." He brought me closer into his chest. "You asked me a question, and I didn't give you a good enough answer."

"I was too hard on you..."

"I like it when you're hard on me. That's why I'm so obsessed with you." He leaned into me and pressed his lips to mine, giving me a kiss so soft I thought his lips were made of rose petals.

When he pulled away, I was a little light-headed. All the anger I had from the night before disappeared. Now, I just wanted him to stay with me forever. I wanted that kiss a million times over, until the sun burned out.

"So I'm sorry and you're sorry." He kissed the corner of my mouth. "Now we can move on."

"Yeah…"

He cupped my cheek before he kissed me again, giving me a more forceful embrace.

I melted under the touch, feeling my entire body get pulled under. I was drowning, but every moment I didn't have air was the best struggle I'd ever experienced.

He guided me to my small bed in the corner and laid me down, his powerful body covering mine. His hands immediately yanked up my dress before he peeled off his jacket. He wrapped my leg around his waist before he crushed his mouth to mine, bruising my lips with the intensity of his kiss.

Like nothing happened, I hooked my arms around his neck and deepened the kiss, falling under the spell he cast. He had a hold on me that couldn't be shaken, and it ran so deep in my veins that it hit bone. He possessed me and claimed me as his, and for the first time, I was perfectly fine being claimed by a man.

*** .

After we had dinner at his place, I went to the sink and started to scrub the dirty dishes. A habit that I had never shaken, I liked to place all the dirty dishes in the dishwasher before I went to bed. Having a clean kitchen in the morning put my mind at ease. And with a kitchen as nice as his, it needed to be kept clean.

"What are you doing?" He shut off the faucet and grabbed the plate from my hand.

"Dishes. You've never done it before?" The corner of my lip rose in a smile because I liked being a smartass.

"Many times." He set the wet plate in the sink. "But you aren't doing the dishes. I'll take care of them later."

"But you always take care of them."

"Because you're my guest." He grabbed both of my wrists and guided me against the kitchen island, making my back press against the counter. He kept his hold securely around my wrists, squeezing them slightly. "Do you understand me?"

"No. I'll never understand you." Sometimes, I defied him just to get a rise out of him. His eyes gave me a smoldering look, and he was even sexier that way.

"I guess I'll have to make you." He lifted me up and set me on the kitchen island. He wrapped my legs around his waist and pressed his hard-on right against me through his jeans. "In case it wasn't clear before, my cock is only hard for you—no one else. So don't ever accuse me otherwise again." His hand fisted my hair, and he got a good grip on the back of my neck. "Do we understand each other now?"

This time, I obeyed him. "Yes."

"Good." He slid his hand under my dress and down my panties in a nanosecond. Large fingers found my clitoris, and he rubbed me aggressively, trying to get me off right in the middle of his kitchen. He looked into my eyes with the same expression of steel and watched me writhe for him. "I love watching your face as you come."

My hands snaked to his biceps, my anchor, and I held on as he continued to rub me down below. It felt so amazing, like a fire burning white-hot. It scorched every inch of my skin and burned me from the inside out.

He pressed his lips to my ear and held his breath, waiting for just the right moment.

I felt the burn between my legs grow until it reached the breaking point.

"Now come."

I obeyed his command and felt my body disintegrate as the pleasure ripped me apart violently. Incoherent screams escaped from my throat, and I wasn't sure what I was saying or what I meant to say. With just his fingers, he turned me into a puddle at his feet. I could only imagine what his big, fat cock would do.

He admired the spent look on my face, the corner of his mouth rising in a triumphant grin. "Hope you aren't too tired. Because it's my turn next."

I'd never wanted cock in my mouth so much in my life. But now it was all I wanted, to feel myself choke on his size until my eyes were wet with tears. "I'm never too tired for that."

**

We lay in his large bed, curled up under the sheets. The cold frost pressed against the windows and made us feel as if we were in a winter wonderland. It had snowed the day before, and fresh powder was on the sidewalks.

236

We didn't need central heating because I had this large man beside me. Big and powerful, his body kept me warm and protected me from the cold. With him, I didn't need clothes or shelter. I just needed Calloway.

"Can I ask you something?" I ran my hand up his chest and to his shoulder, feeling all the grooves of individual muscles.

"Yes."

"When do you work out?" He never mentioned going to the gym, but I knew he must work out. There was no way a man could look like that without serious commitment. If not, then he really was a god.

"Early in the morning before work."

That would explain why he never mentioned it. "I've been meaning to work out...but I've been saying that for years now and haven't actually done anything." I was too busy and too poor for a gym membership.

"Good thing you never eat," he teased.

"I eat," I argued. "Otherwise, I would be dead."

"But you certainly don't eat enough." His hand slid over my flat stomach to my hip. "But I think your body is still sexy."

"Really? I'm not a fan of my legs."

"Why?"

"They're too skinny. They remind me of chicken legs."

"Do some squats."

"I'll pass." Getting hot and sweaty in a gym wasn't my thing. I would never have the commitment to put my mind to it. Besides, everyone would stare at me because they would know I didn't have a clue what I was doing. "I would rather squat on your face."

His eyes immediately darkened at that comment, turning darker than the underworld. "That sounds like a perfect workout."

"I agree."

He pulled me closer then pressed a few kisses to my earlobe. I loved the feel of his heavy breathing amplified in my canal. I could feel his sexual desperation along with his restraint. And when his tongue moved across the sensitive area, it gave me chills.

I wanted to stay in his bed all night long, but I knew the outcome of the evening. Like every other night, I would have to leave. This time, I wouldn't ask any questions about it. He obviously didn't want to talk about it, and I wasn't going to press the conversation. I knew he wasn't sneaking around behind my back. He wasn't that kind of person, and I knew he wouldn't hurt me like that. He must have issues with space—and nothing more. "Can I ask you something?"

"Don't ask if you can ask. Just ask." His hand rested in the curve along my waist.

"Have you ever been in love?" Maybe he'd had a serious relationship with someone and it didn't work out. He slept beside her every night until they had a nasty breakup, and he couldn't sleep with anyone ever again. I wasn't trying to be nosy. I really just wanted to know more about the man I was falling for.

"No." His answer was cold and hard, as if there was no possibility he'd even been close to feeling that way for someone.

"Oh…" Now that my theory was wrong, I didn't know what to think. "Have you had a serious relationship?" That answer must be no too.

"No."

Now I didn't know what to say.

"I was with someone shortly before you came along. But we weren't in a relationship. We saw each other for a while, but there weren't feelings there…like what we have."

"How long?"

He hesitated before he answered. "A year."

My jaw almost dropped. "You dated her for a year, but you were never serious?"

"Yeah. We were mostly monogamous fuck buddies." There was no remorse on his face for what he was saying. And he didn't seem to care about my opinion about it.

"Is that because you haven't found the right person yet?" Calloway was handsome, wealthy, and compassionate. He could have whoever he wanted, and it shouldn't be surprising that he was so emotionally unattached. He could do anything he wanted and get away with it.

"Possibly. But honestly, I've never been looking for something serious. Marriage and stuff like that aren't really on my mind." He watched my expression, seeing my eyes dart back and forth in stress. "I know that's not something you want to hear, but I don't want to lie to you."

"So that means this has an expiration date?"

He closed his mouth like he wasn't going to answer. "No, not necessarily. The idea of losing you terrifies me. I don't want to wake up in the morning without knowing you're mine. I know it's soon, and we haven't been dating long, but...I feel differently with you."

All my anxiety disappeared when he said those words. "I feel differently with you too."

"My past has nothing to do with us, so I'd rather not compare us to it." His hand tightened on my lower back, keeping me in place. "All I know is, I want to be with you—and just you."

My heart warned me I was getting into something dangerous. Calloway was a loose cannon and didn't have the kind of track record I looked for in a man. I would've rather known he used to be in a serious relationship and was looking for marriage and kids...but that wasn't the case. But I knew I couldn't walk away from him, not when I felt this strongly about him. My heart beat wildly in my chest anytime he was near, and I grew weak in the knees every time he kissed me. I'd been searching my whole life for someone like him, a partner who helped the less fortunate. I'd been looking for a man who didn't give up when times grew rough. I'd been looking for a man who could give me that beautiful feeling of bliss whenever he kissed me. For all those reasons, I didn't want to walk away.

I never wanted to walk away.

Christopher walked beside me in the park, sipping his coffee. We both just got off work and decided to meet up for an early dinner. Now, we were walking off the calories we consumed because we stuffed our guts with too much Indian food.

Fall in Central Park was beautiful because the leaves changed to red and gold. Winter was a blank sheet of white. The leaves on the trees were caked in the powder, and the pond was frozen over with ice that was inches thick. But in either case, the backdrop was still beautiful.

"Dude, I hate work right now." His long gray coat stopped at his knees and kept his large body warm. "It never ends. Just when I think I'm caught up, I walk in the next morning and it's a nightmare all over again."

"Yeah, but you love it."

"No. I need to find a sugar mama. You know, a hot little number that makes bank. I could stay home all day and play video games, and when she gets home, she could ride my dick and bring me a present."

I rolled my eyes. "You would never do that."

"Hell yeah, I would. If I met a doctor or lawyer or something."

"You would get bored."

He shook his head. "You don't know me very well. Besides, we'd have kids, so I'd take care of them."

"And when they're at school all day?"

He shrugged. "I'll shop on Amazon."

That time, I actually chuckled.

He sipped his coffee and stuffed his free hand in his pocket to keep warm. "So how's it going with Mr. Dreamy?"

"Don't call him that."

"What? He is."

"Maybe he can be your sugar mama since you like him so much."

He was about to reject the idea when he shrugged instead. "That wouldn't be the worst idea. We both like the Knicks, and he's pretty laid-back."

I didn't know if he was kidding or not. "Things are good. We made up, and everything has been smooth."

"Wow. I'm surprised he didn't dump you."

"That makes two of us." I'd slapped him three times—and deep down inside, I liked it. That made me a sick and twisted freak. I didn't have any

243

inclination toward violence, but that somehow got me fired up.

"Must really like you. I could tell the first time I met him. He doesn't acknowledge anyone else in the room but you. Not sure why. I mean, it's not like you're a supermodel or anything."

"Uh, thanks."

"Whatever you have, he's into it. Looks like you're doing something right."

The last conversation we had was about his lack of commitment. He wasn't looking for marriage and kids. He'd never thought about it before, and even now, it wasn't on his mind. I wasn't sure if I should be worried about it. I didn't need to get married right away, but I also didn't want to waste my time. "I want to ask you something, and I need you to be serious."

"Me?" He chuckled. "Like that's possible."

"Christopher." I used my stern voice so he knew to straighten out.

"Alright." He sipped his coffee. "Lay it on me."

I adjusted my red scarf around my throat to keep the cold from touching my skin. My breath escaped as vapor, and I felt bad for all the homeless on the street. There were shelters, but they were overflowing and unsanitary. "We were talking last night, and he basically told me he's never been in a serious relationship and isn't looking for a serious relationship. He doesn't think about marriage and kids. And the last relationship he had wasn't really a relationship, but a fuck buddy situation."

Christopher kept walking, his wide shoulders looking powerful in his coat. The hair on his face had come in because he hadn't shaved for days, but it probably protected his skin from the kiss of winter. "And?"

"Do you think I should be concerned about that?"

He considered my question before he shook his head. "Not really."

I raised an eyebrow because it wasn't the response I was expecting.

"Let me give you the scoop on men, sis. You know, since you don't have any friends, I have to teach you everything."

I didn't even bother rolling my eyes.

"No man is looking for a relationship at any given point in time. If you do meet a guy who says that, then there's obviously something wrong with him."

"Uh, how?"

"That means they're eager to settle down because they're afraid to be alone. Or they're on the rebound because they were in a great relationship until the chick dumped them. Now they can't function without a partner. Just trust me on this."

He was a making a big generalization.

"For the average guy who says he's not looking for a relationship, that's perfectly normal. To them, they need to find the right woman first. If and when they do, they realize they want to keep their dick in their pants, and they don't want any other guy going near their woman. And it's that moment that makes them realize they don't have any other option but to do the relationship thing. That make sense?"

Oddly, it did.

"The guy flat out told me he was your boyfriend. He told me he was going to be around for a long time. He staked a claim even to me— your brother. So don't worry about all that bullshit he said about marriage. He's hooked on you, and after enough time passes, he'll realize he doesn't want to be with another woman. And that's when you have a stupid and ridiculous wedding."

Calloway did say things were different with me, that he was my boyfriend and we were exclusive. We had strong chemistry and spent nearly all of our free time together. Christopher was probably right. I didn't need to worry about anything. But even if he were wrong, it wouldn't change my mind. I wanted to be with Calloway—even if it didn't last forever.

"And you haven't slept together, right?"

"That's a personal question."

"You want my help or not? Just answer."

"No."

"No, you won't answer?"

"No, we haven't slept together." Christopher teased me about needing him, but he needed me too. He just wasn't so obvious about it. He asked me to go apartment hunting with him, and I even acted as his wingman a few times when he picked up girls. We spent every holiday together even if it was just the two of us sitting in my tiny apartment with a bottle of wine and no dinner.

"You've been seeing him for weeks."

I shrugged in response.

"Then you're set, Rome. He's not going anywhere."

"Why do you say that?"

"If a girl made me wait longer than two dates, I'd lose interest. Sex isn't everything, but if I was exclusive with her and buying all her dinners...I'd expect some action. So if he's this patient with you, then he's damn serious. A guy like him could get laid whenever he wanted. He's keeping it in his pants for you without even getting laid. Basically, this guy deserves a medal awarded by the president of the United States."

Chapter Fifteen

Calloway

I walked into Ruin after midnight and welcomed the loud music against my ears. The heavy metal was just noise to most people, but to me, it was just as comforting as classical music in an art gallery.

I passed by the bar and said hello to a few regulars. Anytime I was inside Ruin, I was surrounded by friends, like-minded people who understood my fetishes and dark desires. There were no questions here, just solutions.

Jackson was sitting at the bar talking to a woman dressed in leather. Skintight pants hugged her curvy hips, and her black jacket was snug around her waist. The zipper was down past her chest, and a noticeable line of cleavage was on display for anyone who glanced in that direction. "This is what I'm thinking. You're the lion, and I'm the tamer. All we're missing is the whip."

We had very different approaches to picking up women. I just made eye contact with them and explored their body with my gaze. I searched for the flushed color of their cheeks and the way their mouths opened slightly in need of a kiss. Then I walked over and pressed my mouth to theirs. The rest was history. "I think you should reverse roles. That's just my opinion."

Jackson looked up at me, pure annoyance on his face. "Maybe you should get on your hands and knees. She'll whip you a few times."

"Nah. I don't want to steal your girl." I waggled my eyebrows at her and walked away.

Jackson left the bar and caught up to me. "You're in a good mood. Vanilla finally put out?"

I didn't answer the question because my cock between her lips was none of his business.

He watched the hardened expression form on my face. "Guess not."

I wanted to change the subject—and change it quickly. "Don't let me keep you from your friend." I moved through the darkness of the club and headed toward my office.

"Whoa, hold on. I need to tell you something."

"Text me." As my little brother, he'd inherited a lifetime of bullshit from me. But he was used to it by now.

This time, he grabbed me by the shoulder. "Dude, I'm trying to tell you that Isabella came in tonight. Not sure if she's still here."

The mention of my ex piqued my interest. "Good for her. I knew she would get back into the swing of things."

"She asked if you were here. So, no, I don't think she's back in the swing of things."

My god, would this woman just move on already?

"I didn't think you were coming in tonight, so I wanted to give you a heads-up."

"Well, thanks."

He patted my shoulder before he walked back to his date.

Now I felt like I was on display, the prey evading the predator. She was probably searching for me right now, knowing I would make an appearance at Ruin during the twilight hours. I walked back to my office and felt eyes drill into my back. That eerie sensation of being watched burned me to the bone. I knew she was there, waiting for her chance.

I got to my office because I'd rather have this argument in private. Everyone knew she and I were no longer an item, and I wanted to keep it that way.

I walked inside and left the door unlocked so I wouldn't have to get up again.

Just as I reached my desk, she made her move. "There you are." Isabella spoke with triumph, like she beat me at some kind of game.

I looked down at my desk and didn't give her the respect of meeting her gaze. "And there you are." I grabbed the stack of folders Jackson left for me and rifled through them. "Just taking care of business. How can I help you?"

Her heels echoed on the black hardwood floor as she approached me from behind. "Just wanted to say hi."

I tossed the folders on the desk and finally turned around. I leaned against the wood and stared at her skintight outfit. She wore a black bra that pushed her tits together and a short skirt, looking like a woman in desperate need of a Dom. Her hair was in luscious curls, exactly the way I liked.

I knew exactly what she was doing.

But my cock didn't even twitch. "Hi." I suspected Isabella would be a nuisance for a while. Instead of telling her off, I tried to be patient. She devoted a year of her life to me, allowing me to possess and control her. While I didn't feel the same way anymore, I still respected her for trusting me for so long. Our history held me back from insulting her like I would anyone else.

"How's your plaything?"

She wasn't my plaything—yet. "Good. Found the right Dom?"

"You're the right Dom, Cal."

Perhaps a year had been too long. I shouldn't have trusted her not to get this attached to me, not to fall in love with me. It was my fault for letting this happen. "Not for you."

Her eyes narrowed in humiliation. "What's so special about this woman? There's no way she's a better sub than I am. I've given you everything, Cal. I've given you a whole year of my life. When you get her out of your system, I'll still be here—waiting for you."

That was the worst thing she could have possibly said. "Isabella, I'm never coming back. Even if I stop seeing this woman, I'll never ask you to be my sub again. We're no different than animals. We stick with one partner for a while, and then we move on. I'm sorry I hurt you. Truly, I am. But you need to let this go—let me go."

***

Rome opened the door wearing a skintight black dress with red pumps. Her hair was volumized and curled, framing her beautiful face and showing off her high cheekbones. Her green eyes dazzled against the dark makeup around her eyes.

She was fuckable.

"You look beautiful." I pressed her against the door just after she shut it, and I pressed both of my palms against the wood, keeping her back firmly placed against it. Like a caged animal, she was cornered with nowhere to run.

She took a deep breath, preparing for whatever would happen next.

Now I didn't want to go out for drinks. I just wanted to stay here, climb on that small bed of hers, and fuck her all weekend. All the fooling around we did satisfied me temporarily, but it didn't satiate my hunger. Only when I came inside her, filled her pussy with my domination, would I finally feel full.

I stared into her eyes so hard I didn't blink. My hands practically shook in aggravation. My true self, the controlling man deep inside, wanted to burst out of my skin and come into his full form. I would always be a creature of the night. I would always be a Dom. It was nearly impossible for me to remain calm and focused. It was nearly impossible for me to grant her any rights. But I wanted her so bad. I battled that dark aspect of myself until he was tucked away, hidden deep inside a locked cage without a key.

I pressed my mouth against hers and kissed her softly, the exact opposite of what I wanted to do to her. I wanted to press my chest hard against her tits and feel her nipples pebble. I wanted to fuck her right against the door and listen to her whisper my name.

She melted under my touch, her bottom lip trembling slightly from the heat. Her tongue entered my mouth and reached mine, lightly playing with it. I wanted a soft embrace, but she immediately took it to the next level. Whenever she wanted something, she just took it.

I loved that about her.

"Let's forget the drinks." I lowered my hands to either side of her waist and pressed my chest against hers. I had one more week of this torture before my cock could finally claim what was mine. A part of me was afraid of the moment when I would finally have her. I wouldn't be able to control my dominant side, to remain calm and gentle. I would grab her by the hair and tell her she was my possession forever, that she wouldn't even make eye contact with another man unless I gave her permission.

And she wouldn't take that lying down.

"We can't." Her hands slid up my arms and rested on my biceps. That was her favorite place to touch me. Her fingers dug into the power of their size and didn't let go. "Christopher is waiting for us."

"He's a guy. He'll understand."

"And he's my brother," she reminded me. "I don't stand up family."

When it came to her, I honestly didn't care about anything else.

"I'll make it up to you later." She brought her soft lips to the corner of my mouth and pressed a gentle kiss there. She let her mouth linger, sending warmth all the way down my spine and to my groin. "You can stick your big cock down my throat, and I'll swallow every drop."

My hands dug into the wood, and I almost knocked down the door.

She gave me a playful smile like she loved the little number she'd just pulled on me.

But she didn't want to play this game—because she would lose.

***

We met at a small bar a few blocks over and sat in a booth in the corner. Christopher had a pretty girl with him, a blonde with straight hair and big boobs. She was eager for his affection, grabbing his arm and kissing him even though Rome was sitting right beside her brother.

I pressed my mouth to her ear. "Gross you out?"

"I'm used to it. He's been doing this since I can remember."

Good thing they weren't actually related.

"Besides, he doesn't ask me to talk to his ladies, so I don't have to put in any effort."

"How thoughtful." My hand reached for her thigh under the table and moved up until her dress was almost to her waist. My fingers slid across the curve of her inner thigh until I could feel the fabric of her panties.

She didn't push my hand away.

"Where did you two meet?" Bridget was her name. She was nice but talked with a high-pitched voice that irritated my ear canal. She continued to hang all over Christopher like they were newlyweds.

I had a difficult time keeping my hands to myself around Rome, but I kept myself in check in front of her brother—out of respect. I liked that guy a great deal. He was real and true, naturally charismatic and laid-back. He treated his sister like an adult rather than playing the part of overprotective brother.

"Well..." Rome glanced at me before she turned back to Bridget. "At a bar. I mistook him for someone else and...slapped him a few times."

"Oh, wow." Bridget placed her hand over her heart in shock. "That's interesting..."

"I like a woman who knows how to throw a punch." I grabbed my scotch and took a drink. "She turned my cheek red, and I couldn't stop thinking about her. We ran into each other at a charity event, and the rest is history."

"That's so romantic," she said. "Christopher and I met at a bar too."

"She didn't slap me," Christopher said. "But she invited me into the ladies' restroom, and we got rough."

She leaned into his side and chuckled.

Rome took a long drink of her wine.

I squeezed her thigh gently, reminding her we could have ditched this whole evening and dry-humped on her bed like teenagers. The idea used to repulse me, but now, I was so hot for her I'd settle for any kind of friction.

Bridget kissed his ear, moving her tongue over the shell, before she excused herself to the restroom. She blew him a kiss before she walked off, tall in her heels with a body that made every guy turn to look at her.

When she was out of earshot, Christopher nodded. "That woman is smokin'."

Blondes weren't my type, but I couldn't deny she was pretty. Rome, on the other hand, was a goddamn goddess. She made every woman in the bar look like a troll. She was a natural beauty, soft skin with perfect curves. She had small but full lips and long legs that fit perfectly around my waist. When she did her hair and makeup, she was a bombshell, making every woman in her vicinity feel uneasy about her own appearance. To top it off, she didn't even realize it. "She's alright."

"You're just saying that because of Rome."

"No, he's not." Rome swirled her glass then took a drink. "His eyes don't stray."

Inexplicably, a white-hot feeling shot through me. Pride, warmth, and strong affection swept through me like a tide. Hearing her say I only had eyes for her turned me on like nothing else ever did.

There was nothing that happened in my playroom that gave me the same kind of satisfaction. It was so hot, so scorching, that my ears turned red from the heat. I didn't want to wait another week to get inside her. I wanted to do that tonight.

Christopher didn't argue with her comment. "You like her?"

Rome shrugged. "I don't know. I guess. You've never asked me that before."

"I was just curious." He ordered an old-fashioned and sipped it quietly, his jaw stern and his eyes dark.

"Is she going to be around for a while?" Rome asked.

"Probably," Christopher said. "At least a month."

"That's a new record." Rome didn't hide her sarcasm.

"She's awesome in the sack." Christopher shook his head like he couldn't believe it. "It'll be a while before I can bang her out of my system."

Rome cringed then grabbed my scotch and took a long drink. "I need something stronger for that..."

I suddenly got the image of pouring scotch all over her perfect body and kissing it away. Drops would move all the way down her stomach to her pussy, and my lips would chase every one, tasting a mixture of sweet and bitter.

"So you do hate her?" Christopher asked.

"Whoa." Rome held up her hand. "Who said anything about hate? I just think she's a little slutty, but who am I to judge? That's what you like, right? And since when did you start caring what I think?"

"I've always cared, Ro." He eyed the bathroom and saw her returning. "Here she comes."

She slid into the booth and practically sat on his lap. "Miss me?"

"Always." He wrapped his arm around her shoulder and kissed her with more vigor than he should for a public place.

Rome turned her body into mine, leaning in close and lowering her voice. "Do you need to throw up too?"

"No. But we can go in the bathroom anyway."

Her pretty smile stretched across her lips when she understood my meaning. "Bathrooms don't turn me on."

"Then what does turn you on?"

"Your bed. I like the way those sheets feel against my skin...so soft."

I wanted her on my bed right this second. "We can make that happen." When I glanced at Christopher, he was making out with Bridget. "I don't think they would notice if we left."

"Probably not," she said with a chuckle.

"Or we can just make out." I didn't care if anyone watched us. As long as none of the guys beat off to her when they got home, I was cool with it. If anything, I wanted to do it—all night long. Even something as mediocre as kissing was extraordinary with this woman.

"Gross. I'm not doing that in front of my brother."

"Honestly, I don't think he would notice."

Rome's eyes left my face and moved to the edge of the booth.

I kept my eyes on her because it was impossible to look away. The light was hitting her perfectly, highlighting her beautiful features and making her eyes look like sparkling emeralds. I thought she was beautiful the first time I looked at her, but as time passed, she somehow became even more stunning.

"Look who it is."

I'd recognize that voice from anywhere. It was cocky and full of arrogance—just like my own. I turned to see Jackson standing there, a woman under his arm. "Just when my night was getting good."

Rome glanced back and forth between us, and she immediately connected the dots. "Is this your brother?"

"You didn't tell me Vanilla was smart." Jackson dropped his arm from his lady and extended his hand.

"What?" Rome had a blank look on her face, having no idea what vanilla meant.

I glared at Jackson and told him to knock his shit off with just my eyes. I wasn't afraid to kick his ass right in the middle of this goddamn bar.

Jackson ignored the question and shook her hand. "I'm Cal's brother. Jackson. Pleasure to meet you."

"You too." She shook his hand then let go.

Jealousy like I'd never known swept through me when she touched my brother. The embrace was innocent, more than just innocent, but I wanted to kill Jackson anyway. I didn't want her touching anyone but me. The impulse was so strong I had to take a deep breath and wait for it to pass. If she were my sub, I would order her never to look at my brother or acknowledge him when he was in our presence.

Like she'd ever cooperate.

"And this is…" Jackson stared at his date as he tried to remember her name. "Uh…we just met. Sorry, beautiful. I can't remember your name."

She was too smitten with him to be offended. "Cassie."

I shook her hand. "Cal. Pleasure to meet you. This is my girlfriend, Rome."

Jackson grinned like an idiot. "Girlfriend?"

I glared at him again. "Yes. Girlfriend." If he made a scene right now, I'd kill him. Like, actually kill him.

Rome picked up on the tension between my brother and me. It was obvious by the look in her eyes. "Would you like to join us?"

Fuck no.

"That sounds like a great idea." Jackson pulled Cassie into his side again. "We're just going to get some drinks."

Goddamn nightmare.

When they were gone, Rome looked at me with a wary expression on her face. "Is that okay?"

It didn't matter if it wasn't. The damage had been done. "We'll find out."

***

Christopher and Bridget left because they were ready to upgrade from making out to fucking.

I wished Rome and I were doing the same.

Jackson and Cassie took the seats across from us. Cassie had tattoos along her right arm and black gauges in her ears. A small tattoo was just behind her right ear, a simple image of a circle. Without asking her a single question, I knew she was one of us—a woman who wanted to be ruled.

Jackson ordered a scotch just like I did, probably copying me to annoy me. Jackson had always lived in my shadow since as far back as I could remember. He thought I was favored among my parents. If he knew the truth, he would understand he was the lucky one. But I would never tell him.

"So…" Jackson leaned forward, fascinated by Rome. He stared at her a little too long and a little too hard. He was clearly attracted to her, understanding my infatuation with her once he laid his eyes on her beautiful face. "My brother is pretty hard up for you."

Rome immediately smiled, a blush coming across her cheeks. "That's flattering…"

If only she knew what he really meant. "Leave my girlfriend alone, Jackson."

"I'm not bothering her." Jackson swirled his ice cubes in his glass. "You talk about her so much, and now I'm finally meeting her in the flesh. I have to say, she's out of your league."

Rome blushed again.

"I like that color on your face." Jackson gave me a knowing look, understanding I would catch his meaning.

"Sweetheart, I apologize that my brother is such a wang."

"I'm not a wang," Jackson argued. "You're the douchebag trying to hide her."

"I'm not hiding her." I was trying to protect her from my brother's nonsense.

"Look, this is a big deal." Jackson stopped looking at me, his gaze focused on Rome. "This is your first girlfriend. And now I understand why vanilla is your new favorite flavor." He waggled his eyebrows at her.

"Vanilla?" Rome asked. "That's the second time you've called me that."

I placed my arm around her shoulder. "Ignore him."

"Have you been to Ruin?" Cassie asked. "Is that where you met?"

My eyes snapped wide-open in terror.

Jackson caught my expression and knew I wasn't ready to tell her the truth. He was an ass, but he wasn't that big of an ass. "No, baby. They met at a bar. Let me tell you the story…" He told her about how Rome slapped me right in front of everyone. She put her back into it because I was red for nearly a day afterward.

Rome turned to me. "What's Ruin?"

I didn't lie, but I didn't tell the whole truth either. "It's a bar my brother works at."

She accepted the story without question.

"My brother likes being treated like a bitch, so naturally, he fell for her." Even though he saved my ass, he was still a dick about it. He gave me a smug look like he was enjoying every second of my unease.

My brother had pissed me off enough for the night, and now it was time to go. "Rome and I have plans." I scooted out of the booth and pulled her to her feet. "We'll see you guys around."

Jackson gave me a curt wave. "Rome, let me know when you're ready for a real man."

Rome wrapped her arm around my waist and cuddled into my side. "Calloway is the only one man enough for me."

That same wonderful sensation from earlier traveled down my spine and entered my groin. I was moved she said that—and not because I asked her to. Now I wanted to get back to my place as quickly as possible and get her naked. I wanted to eat her pussy all night long—make her mine as thoroughly as possible.

***

"You look so much alike." Rome shook her head as she stood at the stove in my kitchen. She made herself a pot of tea, something she usually did after she had dinner. It was a ritual, and I wondered if she did the same thing before bed.

"Lucky for him." I didn't want to talk about my brother, but I couldn't ask her not to. Naturally, she would be curious. I couldn't snap that out of her.

"You guys aren't close like Christopher and I..." Sadness entered her voice.

"No. We're both too headstrong to tolerate one another." We both needed to be in charge at all times, and that need for leadership resulted in major power struggles. He always tried to undermine me, and sometimes, I wanted him to, just so I could punch him in the face.

"Do you prefer to be called Cal or Calloway?"

"It doesn't matter."

"It seems like most people refer to you as Cal."

They did. But I liked it when she used my full name. No one else ever did. "I like it when you call me Calloway. Or your boyfriend. Either one is fine." Or the man you want between your legs every night. Honestly, I'd prefer the last one.

She came to the table and set her steaming mug of tea down. Then she straddled my hips and sat on my lap, her pussy directly on top of my cock. Within seconds, she felt it inflate like a balloon. Knowing just my jeans and her panties kept us apart was a turn-on. Her dress rose up to her hips when she sat down, exposing her gorgeous thighs for me to cherish. "Calloway." She said the name slowly, treasuring the sound of each syllable. "What does vanilla mean?"

I should have prepared for this question. Jackson was an idiot and said it twice like she wouldn't notice. "Nothing."

She tilted her head to the side then placed her hands at the top of my jeans. She unbuttoned the top but didn't touch the zipper. "Calloway, what does it mean?" She pressed her face close to mine but didn't kiss me, intimidating me with her sexuality.

It was fucking hot. "You're a good girl."

She unzipped my jeans so my cock could finally come free. "You think I'm a good girl?"

No. I knew she was. "You wouldn't make me wait four weeks if you weren't." I was used to women who only wanted to fuck. When Rome initially told me she wanted to wait, I was annoyed. But now the wait was a turn-on too. She wasn't the kind of woman who just slept with any man. She was picky about who she allowed deep inside her. I was one of the lucky few who were worthy of her. I was one of the few who were man enough for her.

"Maybe I just wanted to torture you."

I swallowed the lump in my throat, picturing how slick and wet her pussy would be. "Mission accomplished. You've got me on my knees."

She wrapped her arms around my neck and pressed her face close to mine. She brushed the tip of her nose against my cheek before she kissed the shell of my ear. "I thought about cutting the wait down, but since I'm so vanilla, I'm gonna make you wait until the very end."

My fingers dug into her thighs. "Sweetheart…" I clenched my jaw because I wanted to be inside her so bad. I was in the middle of the desert without a drop of water. It was the longest dry spell I'd ever survived. The second I sank into her, I'd fuck her so hard she wouldn't be able to walk.

"Beg me all you like, but I'm a good girl. And this is what good girls do."

***

We lay together in my bed after we fooled around. She gave me amazing head, too awesome for a good girl, and then she massaged my shoulders like I was her king. She was a selfless lover, always giving me what I needed and then something extra.

I knew she would make the sex amazing.

It was getting late, and exhaustion was creeping into my limbs. Sometimes, I considered falling asleep with her, but I knew what would happen. It was a road I couldn't take with her. Eventually, I would have to tell her the truth.

She needed to know at some point.

But I didn't want the questions or the sympathy. I wasn't ready for the long conversation that would follow, the prying into my past that I wanted to forget. It was easy to procrastinate.

She got up on her own and grabbed her dress off the floor. "I should get going…" She wanted to stay. The sigh of longing in her voice made it obvious she wanted to sleep in that bed beside me, her arms linked around my neck as our breathing fell in sync.

But I had to deny her. "You're probably right." I got dressed and drove her to her apartment. I hated taking her home every night because it meant I had to say goodbye until I saw her again. I hated the silence in the car, the heavy feeling of disappointment. We were both tired and we should have both been in bed, not saying bye on a doorstep like inexperienced teenagers.

I walked her to her front door and gave her a kiss. "Goodnight, sweetheart."

"Goodnight. I'll see you later." She got the door unlocked and walked inside.

I didn't want to say goodbye. I wanted to keep her in my arms throughout the night. I wanted to eat her pussy for breakfast and watch her get ready for work in my bathroom. I wanted to make coffee for her in the kitchen before she left for work.

But none of those things would ever happen.

Chapter Sixteen

Rome

I was Calloway's first girlfriend, apparently.

At least that's what Jackson said.

And that's how Calloway introduced me to anyone we came across. Being his first meant something to me. It allowed me to put up with the fact that he wouldn't allow me to sleep over. It helped me forget that I wasn't completely satisfied with the parameters around our relationship.

But I was still falling so goddamn hard.

I didn't want to wait another week. I didn't think I could survive seven days without feeling him inside me. At first, the request was just to protect myself, but now, I didn't want to be protected.

I was ready.

I'd waited too long to get my feet in the water. I'd waited too long to jump headfirst into the unknown. Now, I needed to do it and enjoy it. I needed to do it with Calloway and hope for the best.

And it probably would be the best.

I had a meeting with a donor, so I got off work much later than I normally would. Calloway texted me and invited me to his place for dinner. He didn't usually take me out to dinner because he liked the privacy of his home.

I preferred it too.

I could eat dinner while sitting on his lap, or he could he eat while I sucked his cock under the table. And more importantly, we could eat buck naked.

I was running late, so I had to speed walk to my apartment. When I finally got onto my floor, I was sweaty from busting my ass, and my feet were killing me from the stilettos I wore. Just when I reached the door, I noticed it was cracked—and the lock was busted.

Someone broke in.

"Motherfucker." This happened to me last year, and they took all of my things. My computer and TV were gone, and they took my autographed Stephen Curry basketball. That last one pissed me off the most. The police never found the burglars, and I was angry for weeks.

I stormed into the apartment and saw everything misplaced. The armchair was moved and the bed was pushed up so they could access whatever was underneath. The TV wasn't on the table. It was on the ground with the cord wrapped around it.

They were still in here.

An arm wrapped around my throat and choked me, coming from behind the door. He pulled with all his strength, immediately collapsing my airway. "Scream, bitch. See what happens."

I slammed my heel onto his foot so hard my heel snapped.

"Fuck!" His arm loosened when he cried out in pain.

I threw my head back and hit him square in the nose.

"Shit!"

I grabbed his arm and pulled it across my shoulder before I hurled him to the ground, making his heavy body fall with a loud thud. I only had seconds before he regained his footing, so I turned him over and sat on his lower back, pulling his hands behind his back. "Scream, bitch." I slammed his head into the floor just for kicks.

He got one arm loose and threw my body to the ground. Quickly, he moved on top of me and slugged me hard in the eye. In quick succession, he hit me again, making my mouth ooze with blood.

Now I was pissed. "You fucking asshole." I threw my palm up and hit him in the nose, breaking it. I could hear it crack like a firecracker.

I pushed him down to the floor, on his back like before. This time, I yanked my computer charger off the table and quickly wrapped it around his wrists, making a knot like I learned when it was twelve.

He moaned incoherently, his words rambling out.

I pulled out my phone and called 9-1-1 on speed dial. "Enjoy your time in the slammer, bitch face."

***

The police conducted their investigation, but there wasn't much to look into. It was pretty clear what happened.

"Are you sure you don't want to go to the hospital?" Officer Dean pressed.

"Really, I'm fine." My eye was swollen shut, and my lip kept bleeding. "My only problem is being hideous for a few days."

He didn't crack a smile. "I still strongly suggest it."

"Trust me, I've had worse." This was nothing compared to what I was used to. I'd broken my ribs twice, and there was a metal plate in my skull. It was such a bitch going through airport security.

"That doesn't sound good." He put his notepad in his holster. "The locksmith won't be here until tomorrow. You have somewhere to stay tonight?"

"Yeah." I'd slept on Christopher's couch before. It was pretty comfortable. "Thank you, Officer Dean."

"Of course, Ms. Moretti." He nodded before he stepped away.

When I looked at the front door, I saw Calloway walk inside. With his eyes as big as melons, he walked in and saw the messy scene before him. My stuff was in disarray, and the burglar was cuffed and ready to be escorted out by the police. Finally, his eyes moved to my face, and he saw the blood and bruises. "What the fuck happened?" He charged me like he was about to knock me down. He cupped my face and looked straight at my injuries, his jaw stern with ferocity. "Rome." His hands moved to my shoulders, and he squeezed me so hard it actually hurt.

"I'm okay." I watched the police take the assailant away, his black mask now removed. They marched him out, and I was grateful he was gone. I wasn't afraid of him, but I was certainly afraid of what Calloway would do to him. "This guy robbed my apartment, but he didn't take anything."

"Did he hit you?"

"When I saw him inside, we got into it. He hit me a few times before I broke his nose and pinned him to the floor. Then the police arrived and arrested him. So everything is fine. Honestly, it looks worse than it feels."

He dragged his hands down his face, a vein throbbing in his forehead. He looked like he was about to scream at the top of his lungs. He took a deep breath to steady himself but that didn't dim his anger. "You knew he was inside, and you came in anyway?"

"I was robbed last year, and it really sucked. I wasn't going to let someone take my shit again. Last time, they got my Michael Jordan—"

"What the fuck is wrong with you?" He got in my face again, screaming. "You don't go inside. Rome, he could have killed you."

"I wasn't afraid of him."

"That's not the fucking point." He threw his arms down, furious. "He could have had a gun or a knife."

"Well, I'm protecting my shit."

"Is your shit worth your life?" His hands balled into his fists until his knuckles turned white.

"No. But I'm not letting anyone think they can scare me. If you cross me, I'm coming after you. That's the point."

He dragged his hands down his face again.

"Nothing happened. I kicked his ass, and the police took him away."

"But it could have turn out completely different, and you know it. Why didn't you just wait in the hall and call the cops."

"Because he could have run down the fire escape."

Calloway walked away and started pacing the room, shaking the floorboards with his heavy footsteps. He was about to explode again, yelling in my face and calling me a goddamn lunatic.

I admit my actions weren't the smartest, but I wasn't thinking in the moment. I just reacted. I'd learned to fight a long time ago, and I didn't see a problem using my skills when they mattered. "I'm sorry I upset you, but the past is in the past. Move on."

He turned back to me, his eyes burning holes in my skin. "Pack your shit. You're staying with me."

"They'll fix the door tomorrow. It's not a big deal."

"You. Are. Staying. With. Me."

I wasn't a fan of the bossiness—not like this. "I'll just stay at Christopher's. It's fine." I knew Calloway didn't want me to sleep over, and I really didn't want to be invited just because I had nowhere else to stay.

"You don't understand what I'm saying." He jabbed his finger into his chest with every word. "You aren't living here anymore, Rome. It's not safe, and I can't handle it anymore. You're staying with me until we find something better."

"There is nothing better, Calloway. You think I haven't looked?"

"Trust me, there is."

"But nothing I can afford." I didn't want to make this about money. It was an awkward subject, especially since he was wealthy. I didn't want him to feel bad for me since I didn't even have a savings account. Happiness was measured in different ways. "Really, it's fine. I can stay with Christopher, and the door will be fixed tomorrow. I know you're upset, but you're overreacting."

"Overreacting?" He got in my face with the look of a madman. "You just told me you've been robbed before."

"But it's not that big of a deal—"

"What if someone tries to rape you next? Or kill you?"

Again, he was overreacting.

"My girlfriend isn't going to stay in a place like this. That's the end of this discussion."

"Excuse me?" I hissed. "No, it's not the end of the discussion just because you say so."

"You bet your ass it is." He looked down into my face with the threat of a king. "You will do as I say. You will not question me. When I tell you to do something, all you're responsible for is doing it."

"I'm not a dog, Calloway."

"I never said you were. But you need to listen to me."

"Fuck you." Hell no, I wasn't letting him boss me around like he owned me. "I'm willing to listen to your opinion and advice, but that's it. I make all the decisions for myself. I've never needed a man to do that for me."

"Well, that's about to change." He grabbed me by the arm and pulled me against his body. "You're staying with me. End of discussion."

"You don't even want me there."

"I wouldn't ask if I felt otherwise."

"Are you going to make me sleep outside like a dog?" I hissed. "Since I can't stay in your bed?"

He glared at me, his look hotter than fiery coals. "Get your shit, and you'll find out." He finally released my arm. "I always win, Rome. Fight me all you want, but I promise you that outcome won't change. Save yourself the time and energy, and just do what I say. Now."

"Fuck. You."

He grabbed both of my shoulders and shoved me into the wall. He held my hands above my head and kept me in place, pinning me with his strength. I couldn't even wiggle. "I'm supposed to take care of you. Now let me." His face was so close that his lips brushed against mine when he spoke. "I'm not asking you to stay with me out of obligation. I'm doing it because I want you under my roof where I can look after you. I want you to be in a safe place because you're the most important thing in my life. I have to protect you. If something ever happened to you, I wouldn't know what to do with myself." He finally released my wrists. "Now pack your stuff and let's go."

Chapter Seventeen

Calloway

I set her bags in the entryway then grabbed her face with both of my hands. The swelling around her eyes was fierce, turning black and blue from the popped blood vessels. The guy hit her hard, slamming his knuckles right where it counted. Her bottom lip was swollen, but the bleeding finally stopped.

I felt...dead inside.

"I think we should go to the doctor tomorrow. I'll make an appointment."

"Calloway, I'm fine. Nothing will help the swelling go down other than time itself. And the bruises will go away on their own too. If I take a few pain killers, I'll be good."

"It wouldn't hurt to get an exam."

"I'm not going." She said it with her aggressive attitude then picked up one of the bags from the floor. "I'm going to shower. Which bedroom is mine?" She glanced at the stairs before she turned back to me. Her eyes were glued to mine with the same fierceness she always possessed.

"Mine." My past and my nightmares couldn't control me forever. If I didn't move on, I would be stuck in this vortex forever. A true man needed to face his fears and conquer them. Could I call myself a man if I didn't take my own advice?

Rome knew I didn't want her in there. She could read my expression because she understood it. She'd been studying it every single time we'd been together. Now she was a pro. "I'll just find a vacant one." She walked up the stairs to the next landing until she disappeared.

I watched her go without stopping her. When she was out of earshot, I went into the kitchen and whipped up food for both of us, making an easy meal of spaghetti. All I could think about was having her in my bedroom, and it gave me so much anxiety that I could barely breathe. Just the idea of having someone in the house while I was unconscious terrified me.

Could I do this?

***

She sat beside me on the couch, her arm hooked through mine. She pulled her hair into a ponytail because she'd just washed and moisturized her face. It was the first time I'd seen her without makeup.

And I thought she looked beautiful.

Her skin was just as flawless without foundation on. Sometimes, there was a difference in tone above her cheek and below it, but those negligent flaws didn't mar her obvious perfection. Her eyes looked smaller without makeup, but somehow, they looked brighter. The natural intensity of her eyes made them stand out like diamonds in the dark.

She felt me staring at her, so she turned my way. "Hmm?"

I didn't hide my gaze. I didn't care if she knew I was staring at her. I didn't hide my actions from anyone, and if they bothered her, she could walk away. But I knew she never would. "I like the way you look without makeup."

She rolled her eyes like my compliment was absurd. "Yeah, okay."

"I'm being serious."

"The only reason why I took it off around you is because my face is screwed up anyway." Her lip was still swollen, and her left eye would be dark for days.

Every time I looked at her injuries, I felt rage bubble deep inside me. I'd find out who her assailant was, and even if he went to jail, I'd still find a way to torture him. I'd break through those bars just to strangle him for laying a hand on my girl.

Having her stay with me wasn't the best option, but I knew she would be offended if I got her a new apartment. She would never take my money, no matter how much I pushed her. She had too much pride and self-respect to rely on me for anything. While it frustrated me, it was still a turn-on. Any other woman would take my gifts without blinking an eye over it. But she was too strong to accept help.

Everything about her was contradictory.

"Even with the bruises, you're stunning." My hand rested on the back of her neck, and I massaged her gently, feeling the loose strands of soft hair that didn't make it into her ponytail. My thumb rested against her pulse, and I felt it quicken under my touch. I aroused her, excited her, even if she tried to hide it.

"You're sweet, Calloway…"

"Honest. There's a difference. You know I'll say stuff to piss you off tomorrow."

The corner of her lips rose into a smile. "I know that all too well." She moved from my embrace and gave me a quick kiss right in the corner of my mouth. "I'm going to bed. I'll see you in the morning." She didn't glance at me as she reached the stairs then disappeared.

The awkwardness settled on my shoulders like the weight of the world. Not having my girlfriend sleep with me while staying in my home was the weirdest thing ever, and I knew that's what she was thinking even if she didn't say it. It was strange, to say the least.

With my subs, I didn't sleep with them simply because I didn't want to. And I didn't need to explain that. It was okay to be an asshole because I was the one in charge.

But Rome was different.

I walked to the third story then found the bedroom she was staying in. I lightly rapped my fingers against the door. "Sweetheart."

"Come in."

I cracked the door and walked inside. The guest bedroom had a private bathroom and more space than a single person could ever need.

She was already lying in bed, her tiny frame looking remarkably small in the large bed. The sheets were a mixture of brown and gold, and the accompanying furniture was constructed of fine dark wood. A TV was mounted on the wall between two windows covered by curtains that matched the bedspread.

I sat at the edge of the bed and searched her face in the darkness. Even without a single light on, I could see the brilliance of her eyes. They possessed their own light that shone outward with its own vibrancy.

She sat up and rested her back against the headboard, wearing a loose t-shirt that hid all of her delectable curves from view. Her hair had been pulled from the ponytail, and now her long strands framed her shoulders. There was an obvious kink where the band had constricted her hair. "What's up?"

I had no obligation to tell her a damn thing about my past. Keeping my secrets was a much easier way of life. During my time with Isabella, I didn't tell her a single thing about myself. She didn't know about my father, my mother, or the other things I'd seen in my lifetime. It was all about business with her, fucking and fucking hard. But with Rome, I wanted to tell her. I wanted to give her more of myself than I'd given to anyone else. She'd confided her secrets to me and asked me not to pity her. I needed to do the same. "My father had an unusual style of punishment."

When Rome heard me speak, she stiffened slightly. Her eyes didn't blink, and she watched me with concentration. She didn't even breathe, like making a single sound would chase me away.

"He told me the act of punishment isn't what gets to people. It's the anticipation. Waiting and knowing what's coming is worse than the pain itself. It does crazy things to the body, makes it clench up with anxiety. Your heart palpitates, and you sweat out your entire body weight. The feeling of doom drowns you."

She moved her hands to her lap and kept her eyes on me the entire time.

"When I did something my father didn't agree with, he told me I would be punished. But he never told me when or how. I had to use my imagination to figure it out on my own."

For the first time, she blinked. She waited so long that her eyes started to water.

"My punishments were always served during the night. He waited until I went to sleep, and just when I was in the land of dreams, he would strike. He would yank me from the bed, hitting me with a bat or doing things I won't speak of. The punishments themselves were never the worst part. It was trying to fight sleep because I knew what was coming. It was exhausting myself by trying to stay awake that killed me. It was the suffocating feeling of wondering when he was going to get me. That was the worst part, by far."

Her eyes continued to water, but not because she hadn't blinked.

"That's why I can't sleep with anyone. If someone's lying next to me, I won't be able to sleep. And if I do fall asleep, I'll have nightmares. I need the door locked so I know no one can get to me. When I told you it had nothing to do with you, I meant it."

"Calloway..." She reached for me and placed her hand around my wrist.

I stared at her hand, momentarily feeling bliss run through my veins. It was one of the few times she touched me, and I didn't immediately think of pinning her down against the mattress and having my way with her. All I thought about were her fingertips and how soft they felt against my skin. Her hand was cold in comparison to mine, and the effect was oddly soothing.

But then it disappeared just as quickly as it came. "Don't feel bad for me." I looked into her eyes and gave her a command, a silent one. She had to obey me since I gave her the same respect.

She closed her eyes for thirty seconds, taking my words to heart. When she opened them, her usual look of resilience had returned. She gave me that closed-off expression, hiding her thoughts. "Of course." My request was something she understood too well, and I didn't have to fight her over it. "Thank you for telling me."

"Not sure why I did." I didn't owe her anything. The two of us were spending time together and exploring each other. There was no love involved. Forever certainly wasn't involved either. But my body was constantly aching for hers, and not just the swell of her breasts or her tight pussy. I wanted to wrap my arms around her and protect her from the world.

I also wanted to give her the world.

"I do." She wrapped her finger around mine, making them hook together. Her voice carried like a whisper, softer than the wind and nearly inaudible.

I only heard it because I was staring at her lips.

"We're the same, Calloway."

We're not the same. I was the dark, and she was the light. If she really knew me, understood the type of kinky shit I was into, she'd understand we were nothing alike. Maybe she possessed some of the same heartache. Maybe she understood true suffering. But even then, we weren't on the same level.

And we never would be.

***

When I went downstairs the following morning, it smelled like pancakes and vanilla mixed together. The scent wafted through the kitchen and all the way up the stairs, making the house smell better than it had in years.

She stood at the stove and shoveled flapjacks onto a plate before she turned off the burners.

I didn't want to scare her, so I chose to stare at her instead. She wore a tight, black pencil skirt with a teal blouse. I loved both colors on her because they complimented the shade of her skin. It was darker than cream but lighter than tan. And it was so soft. You could tell just by looking at it.

I wondered how red it could get.

She turned in my direction, probably to walk out of the kitchen and let me know breakfast was ready. She stopped in her tracks and covered her chest like she was about to have a heart attack. "Jesus Christ, you scared the shit out of me."

I loved seeing her flustered, so I continued to stare at her.

"How long have you been standing there?"

"Long enough to check out your ass."

"You check out my ass even when you know I'm looking."

I shrugged. "True."

She set the plate on the table. "Are you hungry?"

"I'm always hungry for pancakes." I wrapped my arms around her waist and kissed her. "And you." The ChapStick on her mouth tasted like vanilla, and I was starting to wonder if she did it on purpose. Her perfume was the same scent.

"Well, I take less time to prepare than pancakes."

"Saves you time." I squeezed her hips and pulled her tight against me, her tits pressed to my chest. I'd never tit-fucked her, and it was on my bucket list. But I really needed to fuck her soon. All this touching and kissing was going straight to my dick.

When she pulled away, she squeezed my arms, her favorite feature. "How'd you sleep?"

I didn't dodge the question because she asked it so casually. It seemed like we were a married couple in the fifties. "Okay." I made sure the door was locked twice, my nighttime ritual, before I was able to fall asleep. A baseball bat was tucked under my bed just in case. I didn't have a gun in the house because those were more work than they were worth. I wasn't afraid of Rome down the hallway. I wasn't afraid of anyone specifically. My father had been gone for nearly ten years, and there was no one else on the planet who could cause me any harm. But the fear was ingrained in my skin like a tattoo. "You?"

"Like a pile of bricks. My god, that bed was so comfy. And those sheets..." She rolled her head back and closed her eyes like she was in the middle an orgasm. "I didn't want to get up this morning. Plus, it's so quiet around here. I'm used to rap music and car alarms in the background."

When she rolled her head back like that, I immediately thought of one thing.

"Unfortunately, I've got to open the office and start a new day." She sighed like it was the most disappointing thing in the world.

If she were mine, she wouldn't work at all. I pictured her living with me, making me breakfast and dinner every day like clockwork. She'd take care of my laundry and hang up my dry cleaning in the closet. And when I came home, she'd give me a hard kiss on the mouth then fall to her knees to suck me off right in the entryway. After I showered and we had dinner, she'd straddle my hips on the couch and fuck me nice and slow, letting my dick enjoy every inch of that wet pussy. She would tell me she was mine and she'd thought about me all day while I was at work. And then, I would tie her up and spank her ass with my belt.

The thought came from nowhere.

She turned away and poured a mug of coffee before she sat at the table and sipped it. The newspaper was sitting there, and she was reading the comics. I assumed she would want to read about politics or national news. Inexplicably, I found her choice to be cute.

I sat across from her and poured syrup onto my pancakes. There were scrambled eggs and bacon as well. I took a bite and hid my surprise at how good it all tasted. Up until that point, she'd never cooked for me.

She kept reading.

I took advantage of her distraction to stare at her across the table, wishing the sweetness in my mouth wasn't from the syrup but her lips instead. I didn't want to go to work. I wanted to stay there and handcuff her to my bedpost.

One day, I would get the chance. But for now, I would just look at her.

***

"How's Vanilla?" Jackson was restocking the bar when I walked inside. The club was closed during the early hours of the afternoon. Everyone had real jobs and real lives they had to get through before they could return to the place that made them feel most alive.

"Don't call her that."

"Why not? It's not offensive." He was dressed down in a V-neck t-shirt and jeans. His smug smile annoyed me because it was so similar to mine.

"It is when another man uses it." Vanilla or not, she was mine. If anyone called her anything, it would be me. "You can refer to her as Rome—her name."

Jackson grinned hard. "My god, you're so far gone."

"I don't know what that means, and I don't care to find out."

"You're so hung up on her, and she hasn't even put out. Dude, you're in love."

I rested both of my hands on the counter made of glass. Blue lights burned underneath to give it an ethereal glow. "Shut the hell up and don't say anything like that in front of her—if you see her again." Which he wouldn't.

"Like she's not in love with you."

"She's not." Way too soon for anything like that. I didn't have to stress about her falling that far. She made it clear she was a difficult woman to impress. She took serious wooing. And I told her I wasn't looking for a happily ever after—which she accepted.

"I know what I saw, man. She's not your submissive. Just like you said, she's your *girlfriend*. Your choice of words, not mine."

"She won't be my girlfriend forever. Eventually, she'll be my sub."

He snorted with a sarcastic laugh. "I've seen this chick. Believe me, she's not the submissive type. She's too classy and conservative. Did you see that dress she wore? It stopped above her knee, and her ass wasn't even hanging out."

"How would you know?" My hands balled into fists, and my eyes darkened to shades of black. The only man who was allowed to look at her ass was me. That's it. Period.

"Loosen up, man. I'm trying to save you some time."

"You don't know her." She was a good girl on the outside, but I knew she had dark substance like I did. She'd lived a life of abuse, and I remembered that look in her eye when she slapped me. She liked it—both times.

"I don't need to know her. It's never gonna happen, Cal."

"I'm done talking about this." I pulled my hands away and stepped from the bar. If I lingered, I'd grab a bottle of Skyy Vodka and break it over his skull.

"Whoa, whoa. Hold on." He stopped stocking the new bottles of liquor and faced me over the counter. "I get your fascination with her. She's totally fuck—"

I threatened him with just my eyes.

"She's very pretty." He cleared his throat like it took all his energy to say that last sentence. "I understand why you want this to work with her. Really, I get it. I just don't want you to get your hopes up. I know I give you shit most of the time, but I really am trying to help you."

"I don't need your help." I'd never wanted a woman the way I wanted Rome, and something in my gut told me to pursue her until I broke her. If I went to someone else, I would never be content. I would think about the woman I couldn't have—the one who really made me come.

"Fine." He raised both hands in surrender. "Do what you want."

"I will."

"So, why weren't you here last night?" His attempt to change the subject didn't really do much.

"She stayed over." I wasn't giving him more than that. If I told him she was staying with me for a while, he'd give me more shit about it.

"She slept over?" One of his eyebrows arched to the ceiling. "I thought you didn't do that?"

Isabella and I would usually hook up at Ruin. There were bedrooms all over the place, and there was a secret playroom just for me to use. She slept in there while I stayed in the other room, keeping space between us but close enough that I would be there if she needed anything.

"Her apartment got broken in to last night, so she needed somewhere to stay."

"Say what?" He actually showed concern, an expression I thought he'd forgotten about. "Is she alright?"

"She's fine. Has a black eye and a swollen lip, but those will heal."

"He tried to hurt her? What a fucking asshole."

"Rome kicked his ass and pinned him to the ground until the police arrived." I was still pissed at her for doing something so stupid, but deep down inside, I was proud of her fearlessness. She wasn't afraid of anyone or anything, and she had the resilience of flowers in winter. She had the kind of spunk and drive that I admired, the same kind I possessed myself.

"Damn...that's hot."

I glared at him again.

"Sorry, but I'm not sorry about that one. That's one badass woman."

"I know."

"So you're letting her go back to her apartment? Sounds like she lives in a shitty area."

"No." No way in hell was I letting her live in a neighborhood like that again. It didn't matter if she could take care of herself. I wanted to take care of her. "She's staying with me until she finds a new place."

That sick and twisted grin came back into his face. "Is she now?"

"It's temporary."

"Uh-huh."

"It is. She needs to pick a nicer place, and real estate goes quickly in the city."

"But we both know you could buy her any damn thing she wants." His arrogance was only growing.

"She won't accept money from me. She's stubborn."

"Whatever you say." All his teeth were showing.

"Say what you want. It doesn't make a difference to me." Her residence in my home wouldn't last forever. When we found her a suitable place, she would leave. I wouldn't ask her to stay. And she wouldn't expect me to either.

Jackson was enjoying every second of this, for unknown reasons. "Maybe I'll get a sister soon. Sister Vanilla."

I grabbed the towel sitting on the counter and threw it right in his face. "Go fuck yourself."

He pulled it off his face with a laugh. "I'm getting to you. And that's how I know I'm right."

***

When I got home, she already had dinner on the table. "You've made yourself at home pretty quickly." Without thinking about it, I hugged her waist and kissed her the second I walked through the door. The action was too normal, too domesticated for my tastes, but I did it anyway—and I liked it.

"Actually, I've kinda fallen in love with your kitchen."

"Really?" I was into some weird stuff, but I'd never had a thing for stoves and microwaves.

"It's so beautiful. Look how big it is." She walked from the refrigerator to the opposite cabinet, taking fifteen steps from one place to another. "And these granite countertops..." She ran her fingers along the surface. "I'm excited to cook in here during my stay. It actually makes me a little happy that I got robbed."

"And it has nothing to do with the sexy stud sharing the space?" I loosened my tie and wrapped it around her neck so I could pull her toward me. My hand immediately tightened on the fabric because the action was such a turn-on. If only I could throw her back on the counter and fuck her while choking her at the same time. God, that would be heaven.

"No." She tried to hide her smile as she teased me, but the corners of her lips pulled up on their own.

I tightened the tie around her neck but didn't restrict her airway—even though I wanted to. "Oh, really?" I slowly pressed her into the cabinet, my hard cock defined in my slacks. I pressed it against her stomach so she would know just how much I wanted to fuck her.

The muscles of her stomach tightened when she felt my thick cock. "Maybe a little..."

Whatever she was making on the stove smelled incredible, but my stomach took a back seat to my other organ. "I want dessert before dinner tonight."

"Bad boy."

The cords in my neck tensed at her wordplay. She was so good at dirty talk, and she didn't even know it. "You should punish me."

"And how should I punish you?" She ran her hands up my chest until they circled my neck. The tie was still hooked around her throat, blue contrasting against her white complexion.

I knew exactly how I wanted to be punished. "Slap me."

The fire of desire lit up in her eyes, but immediately, it was snuffed out. "No. Get on your knees and press your face between my legs."

"Not a punishment." I grabbed her wrist and squeezed it. "Slap me, sweetheart."

Her eyes darted back and forth as she looked into my eyes, trying to determine if I was serious.

"Do it." My breathing came out uneven at the prospect of her small palm colliding against my skin. I wanted to feel that smack, that burn at impact. I wanted to feel her ferocity like last time. "Punish me."

Her hand shook as it remained on my neck. Then she pulled it away and slapped me, but lightly. It was nothing like before. This lacked fire. This lacked intent.

"Slap me like you mean it." I gripped her thighs and squeezed harshly, forcing her to cooperate with my demands. "Now."

Her lips parted slightly as her breathing increased. That familiar flush took over her face, tinting her cheeks until they were rosy. Her green eyes danced in jade fire, the bruising of her skin almost unnoticeable. She pulled her hand back and slapped me—hard.

Fuck, that was good.

My mouth crushed against hers, and I lifted her from the counter at the same time. I carried her into the living room and threw her on the couch.

My hands gripped her skirt and pulled it to her waist before I yanked her panties off, practically ripping them.

My mouth was eager for that sweetness, for that taste of vanilla between her legs. Now that was all I could think about when I looked at her, how soft and sweet she was. The nickname was once used as an insult, but now, it was the sexiest thing in the world.

I pressed my mouth to her entrance and sucked, wanting all of her in my mouth at the same time. I spread her knees wide apart and dominated her, taking exactly what was mine to enjoy.

Rome dug both of her hands into my hair, fisting the strands and pressing my face farther into her pussy. She rocked her hips against me, wanting my tongue deep inside her. When I circled her clit aggressively, she moaned so loud I thought my neighbors across the street might hear.

I grabbed her hips and pulled her ass over the edge of the couch and maneuvered to my knees. After she slapped me, I was eager to come, but I was more eager to make her come. I buried my face between her legs, absorbing her taste and smell, and nearly got off from just visiting her sweetness.

"Calloway..." She leaned against the back of the couch and watched me, thrusting herself into my face. In the beginning, her desires and movements were subtle. But now, she took what she wanted from me, showing her carefree side. She lived in the moment, and if she wanted more, she just took it.

I sucked her clit into my mouth and pulled hard, giving her the kind of friction that would send her over the edge.

And she did. Like she was dying, she screamed at the top of her lungs and came all around me, her pussy clenching against my mouth as the aftershocks took over. She panted and released my hair, giving my scalp a gentle massage in remorse.

I refused to give her any kind of break because my cock was throbbing in pain. I got my slacks and boxers off then yanked her to the floor. I positioned her on her hands and knees before I got the perfect grip on the back of her hair. I shoved my dick in her mouth and pushed as far as I could go, deep throating her until she nearly gagged. Saliva immediately dripped from her mouth and fell down her chin to the floor.

"Look at me." I thrust my hips and buried my cock deep inside her, letting my dark side run wild. It was the closest I'd ever gotten to pure dominance. When she slapped me, she unleashed a force deep within my chest. Now I couldn't slow down or calm myself. I wanted to fuck her mouth until I filled it with all my cum.

She looked up at me, her ass in the air and her skirt bunched around her waist. Her mouth was wide-open like a snake as she took in my length over and over. Even when she struggled, she kept going—because she was a pro.

I looked into her eyes as I kept thrusting, loving the tears building there because my cock was too big for her mouth. I clenched her hair tighter as I shoved myself deep within, stretching her throat and moving across the grooves of her tongue.

Seeing this beautiful woman on her knees, her mouth gaping open for my cock, was a turn-on in itself. My balls tightened hard against my body, preparing for the all-consuming crescendo of pleasure. "It's coming, sweetheart." I shoved my entire length into her throat and held it there.

She held her breath as she waited for it since she couldn't breathe anyway. Saliva still dripped from her mouth onto the floor.

The blinding sensation traveled down my stomach and through my balls, exploding out of my shaft before it hit the back of her throat. I squirted against her tongue and gave her everything I had.

Like the good submissive she was, she didn't choke. She continued to hold her breath until I finished coming deep inside her. Tears fell from her eyes, and her arms shook from holding her weight up.

I wanted to keep my dick in her mouth, even as it softened. The image before me was purely erotic, getting me hard in my dreams. I didn't want to leave the safety of her mouth because it was such a beautiful place. She sucked my cock like she wanted it more than I did. She wanted every drop of my cum—as much as I wanted to give it.

I pulled my cock out of her mouth then wiped her lips with the back of my sleeve. "You're an amazing cock sucker, you know that?" I hated to imagine her having a lot of practice. It made me jealous over men who weren't even in her life anymore. But she learned the talent somewhere— and at least I got to enjoy it.

"Thank you. Exactly what every woman wants to hear." She sat up, a playful smile on her lips.

"But I really mean it—and in a good way." Still on my knees, I pulled her to my chest, my cock against her pulled-up skirt. My hands went to her ass and squeezed her cheeks, loving how firm yet soft they were.

"Well, you're a great pussy eater."

"Why, thank you. I'll take that as a compliment should be taken—with pride." I pressed my face to hers and watched the glow in her eyes.

"I'm really not a great cock sucker. I just love sucking yours."

Heat flushed my body all over again. She said some pretty sexy things, but that had to be one of the greatest. She basically said she only loved having my cock in her mouth—no one else's. And the more I could possess her, the better. "Yeah?"

She nodded.

"I'm glad you feel that way. Because there's a lot more coming."

***

She and I had set up a routine every night. After dinner, we cleaned up together then moved in front of the TV. If there was a game on, we usually watched that. She wasn't a devoted sports fanatic, but she appreciated it. She always knew what was going on and didn't have a problem telling off the players when they screwed up—and the refs when they made a stupid call.

I loved it.

"Do you get paid twelve million dollars a year to miss a shot?" She shook her head, disgust on her face. "I hate it when people feel bad for the players. It's their job. They aren't supposed to suck."

"Just you."

"What?"

She didn't get my joke, so I let it pass. "You're a hard-ass, sweetheart."

"Am not. I just think everyone should reach their potential. And that player didn't."

"I could picture you as a coach. All your players would hate you."

"They wouldn't hate me if they won the finals."

I wrapped my arm around her shoulders and leaned in close to her. "Have you ever considered leaving charity work for professional sports?"

"God, no. I know where I belong. I make a difference now, but I would never make a difference with these idiots."

I chuckled for the hundredth time that night. She was one of the few people who could make me laugh. Her sassiness was cute, and her attitude was somehow sexy. I liked it when she was confrontational. I wanted to fight with her, and I hoped she would bring the heat when we did. When I told her she was moving in with me, she resisted me at every step, but I couldn't take advantage of that at the time. But when she was my sub, I would.

I knew it was just a matter of time before it happened. She slapped me and enjoyed it. I could see the same fire and darkness in her eyes that I carried everywhere I went. It was in there—deep inside. And once she trusted me implicitly, I would pitch the idea to her. Or I would just give her a test drive.

That blow job was an incredible experience, but I wanted her to have a more intense encounter. I wanted to tie her up to my bed, blindfold her, and put her at my mercy. I wanted to take her out of her comfort zone and push her so hard she broke—because she trusted me.

She'd told me things she never told anyone else, and I did the same. It was only a matter of time before the real fun started. We were just days away from the four-week mark, and when that day arrived, I wouldn't hold back. But I would have to stop myself from tying her up and not letting her go. In that case, she might think I was a little crazy.

"Do you have any plans on Friday?"

"Nope. I'm pretty boring." She looked at me, her bruised eye covered with makeup. "Why?"

"I thought we could have dinner."

"Yeah, that sounds nice."

"And then we can come back here and celebrate."

Her eyes didn't change as she stared at me, and I knew exactly why.

"We'll open some wine and light some candles..." I pressed my lips to her ear and kissed her gently, letting my tongue glide along the shell before releasing a hot breath.

She took a quiet breath, her nipples hardening in her shirt.

"And then you'll be mine." My arms tightened around her because I wanted Friday to be now. I wanted to thrust deep inside her and deposit my cum somewhere besides her throat and her tits. I was eager for it, and I knew she was too. No woman sucked dick like that unless they wanted more of it—in different places.

"Maybe we should skip the dinner..."

I could feel the heat from her pussy without touching her. Her chest rose and fell with even breaths, and I knew her excitement was getting to her. She wanted to feel me buried deep inside her, stretching her until her pussy was completely molded around my length. She didn't want a romantic date.

She just wanted to fuck.

And that was fine by me. "No dinner. Just sex."

"Okay."

I cupped her face and pressed a small kiss to her lips, restraining myself from doing anything more. If I laid her back against the cushions, I would lose control and fuck her right then and there.

A quiet moan escaped her lips like she was thinking the same thing. She tucked her hair behind her ear, her eyes lidded with drunken horniness. "I'm gonna go to bed..."

"Yeah, me too." If I stayed with her any longer, I would jump the gun.

And she wanted to jump the gun too.

"Goodnight." She wrapped her arms around my neck and hugged me instead of giving me a kiss. I knew she did it to control herself, but the affection somehow felt better. I loved feeling her small arms envelop my body. She hugged me like a teddy bear, her tits pressed against me, her nipples hard.

The desire left my body as I held her, understanding just how small she really was. With skin softer than silk and eyes brighter than the stars, she wasn't just some woman I was about to sleep with. In a strange way, she was something more. I felt like I was hugging a friend.

My closest friend.

Chapter Eighteen

Calloway

The following two days were torture.

They passed like quicksand, shifting inside the hourglass but never making any true progress. The seconds passed, but I always thought it was more than it truly was. When I glanced at the clock, only five minutes had gone by, but it felt like five hours.

My afternoon at work was uneventful. I had a few meetings, lots of paperwork, and a few events pinned to my schedule. Despite all the action, my mind kept drifting back to that heathen who was about to share my bed.

I couldn't wait to be inside her.

When she first told me I had to wait four weeks, I almost walked away. Guys like me didn't wait for action. It usually came to us. But I wanted this woman in a way I didn't want anyone else, so I toughed it out.

And I was glad I did.

I'd never felt this kind of excitement in my entire life. The anticipation, the buildup, was giving me chills. The fact that this woman had the power to make me wait and still keep my attention was beyond my understanding. Whatever she had, it obsessed me. I was sharing my house with her, and it didn't even bother me. Isabella had never even come to my house, and I was with her for a year.

Rome changed everything.

When I came home from work, the tension was thick between us. I wanted to pin her to the couch and pound into her hard, feeling my balls slap against her ass while I claimed her as mine. When we were near the kitchen table, I wanted to do the same thing, and then eat my dinner off her as well.

She was stiff around me, going out of her way not to touch me. She kept five feet between us at all times. The house felt like a greenhouse, hot and humid. We were both burning, anxious to fuck like the animals we were.

Whenever I brushed her shoulder, she quickly moved away from me like she'd been zapped. Her breathing picked up, and her cheeks flushed. Her lips were slightly parted like her mouth needed my kiss.

The only thing holding me back was my promise. I gave her my word, and I always kept my word. It was the only thing that gave me any kind of value. If I couldn't trust myself, then my woman couldn't trust me. And if she didn't trust me...she would never see my playroom.

I knew our first time together would be vanilla. I knew all the fucks we had after that would be vanilla too. But once the initial rush was over and she was innately comfortable around me, I would whip out the handcuffs and take them for a spin.

And I'd finally make her the submissive she was meant to be.

The moment I laid eyes on her, it was destined to happen. She didn't have a choice. All this time, I'd been searching for the partner my body craved. I'd been biding my time and waiting for the perfect partner. While I didn't believe in forever, I believed in monogamy.

I knew I would never allow another man to touch her.

Ever.

On the last night before the big day, we sat on opposite sides of the couch. She sipped her wine and watched the game with the blanket pulled over her thighs. She didn't wear makeup, her clothes were unnaturally baggy, and her hair was in a messy bun.

I knew what she was doing.

She was trying to be as unattractive as possible.

But it was backfiring. I loved seeing her natural beauty. The bruises had faded away, and now her left eye sparkled just like the right one. Her hair was off the back of her neck so I could see just how slender her throat was. My hand could completely wrap around it, my fingers touching my palm. Her clothes hid her curves from view, but that didn't change anything. I remembered exactly what was under there.

Her brawl with the low-life thief terrified me because I feared for her safety, but her resilience and strength was such a turn-on—and for a very obvious reason. If she could handle that, she could handle anything I did to her. She would be nearly impossible to break. It would be the greatest challenge of my life. The longer I didn't break her, the more I would want her. Since she wouldn't, I would want her all my life.

She finished her wine then placed the empty glass on the table. "I'm going to bed."

I wanted to go with her, but I'd waited this long, so I could wait a little longer. "Alright."

She looked at me like she might kiss me goodnight but thought better of it. "I'll see you tomorrow."

"Sweet dreams, sweetheart."

Like she was trying to get away from me as quickly as possible, she darted out of the room and disappeared up the stairs.

I stayed on the couch with the TV playing on the wall. My cock was hard in my jeans and impatient to get free. I hadn't gotten any action for the past day, and I was eager for a release, but I wanted the real thing.

I wanted Rome.

So I kept my hands to myself and went to bed.

***

The day finally arrived, and my cock was permanently hard. It knew what was coming and it was only a matter of time before I slid inside her slick, wet pussy. Her legs would wrap around my waist, and she would beg me to fuck her as hard as I could.

And I'd oblige.

I left for work much earlier than I normally would to avoid seeing her. As hard up as I was, I didn't think I could keep my promise any longer. Technically, I wouldn't be breaking it. But I didn't want to fuck her then go to work right after. I wanted to have her all night and the rest of the weekend.

I had flowers delivered, and I set them on the entryway table. Before she walked out to head to work, she would see them. They were deep red roses in a crystal vase. There were two dozen of them. Plump and full of life, they reminded me of her. So innocent and pure, but so sexual at the same time.

I left a note.

Tonight, you're finally mine.

***

I was the first one to arrive at the house.

I went into the bedroom but didn't strip off my suit like I normally would. By now, I would normally be in the shower, washing myself down and scrubbing my hair. Then I would get out and throw on a pair of jeans and a t-shirt.

But today, I kept the suit on.

I sat at the edge of the bed and rested my elbows on my knees. The door was wide-open, and I listened for the sound of the front door opening on the first level. The curtains were closed over the windows because I didn't want anyone to sneak a glance at her, to see that perfectly pale skin surrounding her pink tits.

The bedside lamps were on for atmosphere, casting a dim glow throughout the bedroom. I could hear the heating system kick on and off as it tried to keep the equilibrium within the house. None of her things were in this bedroom, but I felt like I shared it with her anyway.

After twenty minutes of waiting, my cock hard from thinking about what I would do with her, the front door finally opened. I could hear the heavy door close behind her. It was hardly noticeable, but I'd been living there for so long that I recognized every single sound of the place.

A minute passed before her heels sounded up the stairs. She took her time, steeling her nerves before she arrived. She knew exactly where I was because her heels continued to clap against the hardwood floor, even when she passed her bedroom.

I'd never relied on my sense of hearing so much. Like I was going into battle, I prepared for the event about to take place. My heart was beating fast, and my lungs ached to breathe deeper. My body wanted to spring into action and work up a sweat. My hands twitched to grab her, to snatch her by the hips and push her beneath me. My hips wanted to thrust hard against her, the head of my cock reaching her cervix because I impaled her with every inch of my cock. She didn't know what a real fuck was before she met me. Now she would know how it felt to be with a real man—six feet and three inches of all man.

She rounded the corner and stopped in the doorway, seeing me sitting at the edge of the bed. A black pencil skirt hugged her hips, and black stilettos were on her feet. No matter how much cash was in her back account, she dressed like a classy woman, priding herself on her elegance. Her hair had been curled that morning, and now they'd come loose. They were wavy, but that made it easier for my fingers to slide through. She wore a navy blue top with a gold necklace around her throat. Her makeup was heavier than usual, and just like I suspected, her cheeks were flushed pink.

She stared at me with a mix of lust and hesitation, her arms resting by her sides. The pulse in her neck thudded wildly, adrenaline spiking directly into her heart. She was nervous, but she was excited above everything else.

I rose to my feet without breaking her gaze. I finally looked down and stared at every inch of her perfection, treasuring the moment. I'd wanted to be inside her since the moment I spotted her in that bar. Every guy that night wanted the same thing.

But I got to have her.

I'd wined her and dined her. I treated her like a lady and gave her the respect she desired. When she wanted to talk, I listened. When she wanted to cuddle, I obliged. But now it was my turn to have what I wanted.

My eyes drilled into her skin, and I felt the dominant side of me fight for control. I wanted to command her to do exactly as I asked. I wanted to demand she drop to her knees and suck me off until I was soaking wet from her saliva. I'd never struggled with my true self so much in my life.

I had to stay under control.

I walked across the room until I was face-to-face with her. I could feel the heat searing from her body as it burned for mine. Her eyes immediately lit up like stars in the deepening sky, twinkling with excitement. Her cheeks were pinker than they'd ever been before because her pussy wanted my cock so badly. Her breathing was uneven, out of whack and all over the place. My proximity made her nervous, but she enjoyed that feeling. "Thank you for the flowers."

Of all the things I expected her to say, that wasn't one of them. I didn't respond because I didn't feel like talking. The only thing I wanted to do with my lips was kiss her. My hands couldn't remain by my sides any longer, and I dug one hand into her hair and pulled her face to mine in a deep embrace.

Immediately, she took a deep breath like I'd just burned her. Her lips froze like they couldn't process the scorching burn. They hesitated in overload, my kiss throwing her off guard. But then she kissed me back with the same vigor and excitement. Her hands snaked up my arms until they rested on her favorite spot.

I already felt myself unhinge. Immediately, I fell into the unbridled lust. My hands glided down her body, savoring the feeling of her hourglass frame. I felt the definition around her ribs and moved down to her waist, feeling the strong curve in her lower back. My fingers glided to her ass, and I squeezed her cheeks hard, claiming her.

Her hands moved to my chest and undid every single button without stopping our kiss. Her kiss deepened as more buttons came loose. When the last one was finally open, she yanked the shirt off and almost ripped it in her haste.

My shirt was on the ground, and her hands were against my chest. Her nails dug into me as she felt the intricate muscles of my skin. She dragged her fingertips across the skin, feeling every groove of my physique. Her hands migrated to my chest, and she sank her claws there too.

I didn't bother unbuttoning her shirt. Instead, I yanked it off harshly, and the cheap buttons at the front popped off. She didn't seem to care that I ruined her shirt because she kissed me harder, practically panting into my mouth.

My hand unclasped her bra then it fell down her arms until it hit the floor.

I was in love with her tits. She had the nicest rack I'd ever seen. They weren't enormous, but they were round and perky, proportional to her size and sexy as hell. I palmed one, and my thumb played with her nipple, moving over it so many times that it began to pebble.

She moaned into my mouth.

Her reaction to me fueled my fire. She arched her back and pressed her body deeper into mine, practically begging me to take her. I gripped her tits harder and squeezed her nipple while I gave her my tongue.

Her hands shot out to my waist and undid my belt with lightning speed. She released the button and yanked down the zipper, letting the slacks come loose and fall down my hips. She broke our kiss to move to her knees and pulled them down to my ankles. Her face found my crotch where my cock was outlined in my boxers. She looked up at me, her green eyes locked to mine, before she pressed a kiss to my shaft through the cotton.

Fuck.

She grabbed my waistband and pulled my boxers off, letting my throbbing cock pop free. It immediately twitched when it knew it was so close to her mouth, right beside that smooth tongue it loved to slide against.

She cupped my balls and massaged them gently before she closed her mouth over my cock, moving all the way down until her throat couldn't handle another inch. She held her breath as long as she could before she pulled back and gasped for air. Her fingers continued to massage my balls like she was worshiping them.

This was better than any fantasy I'd ever had.

I fisted her hair then yanked her upward, silently commanding her to get to her feet.

When she was standing in front of me again, I unzipped the back of her skirt and let it fall to the ground. She wore a black lacy thong, a sexy little number I'd never seen before. She must have picked it up on her lunch break, wanting to feel sexy tonight.

I could have done that for her.

I gripped the back of her thong and fisted it just the way I did to her hair. I pressed my face to hers but didn't kiss her, choosing to stare at her lips instead. I loved the feel of her curved cheeks under my fingertips. She had the perkiest ass I'd ever seen, probably from walking ten floors to her apartment every single day. I couldn't wait to fuck her in the ass, but that would have to wait for another time.

I pulled the thong over her ass and down her legs. She was naked in front of me, wanting me to take her like I'd wanted since the moment I looked at her. I kissed her neck and her collarbone, nicking the skin with my need to devour her. My hands guided her to the bed, laying her down until her head hit one of my pillows. She was the first woman I'd ever fucked on my bed, and that knowledge was oddly erotic. The echoes of her moans would fill my bedroom forever, and I would live on those memories for even longer.

I hadn't done missionary in a long time. And I'd never done vanilla at all. But my cock was anxious for it as if it was the most exhilarating feeling in the world. I felt like a winner for getting this woman to want me. She could have any man in the world, but she wanted me. She wanted me to fuck her now. She wanted me to come inside her.

I could barely keep my breathing under control because I was so excited. Like a teenager about to get laid for the first time, the anticipation was about to swallow me whole. I gripped her hips and positioned her underneath me, tilting her hips so I could slide every inch of my cock inside that little pussy.

I separated her thighs with my forearms, positioning them right behind her knees. My cock pressed against her folds like it had so many times, but this was different. I knew I wouldn't be sliding over her wet clit. This time, I would be inside her, feeling every inch of her. I locked my eyes with hers, seeing the same desire hot in her cheeks.

"Thank you for waiting." She ran her hands up my chest and to my shoulders, her fingertips dragging over me.

"I'd wait forever for you." The words came out of nowhere, and they were too romantic for anything I would normally say. But in the heated moment, I said whatever came to mind. Rome was my whole purpose in life at the moment, and nothing else mattered.

I pressed the head of my cock into her narrow slit, feeling the immediate resistance. When I inserted two fingers inside her, I could tell how tight she was. I knew my thick cock would struggle to get inside. But I couldn't believe just how narrow she was.

She was soaked, her pussy juice leaking down over her asshole and to her crack. Her arousal wasn't the problem. Just my big cock and her tiny pussy. I gently pressed inside her again, my eyes locked to her. My head moved inside an inch or two, feeling the warm flesh of her channel.

Holy fuck.

Her hands moved up my chest until they cupped my neck. Her thumb rested right over my pulse, feeling the blood pound along with the adrenaline. Her breathing went haywire, erratic as I tried to fit inside her.

I continued to push gently inside her, barely getting half of my length within her. But just those inches were enough to give me shivers. It was everything my cock had been dreaming of. Slick, tight, and gorgeous. When I finally stretched her out and we got moving, it would be even better. But I wasn't sure if I could imagine anything better than this. "Your pussy is fucking incredible. You're so tight." My head absorbed all her slickness. Her warm flesh was exquisite, and I never wanted to leave. Of course, she had the pussy of a goddess. My cock must have known it when it first noticed her.

She dug her nails into my neck, holding on like she might get swept away. "You're my first..."

My cock slid another inch, feeling her tightness slowly give way. "First what?" I pressed my face near hers and stared into her eyes, seeing the entire universe in her irises. Absolutely stunning, she was perfection underneath me. Her nipples were pointed, and her chest was flushed with that beautiful pink hue. Her mouth was open from panting, and her hair was sprawled across my pillow. She was on her back with her legs spread to me, exactly as I fantasized a million times.

"The first." She craned her neck up and kissed my lips, her sweet kiss warm and inviting.

More blood rushed to my cock at the touch, but I still didn't understand her meaning. A sense of doom moved over me, covering me with rain clouds that were about to begin pouring. Her words and the inexplicable tightness of her pussy made me think of one thing. "You're a virgin?" I stopped sinking into her. The lower half of my cock hung out, eager to see everything my tip was feeling.

She kept her eyes locked to mine. "Yes."

Another spike of adrenaline rushed through me, hitting me like a freight train. I didn't fuck virgins because of the emotional repercussions. And I wouldn't have pursued Rome if I'd known that. The chances of getting her to submit to me were nearly zero now. But I didn't pull my cock out. I didn't stop.

My body was even more fired up. My arousal increased tenfold as I stared at her, knowing no other man had ever been inside her before. She was really mine, completely and utterly. I should've pulled out and stopped this before it went any further but I couldn't. I wanted her so much now—more than I ever had before. "You want it to be me?"

"Yes." She kissed my bottom lip and sucked it gently. "I've been waiting to lose my virginity for a while, but I hadn't found the right guy to give it to. I want to give it to you."

Fuck. Fuck. Fuck.

How was that possible?

She had to be at least twenty-four.

This woman could have had any man, but she only wanted me. And she wanted me to be the first one to fuck her.

I was lost.

Nothing could stop me from doing this now. Not even a gun pointed to my head.

I slowly sank farther into her, enjoying the unexplored territory. Soon, I would reach her cherry and pop it. The idea of her blood covering my dick just aroused me even more. I wasn't even sure if I would be able to move without coming.

I felt her nails dig into me harder like she knew what was about to happen. I kissed her again, keeping her aroused before I gave a firm thrust and broke through.

I moved farther into her and sheathed my dick in her tiny channel. My girth stretched her walls, pushing them to limits they'd never experienced before. The farther I went, the more she tensed underneath me, feeling fuller than ever before. My cock moved until I felt the thin layer of hymen.

Feeling that small barrier made me feel like a king.

I rubbed my nose against hers, something I'd never done with a woman, and then gave her a small kiss on the mouth.

Her lips trembled against my mouth when she felt her cherry pop. She didn't cry out in pain, but she tensed underneath me like the shock was unexpected. Her nails practically cut into my skin because she was gripping me so firmly.

I wanted to come so hard.

My cock moved completely inside her, my balls pressed against her entrance. Every inch of her was heaven. I'd never fucked pussy this good. I'd popped a few cherries when I was young, but I wasn't experienced enough to really understand what I was doing. I could make this pleasurable for her instead of a painful experience. I could make her come despite the pain my enormous dick caused.

She wrapped her legs around my waist and hooked her ankles together. Her eyes were locked to mine and she breathed with me, her nipples brushing against my chest when I moved. My name was on her lips, but she didn't say it.

I rocked into her slowly, my cock giving her pussy time to acclimate to my size. She was supernaturally tight, but she was so wet that this could work. I had to keep myself focused. Otherwise, I would give out early and ruin the fun before it even began. The fact that she was a virgin screwed up all the wires in my brain and my cock. It should have disturbed me, but it only turned me on like nothing else ever did.

I kissed her as I moved, my arms pinned on either side of her head. Every inch of my cock was buried deep inside her, our mutual lubrication mixed with tiny drops of her virginity. I breathed into her mouth as I moved, concentrating on her so I wouldn't release.

When I tasted salt, I knew her tears had come loose. I pulled away and looked at her, seeing the thin film covering her eyes. "Want me to stop?" It would take all my strength to force myself to pull out of her, but I would do it if she asked me to.

"No." Her fingers moved through my hair. "It just hurts a little. But it feels so good."

My spine tightened at her response, and my hips continued moving. Her tears turned me on because I was a sick son of a bitch. She experienced the right kind of pain, the pain that felt good. I wasn't whipping her or spanking her, but my cock was causing enough discomfort to make her feel the sensation submissives craved. The pain was noticeable, but it was dull in comparison to the pleasure. My cock was too big for her, and her pussy was too small for me. But our mutual desperation made it possible—and mind-blowing.

I looked down at her and relished the moisture in her eyes. Her cheeks were still flushed pink in desire, and her pussy was soaked. All of those things made her the sexiest thing to ever lie beneath me. "You're so fucking beautiful." My cock slid all the way inside, but I pulled out again, just my head remaining within. I slid back inside her, my cock constricted on all sides. It was the most intense pressure I'd ever felt, better than any sex I'd had with any woman. "It hurts." I grabbed the back of her hair and yanked her head back so I could kiss her neck. I slathered the area with kisses then nipped at her collarbone, possessing her completely. I branded her with my kisses and my cock, wanting the world to know she was only mine to enjoy.

She dragged her nails down my back, making tiny valleys across the surface of my skin. Her hips slowly moved with me, taking my cock with resilience. Her breathing increased, and her moans echoed in the room. The initial pain of my intrusion slowly began to wear off, and she enjoyed the entire fullness of my cock. "I think I'm gonna come..."

I positioned myself on top of her and looked down into her eyes, claiming her with just a look. "No. You are going to come." I rocked into her harder, quickly giving her more of my cock. Her first time was going to be incredible, and she was going to have a mind-blowing orgasm that made her come back to me for more. "Now come for me."

"Oh god..." She gripped my shoulders before she arched her back, my cock pounding into her furiously. The sheets beneath her were soaked with her lubrication, and I could smell the heavy scent of sex in the bedroom. My room had never smelled like this. I never wanted the smell to go away. Her hands snaked down to my ass, and she pulled more of my cock within her, wanting me so deep my balls smacked her ass. "Yes...right there."

Fuck, she was gorgeous.

Her pussy was getting tighter as she prepared to come. She squeezed my dick so hard she practically bruised it.

"Fuck yes." Her nails almost drew blood as she squeezed my ass. Her head rolled back, and she screamed through the pleasure. Her eyes were wide-open and staring into mine, her mind high in the clouds. "Fuck, you feel so good..."

I wanted to make this last, but that was impossible after her little performance. "I'm gonna come inside you." I wasn't going to ask for permission because this pussy was mine now. I owned it just like I owned her. I'd be coming deep inside her every single day whether she wanted me to or not. I passed the realm of obsession and fell into something deeper, stronger. Now, I wanted to possess her completely, make her mine forever.

"Yes..."

I pumped into her roughly, no longer being delicate with her soft pussy. I pounded into her hard and shook the headboard. Her tits bounced up and down as I rocked into her with enough force to break the bed. Within seconds, I reached my threshold and felt the hot goodness deep in my balls. Like a raging fire, flames moved up my shaft until they finally reached my head.

I shoved myself as far as I could go, right at her cervix, and I released. "Jesus Christ." I growled like a bear and moaned at the same time, dumping myself deep inside her. I gave her so much cum I didn't think she could contain it all. I spilled more than I ever had in my life, filling her up like a car at the gas pump. I topped her off until my cum started to seep from her entrance and drip down her ass.

Fuck, I was ready again.

Rome ran her hands up my neck until she cupped my cheeks. She gave me an otherworldly look, like I was the focus of her whole universe. I couldn't decipher the look she gave me, but I knew it was full of satisfaction and joy. There was no regret for the decision she made. She didn't second-guess her choice to give herself to me. She was happy. And even when the fun was over, she was still happy.

"You're mine now." I said it before, but I meant it in a different way. Now, I meant it so literally I wasn't sure what the definition was. All I knew was, I didn't want to share her with anyone. And the idea of being with anyone else repulsed me. I was devoted to this woman, worshiping her like a goddess who had the power to rule me. If she asked me to bow to her, I would. If she asked me for anything at all, I would oblige.

"I know."

My cock hardened again while inside her, feeling the wetness directly against my tip inside her pussy. It was quickest I'd ever recovered from an orgasm, but this woman made my body reach new heights. "Are you sore?"

"A little. But I want to do it again anyway."

I pulled out and watched my cum drip out of her pussy. The sight was the biggest turn-on in my life. I felt it with my fingers before I shoved it back in, wanting her pussy to be stuffed with it. No man had ever released inside her, and now it was a shrine for my cum. I pointed my hard dick at her opening and stretched her all over again, her pussy having to acclimate to my size once more. "I want to do it all night."

Chapter Nineteen

Rome

Maybe this wouldn't last forever, but I didn't regret my decision. I'd been waiting a long time to have that special moment, and no guy I met was ever the right one. But with Calloway, it didn't just feel right.

It felt perfect.

I knew the first time would hurt. I knew it would be painful. But that wasn't how it felt. His cock felt just as good as I'd hoped it would. My body struggled to accept him, but he somehow made it work.

And it was the most satisfying experience of my life.

Now I lay in bed with him, the sheets soaked with sex and the air heavy from our heat. He spooned me from behind, his powerful chest pressed against my back and his breathing in sync with mine.

I felt my mind drift away as sleep came for me. But I knew I couldn't let myself slip away while I was in his bed. My room was down the hall, and it wasn't a far walk. I slipped from his arms then sat at the edge of the bed. His shirt was on the ground, so I leaned down to pick it up.

"What are you doing?" He sat up, his hair messy and his eyes sleepy.

"I'm going to bed. I'm exhausted." My body and mind were in desperate need of a good night's rest. In the morning, we could pick up where we left off. I didn't even eat dinner that night, but those orgasms were enough to keep me satisfied.

He grabbed me by the wrist and pulled me back to bed. "You're sleeping here." With his powerful arm, he dragged me across the bed and back to where I was lying before.

"It's really okay. I'm not upset." When Calloway explained his situation, I completely understood it. Some scars never healed, no matter how much time had passed. I didn't take his need for solitude as an insult. I knew it wasn't about me at all.

"I said you're sleeping here." He kissed my shoulder and tightened his arm around my stomach.

"But you said—"

"I know what I said. But I'll be fine."

"The door isn't even closed…"

He kissed the back of my neck and let his breaths fall across my skin. "I trust you. Just as you trust me." He buried his face in my hair then didn't move again, drifting off to sleep immediately.

My heart filled with unexpected warmth. I hadn't expected him to get over his past so easily. It was a problem he'd possessed for years, and fears like that didn't disappear overnight. But I didn't leave his side. I stayed next to his warmth and fell asleep immediately—feeling safer than I ever had in my entire life.

***

When I woke up the next morning, I was in the exact position I'd been in the night before. Calloway's thick arm was still hooked around my waist like I might try to escape in the middle of the night.

I glanced over my shoulder and saw his open eyes.

They were heavy and lidded with sleep, and his hair was messier than it was last night. The stubble on his face was thicker than the night before, but I liked the way it sprinkled his face. "Morning, Vanilla." He kissed my cheek then my lips.

I melted at his touch immediately, loving such a warm greeting first thing in the morning. I gently rubbed my ass against him, feeling his hard-on directly between my cheeks. "Vanilla?"

"That's your name."

"I thought it was sweetheart."

He rubbed his cock between my cheeks, his lubrication seeping out of the tip. "Vanilla is better."

"Because I'm a virgin?"

He kissed me then pulled my bottom lip into his mouth aggressively. "*Were* a virgin. Now you're just mine."

"I wanted to sleep with you after our first date." I struggled to keep my legs closed and remain patient. I wanted to jump head first into waters without knowing their depth. I wanted to go in blind and not care about what happened. "That's why I asked you to make me wait."

"I'm glad I did." He kissed the corner of my mouth. "You were worth it, Vanilla."

My heart fluttered with warmth.

"How do you feel?" He moved his hand between my legs and massaged my entrance. The corner of his mouth rose in a smile when he realized I was already wet.

I didn't feel any shame. "A little sore."

"We can take a break. I can kiss all those sores away instead."

"No." I didn't want a break. I wanted to spend the entire weekend making love and forgetting about the rest of the world. I wanted to feel him inside me every second, full of his cum. "I want you."

His arm tightened around my stomach until he nearly crushed me. "You're a dream, you know that?"

"Me?"

"Yes." He kissed the shell of my ear. "When I first saw you, I was a goner. And now... I don't even know what I am."

"Because I was a virgin?" I understood why that would turn some men on. He was the first to have me without having to compete with anyone from my past. To me, it didn't really matter. I didn't wait out of principle. With the progression of my life, I didn't have time for romance. And even when I did, I didn't know how to trust anyone. For whatever reason, Calloway was different. I detected something special inside him, some connection we both shared.

"That has something to do with it. But there's more." He kissed my lips then sat up. "As much as

I want to start up again, I need to eat. A man needs protein."

"Want me to cook you something?"

"No." He opened one of his drawers and pulled on a t-shirt and sweatpants. "I'll make you something."

"You don't have to do that." I sat up and pulled the sheets with me because I was cold without them.

He leaned over the bed and kissed me. "I know I don't. I want to."

***

We had breakfast at the table. I was dressed in one of his large t-shirts with his boxers underneath. The smell of Calloway enveloped me and made it seem as if his arms were permanently wrapped around me even when he was ten feet away.

He ate his breakfast but kept his eyes trained on me the entire time. Like he was watching TV, his attention was glued to me in fascination. His mouth slowly moved as he chewed his food, but the intensity of his gaze refused to dwindle.

"How did you sleep?" I didn't remember him waking up in the middle of the night. In fact, I was certain he didn't move at all. His chest was pressed into my back the entire time. When he breathed, so did I.

A slight reaction of surprise stretched across his face, like he hadn't considered the topic before that moment. "Actually, I slept pretty great..." His eyebrows furrowed in confusion as he tried to figure out exactly what happened. His eyes broke their contact with mine as he continued to think about it in silence.

Maybe all he needed to do was stop thinking about it to feel better. Whenever I had a clear mind, I stopped focusing on the bad and started focusing on the good. Maybe last night was a distraction for him. Maybe I was a distraction for him.

***

Monday arrived quicker than either of us was ready for. I got up and got ready for work, and he did the same, both of us in a terrible mood. I didn't want to go to the office and work until five. What I'd rather have been doing was staying home with Calloway—particularly in bed.

Judging by his sour mood, he felt the same way. He sipped his coffee in silence and read the paper as he finished his eggs. His phone was on the table, and his suit made him look more like the powerhouse he already was.

Then there was a knock at the door.

"Who would stop by at this time of day?"

He set the paper down and rose from the table. "Grab your stuff, Vanilla."

"Why?"

He walked to the entryway without giving me an answer.

I grabbed my purse and followed him, unsure what was waiting behind the door.

A man in a black suit stood there, a town car parked at the curb. "Ms. Moretti, are you ready to go?"

I eyed Calloway, unsure what this was about. "Go where?"

"To work," the man answered. "I'll drop you off and pick you up."

My eyes narrowed on Calloway. "What's this about?"

He didn't give any kind of look of apology. "I don't want you taking the subway anymore."

"What's wrong with the subway?" I'd been riding the rail for years. I usually got a seat next to someone relatively normal, and when I read my paper and minded my own business, it was just fine.

"Nothing. I just don't want you on it."

I felt awkward having this conversation in front of a stranger. "Excuse us for a second." I shut the door in his face even though it made me look rude as hell. "Calloway, what the hell is this about?"

"I don't want you riding the subway." He kept his tone the same, but his eyes darkened. "He'll drive you to work and pick you up. If there's somewhere else you need to go, he'll take you."

"Calloway, I don't need a butler."

"He's not a butler. He's a driver."

"Whatever." I was losing my temper and losing it fast. "I don't need that either. I've been taking the subway since I've lived here, and I like it. I'm more likely to take a cab than a private chauffeur if you really want to press your argument."

"You aren't taking a cab either." In his suit and tie, he looked absolutely terrifying. He had all the power and control, and he wasn't afraid to use both. Like a wall, he loomed over me and threatened me with his silence.

"I'm doing whatever the hell I want. You aren't the boss of me."

"Wrong."

My hands immediately balled into fists. "Excuse me? We just had a pretty incredible weekend, and you're going to ruin it with this bullshit?"

"It's not bullshit." He stepped forward and cornered me into the wall, his palms locking me in place as they created barriers on either side of me. "The subway isn't safe for a beautiful woman like you. Neither is a cab. You're going to get into that car whether you walk your ass inside or I put you in there. What's it gonna be?"

I crossed my arms over my chest, threatening him with my own fire. "The subway is perfectly fine. I've been riding it for years."

"Those days are long gone."

"Calloway, no."

This time, he grabbed both of my arms and pinned them over my head. I wasn't fighting him, but he restrained me anyway. "This is a fight you can't win. This is a fight you'll never win. I'm taking care of you. I'm protecting you. This is my job, so just accept it and be grateful."

"Be grateful that I'm being controlled?"

"Not controlled. Just taken care of. Frankly, if I had it my way, you wouldn't even have a job."

I raised an eyebrow. "So I would sit at home all day and wait for you?"

"Exactly."

"What the hell has gotten into you?"

His eyes shifted back and forth as he stared into my gaze. His thoughts were unreadable, but his mood was unmistakable. "I don't know, Vanilla. But I know I'm not letting you take the subway or a cab. That's final."

Chapter Twenty

Calloway

"Thanks for calling me back." Jackson was in my face the second I walked inside Ruin. "Oh wait, that's right. You never did." He trailed behind me as I made my way to the back office.

"What did you need?" I didn't fall prey to his whining. I used to when we were kids, but I learned at a young age it was better just to ignore him.

"Business stuff that I already took care of."

"Looks like you didn't need me after all, then."

"You're right." He continued to follow me, his voice chasing me. "Which makes me wonder why you're in charge around here anymore. You haven't been here for a week."

"You know Rome is staying with me."

"How long does it take to find an apartment?"

"Pretty damn long in the city." And I didn't really care if she found another place or not. In fact, I hoped she didn't. I got the door unlocked then walked inside. The lights automatically came on to a low level. I walked to the desk and immediately searched through the drawers.

"What are you looking for?" Jackson watched me, his arms across his chest.

"Don't worry about it." I rifled through the pens and notepads, searching for the black box I'd tossed inside nearly a lifetime ago.

"Did you fuck her yet?"

Talking about my personal endeavors with Rome suddenly made me uncomfortable. I didn't want to mention them to anyone, especially my perverted brother. "Instead of being obsessed with my sex life, you should concentrate on yours."

"My sex life is all over the place. Yours is the one that's pathetic."

It didn't feel pathetic this weekend.

"I still think she's a virgin." He stared at me and asked the question without actually asking it.

I refused to answer. "I guess you'll never know." I opened the last drawer and finally found what I was looking for. I popped the lid and saw the two rings inside. One was thick and made of solid black obsidian. The other was slimmer with a black diamond in the center. I grabbed the thicker one and placed it on my right ring finger.

Jackson watched me, both of his eyebrows raising. "Oh, shit."

I closed the box and placed it inside my pocket.

"She's your submissive now?"

"No." But I wanted the world to know I wasn't available. When enough time had passed and people knew Isabella and I weren't getting back together, women would begin to make passes at me. But this ring was like bug repellent. It would keep the gnats away.

"Then why are you wearing it?"

"Even though she's not my submissive now, doesn't mean she won't be very soon."

***

I was just about to leave the office when Bruce called me. He was Rome's personal driver, and I paid him a lot of money to take her wherever she wanted, safely tucked in the back seat of a luxury car with windows so tinted it was like staring into deep space.

"What's up, Bruce?" I crossed my legs under the desk and adjusted my tie with my fingertips.

"Sorry, boss. We have a problem."

I stiffened in my chair, anticipating what that problem was.

"She ducked out from the back exit of the building. The front door is locked, and she's gone. I suspect she's on her way back to the house now."

I wanted to strangle her.

"I'm sorry, boss," he repeated. "She was in a bad mood this morning, but I didn't think she was a flight risk."

"Don't worry about it, Bruce. Thank you." I hung up and tossed the phone on the table, a migraine forming deep behind my eyes. I loved Rome's feistiness, her strong sense of independence and no bullshit. I found her attitude beautiful, even charming. But when she didn't listen to my direct orders, it pissed me the fuck off.

She needed to listen to me.

I felt my hand shake at her disobedience. I wanted to spank her ass hard enough that her cheeks welted like my hand had been the leather bite from a belt. With Isabella, I told her what to do every instant we were together, and she obeyed. It was a year of perfection, of a perfect Dom with a perfect sub. Now, I had a woman who was a loose cannon, exceptionally beautiful and satisfying, but a huge pain in the ass.

I wanted to come clean and explain my needs. I wanted to ask her to be my sub, to trust me to take us to a world of pleasure she would grow to appreciate. But I knew it was way too soon for that. She lost her virginity to me just a few days ago, and there was no way in hell she would listen to my proposition with an open mind.

I had to steady my hand longer.

I had to be patient.

I had to gradually combat her.

I had to restrain her.

And I had to control her.

***

When I walked into the house, she already had dinner cooking in the kitchen. The aroma of pot roast filled the air, the delectable scent of potatoes and spices heavy on my sinuses. For coming from an apartment with a microwave for a kitchen, she knew how to whip up some incredible things.

But even if she were naked, I wouldn't appreciate it.

I tossed my heavy coat on the stand in the walkway and slammed the door behind me, wanting her to know I was there—and I was pissed. I marched into the kitchen, eager to grab her by the hair and push her to her knees. I wanted her to suck me off as a punishment, to let her knees ache against the tiles as she deep-throated me until she choked.

I rounded the corner and stared her down, my expression a formidable storm.

She glanced at me, and as if my threat meant nothing, she continued her work at the stove. "Dinner is almost ready." She kept her voice steady like there wasn't any kind of problem.

The more she defied me, the more I wanted to control her.

And that was bad news for her. "Did you take the subway?"

She stirred the pot before she turned off the gas on the stove. The contents simmered with heat, bubbling at the surface. She turned to face me, her hand on her hip and her eyes guarded with steel armor. She wasn't afraid of me.

But she should've been.

"Yes." She continued her defiant attitude, not wincing or breaking her gaze. "And I'm going to take the subway tomorrow."

I took a deep breath because I felt my hands shake. An image of me grabbing her by the throat and shoving her into the wall filled my mind. I'd get in her face and command her to obey me, and if she didn't, there would be consequences. Then she would apologize and call me her master.

I was so fucking hard.

But I couldn't do that. Not without her explicit permission. "You aren't taking the subway. Don't push me, Vanilla."

"I'll push you all I like." She stared me down like a general in the midst of war. Corpses, weapons, and smoke didn't make her blink an eye. This woman was fearless.

But I was fearless too. I rushed her quicker than she could process, and before she could take a step back, I grabbed both of her wrists and pinned them behind her back. Then I grabbed her by the nape of her neck and shoved her into the living room. When I reached the nearest couch, I threw her on the cushions then pressed her down with my body. My cock was pressed right into her ass, and her wrists were pinned together against her lower back. My hand fisted her hair, keeping her head up.

She tried to fight me but couldn't wiggle free. "Get the hell off me."

"No." I dug my cock into her harder, feeling my blood burn with desire. I hadn't felt this high in so long. My domination was coming forth, powerful and blinding. It was a drug I was addicted to, and now that I broke my abstinence, it felt so good. "You're taking the car tomorrow. Do you understand me?"

She bucked her hips and tried to throw me off. "No."

My mouth went to her ear, and I kissed the shell, breathing hard into her canal. I wasn't sure if I wanted her to submit or fight. Her resistance was arousing, but the thought of breaking her was a turn-on too. I nipped at her earlobe then brushed my tongue across her opening. "Do you understand me?"

Her body stopped fighting, but she retained her silence. With her hands still pinned to the deep curve in her back, she held her neck up with her strength. Her legs shot out directly underneath her, her heels still on. She breathed hard but didn't say a single word.

"Vanilla, answer me. And give me the right answer." I undid my slacks and pulled my boxers down until my cock was free. Lubrication leaked from the tip. A drop bubbled before it fell onto her black skirt.

She didn't fight me anymore, but she didn't want to surrender. Every bone in her body screamed against the loss. But she knew she had to submit. She had to let me win. Because if she didn't, this battle would continue forever. "Yes."

Fire burned deep inside my gut before it reached every limb and every nerve. Victory tasted so good, and the visit to my dominance was unbelievably thrilling. I had the control. I had the authority. It was like being reunited with a very close friend. "Yes, what?"

Her voice came out as a whisper. "I understand."

I yanked her skirt up to her stomach and pulled her thong aside. My hands still pinned her wrists down even though she wasn't fighting me anymore, and my cock slid into her opening and was greeted by her sheer wetness.

Fuck yeah.

It was still a tight fit despite all the fucking we did over the weekend, and I had to slowly sink into her until my shaft was completely sheathed. My hand never released her wrists. I loved her pinned down like this, submitting to me because she knew she lost this battle. I was her king, and she needed to bow to me.

I pressed my mouth to her ear and thrust into her, feeling her tiny pussy resist my thick intrusion. With every movement, I felt like I was home. This was my place, where I claimed her to be mine and mine alone. No other man had ever marked the territory. I conquered it.

I owned it.

"Vanilla." I breathed into her ear as I rocked into her, taking it slow because she wasn't ready to fuck hard—at least, her pussy wasn't. "I just want you to be safe." My cock was invigorated by her slick pussy. It was never happier than it was when it was impaled deep inside her. My heart was working in overdrive, and I could barely contain my excitement. "Let me keep you safe." I moved my face to her mouth and kissed the corner of her lips.

She sighed when she felt my touch. Then she turned into the kiss and caressed my lips with hers, giving me those sexy and purposeful kisses I'd come to adore. Her embraces were like dynamite. Every single one was an explosion. "I know. It's hard for me to let someone take care of me."

"I'm not just someone. So please let me." I kissed her harder and sucked her bottom lip into my mouth. One of us had to give in if this relationship was going to last. And I certainly wasn't the one who was going to cave. She would need to take down her walls and let me in completely. She would need to submit to me.

She had to.

She rocked her ass back into me, loving every inch of my thick cock. She took it like a pro despite her inexperienced state. After she cried the first time we fucked, she didn't cry again. Now she wanted me inside her every second she could get.

Her lips trembled against mine before she spoke. "I'll try."

I moaned into her mouth because that was the first sign of submission. She considered giving me control. For the first time, she yielded to me. She gave me what I wanted, and she allowed me to fuck her against my couch with her wrists pinned to her back. She allowed me to do things she would never allow anyone else.

I knew I would get what I wanted—soon.

***

"Thank you for dinner." I'd never considered hiring a maid because I didn't want to share my space with anyone. I didn't want anyone to see the things buried deep inside my drawers and in the back of my closet. In the state of New York, I had a well-known face. If people knew I was the owner of the biggest BDSM club on the East Coast, people wouldn't exactly trust me anymore. I would just be a freak—as I'd been called before.

She sat across from me and took small bites. She always chewed like a rabbit, barely moving her mouth and eating so little it didn't seem like she ate anything at all. Her attitude toward food couldn't be shaken, and with every bite she took, her guilt only increased. "You're welcome. Thanks for letting me stay here."

I wasn't letting her stay there. She was letting me let her stay there—big difference.

Her eyes moved to my hand on the table. She spotted the black ring because it contrasted so sharply against my fair skin. It was thick and bold, looking like solid rock. The ring had a certain heaviness to it. The second I put it back on, I had to get used to the difference. But the weight felt good because it represented something beautiful. "Interesting ring."

I didn't glance at it. I continued to eat quietly, my eyes enjoying the feast sitting across from me.

"I've never seen you wear that before."

"It's something I've had forever."

"I like it."

Good. Because she'd be wearing one soon. "Thanks."

"It's the thickest ring I've ever seen."

Because I'm thick too. "Would you like to see it?" I pulled it off and pushed it across the table toward her.

She eyed it without picking it up.

The ring was thick with power, the Dom ring that everyone in my world respected. It represented strength and authority, and the submissive ring was just as powerful. It represented consent, beauty, and trust. The ring bearer relinquished all control to another human being. The mutual respect, friendship, and trust had to be unshakeable for such an arrangement to succeed.

She finally picked it up, her fingers brushing along the cool metal. She examined it closely, looking for a marking within the material. She studied it for nearly a minute before she finally returned it.

She felt the power. It rang quietly in her ears. I could see it in her eyes as well as her plump lips. Electricity coursed through her at lightning speed, burning her fingertips once she felt the cool metal. She wanted that feeling again—and again.

I couldn't wait to place her ring on her finger.

She returned to eating, her gaze averted in quiet thought. Whatever she was thinking was a mystery to me.

But I strongly suspected she was thinking of something she didn't understand—just yet.

***

I dragged her hips to the very edge of the bed, half of her ass hanging off above the hardwood floor. Her legs were spread to me, wide-open so I could fit my enormous dick inside that narrow slit.

She was flexible, able to pull her knees against her ribcage. My hands hooked behind her knees, my fingertips brushing against the skin over her ribs. I could feel her beating heart flutter wildly in her chest. She was eager for me, to be fucked again even though we'd just screwed before dinner.

She had the same appetite I had.

I tilted my hips until my head found her entrance. I slowly slid inside, feeling the usual pool of moisture greet me with excitement. I pushed through the slickness, stretching her walls like I did every other time. My cock would never get used to how tight she was. After taking her virginity and fucking her a few times, she still hadn't stretched out.

I hoped she never did.

She laid her head back and breathed through my entry. Her tiny waist tightened as I moved farther within her. The strong muscles of her thighs tightened, and her nipples were hard and pointed to the ceiling.

I felt like a king every time I was inside her. She lay back and allowed me to have her, to possess her in a way no man ever had. That made me feel more like a man than anything else in my life. Seeing those green eyes burn just for me was an unbelievable turn-on. She turned down every other man in her life—except me.

I moved until my balls touched her ass. She took every bit of my nine-inch length, gripping the sheets underneath her and panting through the pleasure and the pain. I had a remarkable package, something all the women at Ruin whispered about because Isabella told them what I was packing. I knew some women hit on me solely because they wanted to feel every inch of my impressive thickness. But I knew I was too big for some women—like Vanilla. It would take some time for her to get used to it, but at least she enjoyed it.

I slowly thrust into her, my cock pushing through the moisture between her legs. So sticky and thick, her lubrication was similar to mine. I could smell it every time I pulled out, and the scent of her arousal just turned me on more. I kept my pace slow because every touch was enjoyable. I'd never tried vanilla before Rome, but I'd come to realize I enjoyed it—at least, with her. If it were anyone else, it was questionable.

Her hands slid over mine until she locked her small fingers around my wrists. She held on tightly, her tits shaking with every thrust I made. My cock sank deep inside her, nearly hitting her cervix every time, but she continued to enjoy it. She made quiet, sexy sounds as I fucked her at the foot of the bed, and as things heated up, those sounds were no longer quiet. "Calloway…"

I closed my eyes as I treasured that sound. She said it with such desperation and need. I was the only man she wanted on this planet, and she clung to me like she needed me just to survive. She fought me so hard, but in the end, she trusted me. She gave herself to me, taking in my furiously hard cock as her first experience. "Say it again."

She opened her eyes and stared into mine. "Calloway."

I moved my hands underneath her ass and gripped her cheeks. Then I thrust into her harder, our bodies smacking together as I pounded into her. Her pussy juice made the sexiest noises as my cock slid into her over and over. "Vanilla." I buried myself entirely within her, feeling my body grow weak from the extreme pleasure. I could do this all day, every day. I could never leave the house again and fuck her until the end of my days.

"I can't believe I waited this long." Sweat formed on her chest, mixed with the red tint from her arousal. Her mouth was gaping open because she continued to moan from deep in her throat. Her entire body writhed for mine, her hands continuing to grip the sheets for dear life.

"You were supposed to wait this long." I moved into her harder, claiming her pussy as my territory. I didn't realize I'd been looking for her all my life until she walked in it. Now that I had her, I knew I would never want anyone else. She even made vanilla sex satisfying. Whatever she possessed, I needed it. Her virginity was mine because I was meant to take it. Everything that was hers was now mine.

Her moans turned into screams, and she came around my dick, gripping my cock tightly as her cum slathered me on all sides. "Oh god…" Her head rolled back, and she tugged on the sheets so hard they came loose from the mattress. "Fuck…that feels amazing."

Now it was my turn. Having an orgasm wasn't my favorite part of sex when it came to Vanilla.

Every single moment was my favorite part. This was just the icing on top. I shoved my dick hard into her and released my seed. I filled her up to the brim, giving her more cum than she could handle. I left my cock inside her until I began to soften. Then I slowly pulled out, the white stickiness beginning to drip out. I watched it fall, feeling my possessive desires only begin to grow.

Satiated and exhausted, she stared at me with lidded eyes. Every time I made her come, she was wiped out like she'd just run a marathon. Her tits began to soften, and her breathing slowly returned to normal.

I picked her up then crawled on the bed with her held against me. I placed her on the sheet then lay beside her, leaving the covers off because I was too hot. I didn't bother cleaning off because I figured we would have another round.

She was warm, and when she cuddled into my side, I wanted to back away. Sweat clung to her skin and combined with mine. But I didn't want to push her away. I'd rather suck it up than feel the coldness of her being on the other side of the bed. So I wrapped my arm around her and closed my eyes. Before I knew it, I was asleep.

***

Strong hands gripped me around the neck and dragged me out of bed. The veins in his arms protruded outward like strings inside a spider's web. He squeezed my throat so hard I couldn't breathe. When I tried to take a breath, I choked instead.

"You did this." He kept one arm around my throat before he slugged me in the face. My nose broke and blood oozed into my mouth. The metallic taste flooded my mouth and burned my tongue.

"You." He punched me.

"Worthless." He punched me again, hitting me in the eye.

"Piece." Hit. "Of." Knuckles to my cheekbone. "Shit."

I jolted upright and gripped the bed beside me for balance. My eyes snapped open, and I looked around the bedroom for the man I knew to be long gone. The shadows were dark in the corners, and only the light from the bathroom could be seen in the dimness. I breathed hard through my mouth and noticed the sweat soaked around my neck. On instinct, I touched my nose to see if it was broken.

It was just a nightmare.

It was the first one I'd had since Vanilla started sleeping with me. Stupidly, I thought they were long gone, like she was some kind of dream catcher that could chase away my nightmares.

It was a stupid thought.

I got out of bed without stirring her and made my way down to the kitchen. I had a cabinet dedicated to the good stuff—scotch, gin, brandy, and bourbon. Bourbon was my poison for the night, so I poured a glass with massive ice cubes.

I sat at the kitchen table and stared out the back door that led to the yard. There was grass, flowers, and a few trees. The moon was unnaturally bright that evening, especially in the city, and I could see it shine through the clouds.

I wouldn't be able to get back to sleep. The images didn't fade from my mind even after I woke up. Now they were branded on my eyes, visible whether my lids were closed or not.

I drank more bourbon than I should have and let my mind slip away. When there was enough liquor in my veins, I stopped feeling the pain from my memories. I could think about them without the aftershocks. I remembered telling my mom the truth about my father. I remembered when her mind began to fry from whatever illness she was cursed with. I remembered the way my father blamed me, called me a traitor and wished I were dead. I remembered all of it—without feeling a thing.

No matter how much time had passed, I couldn't escape what happened years ago. Jackson didn't know anything because I refused to involve him. He thought I was the favorite son, but little did he know he was the one most fortunate. I protected him like a big brother should, and as a result, I got my ass kicked too many times.

I still hated my father.

He was dead. Buried in the ground. But I still possessed the rage.

Would that ever go away?

Was that why I was the way I was? I spent so much time trying not to be like him that I turned into a younger version of him. I needed control just the way he did. I needed others to submit just the way he did. There wasn't enough booze in the world to deny what was right in front of me.

I was my father.

"Calloway?" Vanilla's sweet voice came from behind me, her concern genuine and strangely beautiful.

I didn't want her to see me like this. I was in a dark place, a place much darker than she'd ever seen. "You should get to bed, Vanilla. It's late." I drank my bourbon and continued to stare out the window. I didn't turn around to look at her.

"Are you alright?" She came closer to me until she stood right behind my chair. Her hand moved to my shoulder.

I forced myself not to flinch. "I'm okay. But I want to be alone." I kept my voice steady even though the rage was about to break through. "Go to bed. Now." I gripped the glass and felt the condensation against my palm.

She remained put, her hand still on my shoulder. "Are you sure you don't want to talk about it? I get bad nightmares too."

The alcohol was fire in my veins, and I wasn't the same man she knew so well. "If I wanted to talk about it, I would. But I don't." My tone was clipped, full of anger that burned the ears. "Leave me alone."

She finally pulled her hand away. "You want me to let you take care of me. Well, this is a two-way street, Calloway. Let me take care of you, and I'll consider letting you do the same for me."

***

All day at work, I was hungover.

Fortunately, no one noticed. And if they did, they didn't give me shit about it. After all, I was their boss. They didn't want to get on my bad side. If they did, they wouldn't see the light of day again.

Vanilla went to work early that morning, so I didn't see her. But Bruce told me she took the car to work, so she didn't test me. After what she saw last night, she probably realized I was a bear in a den. Provoke me, and you might die.

I didn't want her to see me like that. She must have woken up when she got cold and realized my body wasn't there to keep her warm. If only she hadn't gotten up to explore, she wouldn't have seen me at a low and intoxicated point.

I probably should have apologized.

But I wouldn't.

After work, I went home and found her in the kitchen like usual. She was making something in the slow cooker, and judging by the smell, it was another delicious creation. But I didn't have an appetite. All I really wanted to do was take some pain killers and go to sleep.

I walked into the kitchen to greet her. "Something smells good."

She looked at me over her shoulder, but she returned her attention to the dish. When she didn't say anything, I knew I was getting the silent treatment.

"How was your day?"

"I just want to be alone right now. Go away." She mocked the words I'd said to her the evening before.

And they hurt. "I was wasted, Vanilla. I didn't want you to see me like that."

"Then don't drink. Problem solved." She placed the lid on top of the pot then turned off the heat. "It's ready if you're hungry."

I wasn't. "I'm a man. And men drink."

She rolled her eyes exaggeratedly. "Don't make excuses for your actions. That's such a turn-off."

"What would you rather I say? I like to get drunk so I can't feel? That I like to get drunk so I can't remember my nightmare the next morning?"

She stilled at the counter, her eyes downcast.

"That if I don't drink until I pass out, I'll just have the nightmares all over again? That it stops me from leaving the house and doing something I'll regret? That it helps me cope with a past I can't change? Would you rather me say all that?"

She continued to stare at the ground, unable to meet my gaze.

"I didn't think so." I walked away and headed to the stairs. After a shower, I would go into my office so I could think without her judgmental eyes drilling into my face.

Her heels echoed behind me and stopped before she reached me. "Actually, yes."

I slowly turned around and stared at her short frame. A little over five feet, she was a tiny woman. But she had the curves and the style to make her look like the tallest woman in any room. Her slender figure didn't make her appear weak. The fire in her eyes and her stance made her formidable.

"I would much rather have an honest conversation about what's happening than watch a drunk man sit alone in the dark." She gave me a fiery look before she turned around and walked back into the kitchen. She always had to have the last word.

And I always had to have the last word.

I marched back inside and cornered her against the counter. I didn't touch her, but my proximity was enough to make her press back against the cabinet, keeping as much distance between us as possible. "What do you want from me?"

"I made that clear."

"No. You didn't."

Her hands gripped the edge of the counter but her back remained perfectly straight. Even if she was afraid of me, she didn't show it. "For one, I want an apology."

"For what, exactly?"

"For you being a shithead last night."

My mouth remained shut.

"And two, I don't want you to shut me out."

I couldn't do either one of those things.

"Calloway, you want me to do things for you that I don't agree with. And I do them to compromise. I do them because I want to be closer to you. But I won't keep making sacrifices unless you make some too. So what's it gonna be?"

Times like these made me miss Isabella. With her, I could get away with whatever I wanted and never have to deal with the repercussions. If I told her to shut up, she did. If I told her to leave me alone, she obeyed. Like an animal, she followed my commands without ever complaining. Rome was nothing like that and probably never would be. She forced me to confront things I'd rather not think about, and just when I thought I was getting my way, she turned my world upside down.

"I didn't hear you." She continued to peer into my face, giving me that ice-cold expression. She laid down the law without seeming bossy. She was too intelligent for her own good, too strong for any opponent. She made me feel more like a man because I had to combat her. But she also made me feel less like a man because I couldn't control her. "Hello?"

I forced myself to say it. "You're right. I should be more honest with you." If I wanted her on her knees with her hands tied behind her back, her mouth gaping open and ready for my cock, I had to compromise. I knew she wasn't the ideal sub the moment I looked at her. In fact, she was just the opposite. But that didn't make me want her less. Like star-crossed lovers, we were from different worlds. But I wanted her so much it hurt.

"And?"

I wasn't going to apologize. No way. "And that's it."

"That's it?" She put one hand on her hip, her attitude rising.

"I drink alone. I won't apologize for that. You should have left me alone when I asked you to. Your fault. Not mine."

"Don't be an ass, Calloway. I know you're better than that."

I stared her down because that was untrue. "Looks like you're getting to know the real me."

She shook her head in disappointment. "You can put on this act if you want, but I see right through it."

No, she didn't.

"You know I'm right, but you can't admit it. You're stubborn and a bitchface."

Bitchface?

"But let me give you some advice, Calloway." She stepped closer to me, crossing her arms over her chest. "A real man admits when he's wrong. He acknowledges his flaws and doesn't hide behind his pride. Drop the ego and man up." She looked me up and down like she wasn't impressed with what she saw then walked away.

This time, I let her have the last word—because she'd earned it.

***

After a few hours in solitude, I emerged from my office and went downstairs to find her. She was sitting on the couch with her folders scattered around her. She was working from home tonight with a glass of wine in hand. She was still in the same clothes she wore to work, her heels slipped off and resting on the ground.

I walked to the couch, my heavy footsteps announcing my approach.

She didn't look up.

I sat beside her and stared into her lap. She had budget reports and different case studies scattered across the pages. Sticky notes with illegible script were posted everywhere. She thrived in disarray.

She continued to ignore me—and she did it well.

"Put your stuff away. I want to talk to you."

"You don't always get what you want just because you demand it." She didn't falter in her writing.

My dominant side was coming out even more lately. The second we'd started fucking, I couldn't control myself. I wanted to command her to do many things. In some ways, I was already treating her like my submissive even though she wasn't ready for the job. "I came down here to apologize. Please give me the opportunity to do it correctly." It hurt my chest to talk like that, to ask for something instead of just taking it. She brought me out of my comfort zone and made me experience a world I despised—one where I wasn't in charge.

"That's better." She closed the folder and tossed her things aside. Then she looked at me expectantly, her arms over her chest and her tits perky from her posture. A cleavage line formed right down the center, perfect for my cock to fit in.

But now wasn't the time for that. "I shouldn't have talked to you that way. I shouldn't have gotten drunk like that. I'm sorry." I forced myself not to grit my teeth. I didn't want to be an asshole and drive her away, but I didn't want to give up everything I believed in at the same time. Keeping Vanilla was a lot more complicated than I thought it would be.

"It's okay." She accepted my apology with sincerity, and she finally looked at me with those obsessive eyes I'd come to adore. "I just hope you'll talk to me about these things instead of hitting the bottle. Whenever something is getting me down, I usually talk to Christopher about it. Makes me feel better."

"I guess I could give it a try."

"I meant what I said. We need to trust each other if this is going to work. So we need to be honest. I know that's hard because you have your issues, and we both know I have mine. But we need to try."

I was willing to do anything to keep her. That was something I knew with unwavering certainty. "Okay."

Softness entered her eyes, and like nothing happened last night, she forgave me. She put it in the past and moved on with the snap of a finger. Her ability to forgive so easily astounded me. In fact, I was in awe of her. I would never forgive my father for what he did to both my mother and me. But since he was dead, he could never earn my forgiveness anyway. "So, do you want to talk about it?"

Not even in the slightest. "I'm not ready, Vanilla. But I will be eventually."

She accepted the response without question. "That's okay." She scooted into my side and wrapped her arm through mine. Her affection warmed me and chased away the winter chill that seeped into my bones. "I'm always here when you need me."

"I know." My lips found her forehead, and I pressed a kiss to the skin. "And you know I'm always here for you too."

Chapter Twenty-One

Rome

I installed a bell over the door so I would know when someone walked into the office. After Calloway first walked in on me gossiping about him to Taylor, I was mortified. He overheard my most intimate feelings, and I couldn't hide my embarrassment.

And I didn't embarrass easily.

My relationship with Calloway wasn't black and white. Some days were good, and some were bad. But I carried a lot of baggage, and I was beginning to understand he carried even more. Both of us were broken, and I didn't think two broken people could fix each other. But maybe in our case we could.

I wanted to know what his nightmares were about. I wanted to know what made him so angry. I wanted to know what would make him drink nearly a full bottle of bourbon on his own in the middle of the night. I knew it had something to do with this father, but I suspected there was more to the story.

But I hadn't told him everything about myself either. I guarded my past securely. The only person who knew every little detail was Christopher—and that was because he was my brother. My closest friend was Taylor, and she only knew a fraction of what I'd been through. By keeping everything to myself, I didn't earn anyone's pity. At the foster home, I'd gotten that look from so many parents that walked by me and had no interest in adopting me.

I hated that look.

But Calloway made me open up more than I ever did with anyone else. I told him about my past, my time in foster care, and those long days inside the basement. He gave me that look of pity, but when I asked him to stop, he did.

With enough time and work, I really thought we could have something amazing.

I cared for him in ways I'd never anticipated. He was deep in my heart, and my obsession didn't derive from his gorgeous body and his awesome skills in the sack. Those were just bonuses, like winning the lottery power ball.

Sometimes, he became too aggressive, as if he could boss me around. It rubbed me the wrong way when he expected me to listen like I was some kind of pet. But when he took control in the bedroom, I didn't seem to mind at all.

When I pushed back, he would eventually yield, and when I stood up to him, he respected me. Even when he was in his darkest mood, he would listen to me if I asked him to. He was a complicated man with difficult emotions. He wasn't easy to understand, but neither was I.

In the midst of all the events over the past few weeks, I'd fallen even harder for him. It was so strong that I didn't care about the driver who picked me up and took me home every day. I didn't care about his issues sleeping with me in bed. I didn't care that every time we had sex I was a little sore because his dick was so big. I didn't care about any of the negatives because he was everything.

I wasn't even sure how I got there.

The bell rang overhead, and I snapped out of my thoughts. I was sitting at my desk and had completely forgotten what I was doing because I'd zoned out. Calloway began as a small thought and then grew until he filled my entire brain.

I glanced at my computer and realized I was in the middle of writing an email to a donor. I couldn't remember what I'd already wrote, but I would come back to it later. I looked up from my desk to address whoever stopped by.

In a heavy black coat with a gray suit underneath stood a man I despised. His brown hair was shorter than it used to be, almost buzzed along the scalp. His facial hair was thick like he hadn't shaved in over a week. The same evil twinkle was in his eyes, the sparkle of mischief. His smile wasn't cute. Somehow, it was terrifying. When he turned that look on me, I wanted to throw my computer at his head. "There's my girl."

Why did murder have to be illegal? "Hello, Hank. How are you?"

"Good. But better now."

I kept the derision out of my voice because being indifferent would probably get him out of there quicker.

"I went by your apartment the other day. Looks like you moved."

"Yep." I wasn't going to elaborate on my living status. I didn't want him to follow me, but if he did show up at Calloway's doorstep, I'd love to see what would happen to him. "So, were you planning on making a donation to For All? If not, I've got things to do."

He chuckled like I'd made some kind of joke. "Right to the point. Like usual."

I dropped my civility because I couldn't handle it anymore. "Get out, Hank. Otherwise, I'm calling the police."

"So they'll do what?" He smiled in his typical, cruel way. "Bring me lunch?"

I'd filed a restraining order against him a year and a half ago, but the judge denied it. Hank had so much power in government I was defenseless against him. The justice system failed me horribly, and I had no rights or protection against this man. I was on my own—literally. "So I don't bash your skull in." I grabbed the bat sitting under my desk and stood to my full height, gripping the handle with both hands. He might be able to overpower me, but I would get a lot of good swings in before that happened. "You want to rumble, asshole? Give me your best shot."

His smile dropped, and he became uneasy. He was at a disadvantage by not knowing what other weapons could he hiding around. "Hadn't seen you in a while. Just wanted to check on things."

"In case you haven't noticed, I'm good."

"Where are you living?" The question came from nowhere. It must have been something he meant to ask before he even walked in.

Like I'd ever tell. "None of your concern."

"You aren't in the system anywhere. Your mail is still going to your old address."

I hadn't had a chance to forward it. But now, I'd make sure to send it to a PO box. "Get the fuck out before I kill you." I'd never meant a threat more in my life. I would accept a lifetime of imprisonment as long as this asshole was off the streets. Sons of bitches like him preyed on the weak—like I used to be. They took advantage of a person's lack of power and exploited it as much as possible. I would never forget what he did to me, how he broke my arm in two places.

Hank gave me a threatening look as he backed up to the door. He was afraid of me—to some degree. He knew I had the rage and self-defense skills to kick his ass if necessary. The only way he could go head-to-head with me was if he had a gun. I could handle anything else. "I'll be seeing you, baby." His back hit the door, and he opened it as he kept moving. He stepped out, and the door shut behind him, the bell ringing.

"In hell."

Chapter Twenty-Two

Calloway

I walked inside the house then immediately enveloped Rome in my arms. She was in the kitchen like every other night, and this time, I didn't care about dinner. I pressed her against the counter and kissed her hard on the mouth, my cock stiff and eager to be inside her. My tongue darted into her mouth and danced with hers, a seductive tango.

She gripped my biceps and crinkled the material of my suit. Her sweltering tits pressed against me, hard through the blouse she wore. When her nails dug into the fabric, she moaned into my mouth, a sound sexier than anything else I'd ever heard.

"Missed you." I was a dick to her last night, and I knew it. The fight we had was stupid, and if I wanted to be man enough to keep her, I'd have to straighten out. I wasn't willing to break for her, but I was willing to bend.

"Missed you too."

I hiked up her dress then set her on the counter. Her panties were brushed to the side, and I pulled my cock out of my slacks and boxers to slip inside her. As I anticipated, she was soaked. I slipped inside her and felt her stretch, feeling every inch of heaven as I slid inside. "Now I missed you even more."

She wrapped her arms around my neck and kissed me harder than before, her pussy taking the pounding I gave her. We'd been fucking for weeks, and I was finally beginning to break her in. Her pussy accommodated my size better, and she seemed to enjoy it even more. I loved conquering her as virgin land, as an untouched paradise no man had ever enjoyed before. I wanted to be the only man inside her for the rest of time.

***

We ate dinner together in our underwear. I wore my boxers at the table, my chest and arms bare. She wore my collared shirt with her panties underneath. With her messy hair and puckered lips, she looked like a goddamn fantasy.

"How was work?" I wanted to fuck her again, but I would give her a break—a short one.

She took a bite of her food and slowly chewed it before she swallowed. "Good. Pretty boring." She looked down at her plate as she stabbed another piece of meat with her fork. "How was yours?"

"The same. Boring."

"Too bad we can't be bored together." She waggled her eyebrows at me playfully.

I liked it when she flirted with me. "I have a feeling the workday wouldn't be boring."

"Me too." She took a few more bites of her mediocre meal before she pushed the dish away. "I have some good news."

She was ready to try anal? "Hmm?"

"I found an apartment." She grabbed her laptop from the opposite side of the table and flipped it open.

A brick fell into my stomach.

"It's in Chelsea. It's a little closer to work than my old place, and the neighborhood is decent. It's more expensive than my other apartment, but I think I can swing it." She turned the computer so I could see the screen.

It was a simple gray building with dirty windows. I recognized it because it was next door to a Chinese restaurant I'd been to a few times. When she described the neighborhood as decent, she didn't use the appropriate word. A beautiful woman like her shouldn't be living in such a vulnerable place. The second I looked at her, I became obsessed with her. I could only imagine every other guy experienced the same sensation the moment they laid eyes on her. And I'm sure most of them didn't understand the word no.

"I put my application in this afternoon."

Now I was pissed. "Without telling me?" I lost this argument before it even began, and I knew it. I needed to keep my dominance in check, to take it down a few notches before I showed her who I truly was. But when I got angry, I couldn't keep it back.

"What do you mean?" Her eyebrows narrowed in a quizzical way. "I assumed I wouldn't be living here forever."

"But you could have asked for my advice about finding the right place."

"Calloway, I'm a big girl. I can find my own apartment."

I breathed through my nose so I could keep my respiration in check. "Obviously, you can't. Because that place is a dump."

Her jaw nearly dropped. "First of all, you haven't seen the inside. And second of all, fuck you. Not everyone is a millionaire."

"It's not about money. That place isn't safe. I've been there before, and there's a bus stop right across the street and a homeless shelter just a block over."

"What's wrong with homeless people?"

I wanted to flip the table over. "Nothing. I spend my life helping the less fortunate, and you know that. I just don't want you in a dangerous situation."

"Homeless people aren't dangerous."

I wanted to slap her. "Not all of them. But some."

She leaned back in her chair, her arms crossed over her chest. "Frankly, this is all I can afford. I'm okay with that, but you need to get off your high horse."

"It's not about money." It'd never been about money, and I wished she would understand that. "Let me get you a nice place. I have a great real estate agent that knows all the nooks and crannies of this city."

"I'm not looking to buy, and you know it."

"But I can buy something for you."

Now steam was coming out of her nose. Her eyes narrowed in fury, and she looked like she wanted to flip the table over—and then throw it at me. "I don't need your charity, Calloway. I told you I don't want your pity, so stop giving it to me."

"I'm not pitying you." Sometimes I wished she were like other girls. Isabella would take gifts from me without blinking an eye. If Rome were really my submissive, she would accept an apartment without a single argument. "I understand where you're coming from. I really do. But you need to understand where I'm coming from."

"And that is?"

"Rome, you're mine." She was mine in more ways than she realized. If I showed her exactly what that meant, she might take off. "I want to take care of you. I want to keep you safe. That's all I want. And I'm not a bad guy for feeling that way."

Her anger dimmed, but only slightly.

"That's who I am, Vanilla. I like to take care of people. It's not charity or pity. You're very important to me, and my lady shouldn't be walking past bums as she tries to get into her apartment. She shouldn't have to listen to gunshots in the middle of the night. She should live in luxury like the queen that she is. I'm a king, and I take care of my queen."

"I only want to be a queen if I make myself a queen."

"What's the difference?" I admired her independence and resilience. It was one of the reasons I was attracted to her in the first place. But times like these made me realize it was biting me in the ass.

"There's a big difference."

How did I defeat an opponent more stubborn than myself? How did I overrule someone who resisted oppression? How did I govern someone who didn't believe in rules? "You know I'm a man who gets what he wants. And I know you're a woman who gets what she wants. I think we're going to have to compromise here."

She shook her head slightly. "I'm not letting you buy me an apartment."

"Okay. Then what's the compromise?"

She looked away because she didn't have one.

"How about I buy it for you, and you pay me rent?"

She sighed in annoyance. "I'll never be able to afford a place like that. Don't you get it?"

"You can pay me whatever you were paying before. That's a compromise."

"I don't want a dime from you, Calloway. I'm with you because of who you are, not how fat your wallet is. I'm sorry, but I respect you too much to take anything."

Her words were kind, but I couldn't appreciate them. A lot of women wanted me because I was powerful, good-looking, and wealthy. They wanted to be showered with gifts and live with me in a penthouse in Manhattan. I knew some women didn't care who I was underneath my layers. That was why I chose the lifestyle with Ruin. It was much easier, much simpler. But then Rome came into my life and screwed everything up. "I appreciate that, Vanilla. I do. But I'm offering it to you, so it's not disrespectful. It'll ease my mind if I know you're safe when I'm not around. You'll never understand how much it hurt me to see you with a black eye. I can't let that happen again."

"That was a fluke." Her anger continued to slip away as the conversation continued. Now her voice came out quiet, like a gentle whisper in the breeze. "I can take care of myself, Calloway. Really, I can."

"But you don't have to."

She looked at me again, her green eyes soft.

"I know you've been doing it your whole life because you had to. I know you struggled and prided yourself on standing on your own two feet. I know it's hard for you to take down your walls and let anyone in. But I'm not just anyone, Vanilla. You don't have to keep struggling. There's nothing wrong with taking the easier road sometimes."

She looked away, her eyes no longer trained on me. "You're a great guy, Calloway. You're sweet and kind, and I understand how lucky I am to have someone like you. Whatever we have...I love. When I'm with you, I feel things I thought I would never feel. I feel safe, protected, and cherished. And sometimes, I think I've found a partner who really understands me."

The words went straight into my heart, throbbing in both pain and pleasure. I knew she was serious about me if she slept with me, but she didn't confess her feelings very often. She only gave me looks and kisses. Now she was giving me more.

"And I think I've found a man just as broken—but just as strong."

My hand balled into a fist to stop myself from reaching over the table and grabbing her. I wanted to hold her in my lap and force her to straddle my hips. I wanted to hold her close to me and kiss her until her lips were bruised.

"And that's why I can't take anything from you. I don't want to ruin what we have. Allowing you to buy me something just complicates things. And even if I pay you rent, that still makes everything awkward. I appreciate what you're trying to do, but neither of those is an option."

So much for a compromise. "Then live with me." In the back of my mind, I knew it was a stupid decision. I enjoyed having her around, but if it became permanent, we would have problems. If she didn't want the things I wanted, it would be painful when she left. But that didn't stop me from making the offer. "There's no exchange of money, and I'm not giving you anything. And you're safe. It's the best compromise."

She watched me with her pretty eyes, her features soft and unreadable. When she didn't say anything for nearly a minute, I knew her response wasn't what I wanted to hear. "I can't live here."

The disappointment hit me harder than I expected it to. In fact, I was devastated. I'd become used to her being around the house. I'd become used to her sharing my bed. I'd become used to seeing her every minute of the day when I wasn't at work. I never would have asked her to live with me to begin with if she had somewhere else to go, but after it happened, I didn't regret it. Now, I regretted her leaving. "It's a big place. Plenty of space for both of us."

"Calloway, I've loved staying with you. You know how I feel about this gorgeous kitchen."

I smiled automatically.

"But I can't stay here."

"Give me one good reason."

She was quiet as she tried to find the right response. "Because I want this to work. It's too soon, Calloway. Despite how we may feel about each other, I don't want to ruin it by moving too quickly."

It'd been nearly two months since we met. It wasn't that quick.

"So I'm going to get this place and move out." She didn't say it with victory but with calm acceptance. "If things go well, maybe I can move back in. But for now, I think this is the best thing for both of us."

I could accept her leaving my house, but I couldn't accept her moving into a place where she could get stalked and raped. "I accept that, Vanilla. But I don't accept the place you've chosen to move. Compromise with me here."

"Calloway, I can't afford anything nicer. That's the bottom line."

And she wouldn't live with me, the only other possibility. Frustrated, I looked away. If I didn't resolve my anger, I would say something I would later regret. Keeping my mouth shut was the best choice at the moment.

She must have been able to read my emotions because she didn't say anything more on the subject. In silence, she stayed on her side of the table and stared at me. Her eyes were full of remorse for upsetting me.

But she didn't need to pity me.

Because I always got my way.

***

Christopher walked out of his building, and my driver intercepted him at the sidewalk. Wearing a black suit with a thick overcoat, he looked like every other rich guy on Wall Street. He fit the bill perfectly, with his combed hair and shiny dress shoes. He was young and full of ambition, like so many young people in the city.

My driver guided him to my black car, and Christopher got in the back seat.

He took one look at me, his charismatic smile on his face. "Are you James Bond?"

I chuckled. "Pretty much."

He eyed the sleek car with black leather upholstery. "Hope I have a driver someday. Must be nice."

"You will." I rolled up the divider window so we would have some privacy.

Christopher nodded like he knew what this meeting was about. "I get it. Rome is annoying the shit out of you, and you want me to take care of it. It's cool. I figured she would get under your skin sooner or later."

Quite the contrary. I never wanted her to leave. "You're right about the subject, but not the problem."

"Then tell me how I can help. I could always knock her upside the head for you. You know, older brother privileges."

I smiled again because it was so easy to talk to Christopher. Rome was different because she was so serious all the time. She worked so hard to be tough that sometimes she forgot it was okay to crack a joke once in a while. "She's been living with me for a while since that guy broke in to her apartment."

"And you haven't killed her yet. I'm surprised."

I ignored the jab. "She wants to move out. She found this run-down place that makes my skin crawl. It's not safe, and I don't want her there."

"Then tell her. Why are you talking to me about it?"

"You know how stubborn she is." I didn't need to explain that part.

He rolled his eyes. "I feel ya."

"I offered to buy her a place, but of course, she said no. Then, I offered to let her live with me permanently, but she said—"

"Damn." He looked at me with wide eyes. "I knew you were into my sister, but I didn't realize how far it went. I can actually hear wedding bells."

I sidestepped the accusation. "Yes, I really care about her. I'm not going to ask her to marry me, but I definitely want to take care of her. But that's the problem. She won't let me." That answer was political enough.

"So what does this have to do with me?"

"I want you to ask her to move in with you."

He gripped his chest and laughed like a madman. "Good one."

"I'm serious."

He kept laughing because he thought it was some kind of joke. "Yeah, okay. I'm gonna ask my annoying-ass sister to live with me…"

"I'm willing to make it worth your while."

"Look, I care about my sister. I'd do anything for her—no questions asked." He finally turned serious. "But she can take care of herself. I need my privacy because I have a lot of shit going on—dirty shit. And I don't want her in the way. She wouldn't want to get in my way anyway."

"But I can offer you something."

He shook his head. "I can't be bribed."

"It's not bribery, exactly."

He fell silent, listening for my offer.

"I'll buy you an upgraded apartment from what you have now—twice the value. You let her live with you. Take her rent as profit and pay whatever you're paying now for your own apartment. I'll take care of the rest."

Christopher considered the offer in silence.

"When she moves out, because eventually she will, you can keep the place." Now that was a deal no one could turn down.

"Any other stipulations?"

"No."

"I don't have to be nice to her?"

I tried not to smile. "You can be normal."

He turned away and rubbed his chin. "My god, you must be in love with her. I don't care how rich you are, no one would do something like this unless he found his future wife." He continued to rub his chin as he considered the offer.

She wasn't my future wife, but she would be something better than that. "What do you think?"

"I'm interested. But I'm not sure how I'm going to get her to live with me. I'm sure she doesn't want to live with me as much as I don't want to live with her."

"Tell her you need her to cover a portion of the rent."

"But she knows I don't need her money."

"If you get a bigger place, she would believe it." And she would live in a nice place, which would make me happy. And if anyone gave her shit about it, Christopher would be there to look after her.

"I guess I could give it a try."

"So we have a deal?" I extended my hand to shake his.

He eyed it. "You're really serious about this, huh?"

"Absolutely." I'd never been more serious about anything in my life.

He shook my hand. "Alright. We've got a deal."

"Thank you." Eventually, he would understand how much this meant to me. Without him, I'd have to lose sleep every night while wondering if she was okay. "If you ever need anything, let me know. I always repay favors."

"You're the one doing me a favor, man."

The apartment was nothing to me. It barely affected my bank account. But I wouldn't say that and sound like an asshole.

"My sister finally found the right guy to take care of her. So you're the one making my life easier."

Chapter Twenty-Three

Rome

When we got into the elevator, I knew this place would be fancy. Christopher always had a taste for luxury. Even when we were kids, he said he would be rich someday. He carried on about designer clothes, expensive cars, and nice apartments.

Christopher stood beside me as the elevator rose to the top floor. "I think you'll like it."

"What was wrong with your old place?" It was a mansion in my eyes. He had a bedroom, a separate kitchen, and even a dining room.

"I just wanted an upgrade."

The doors opened and we walked down the hall to his door. The hallway looked like it belonged to a fancy hotel. Paintings were on the walls with art lights, and there were lamps outside each door. He got it unlocked before we stepped inside.

As I expected, it was gorgeous. It immediately made me think of Calloway's place. With hardwood floors, walls with original moldings, and so much space he could have thirty people over for a dinner party, it was a dream come true. "Wow...it's beautiful."

"I know. I love it." He walked around with his hands in his pockets and admired the windows that showed the city beyond.

I was so proud of my brother. He worked so hard and never gave up. When he put his mind to something, he succeeded. He took out loans for college and spent a year in poverty to pay them back. Now, he was on top of the world, and no one deserved it more than he did. "I'm so happy for you."

He came back to me, mischief in his eyes. "There's actually something I wanted to ask you."

"Hmm?"

"The rent is a little too high, so I'm looking for someone to share the rent with. You interested?"

I laughed because it was ridiculous. "What makes you think I could afford to live here?"

"I only need like five hundred bucks a month. And that's mainly to cover utilities. I need the cash to buy drinks for all my ladies." He waggled his eyebrows.

"You're serious?" He actually wanted to live with me?

"Yeah. I know you'll be at Calloway's most of the time, and the bedrooms are nowhere near each other. There's plenty of space for both of us."

There was no question that this place was a mansion. "I'm just surprised you don't want a different roommate, maybe a guy who can pay you more for rent."

"I'd rather have someone I know. Someone who understands me and won't get in my way. So, what do you say? Unless you're going to stay with Calloway?"

Christopher didn't realize how much his offer helped me out. I didn't want to stay with Calloway, but I didn't like the apartment complex I intended to move into. I put up a front with Calloway, but the place was tiny and dirty. The walls were paper-thin, and I could hear everything from the neighbors. He would be happy I was living in a nicer neighborhood and under the protection of my brother. It killed two birds with one stone. "No, I'm not staying with him."

"Then, what do you think?"

"Christopher, I would love to. But maybe you should think about this." We hadn't lived together for a long time. We both needed our space and independence.

"I'm sure. Are you in? You need to tell me now because if you aren't, I need to find someone else."

I didn't hesitate. "I would love to live here." It would be a struggle to get used to having a roommate, especially my brother, but we could make it work. "I think we should lay down some ground rules. But other than that, we should be fine."

"Have your dates at Calloway's, and I'll have my dates here. Problem solved." He clapped his hands in triumph. "Let's get your bags."

***

I walked inside the house and saw Calloway in the kitchen. "You're cooking?"

"Yep." He turned off the stove and dished out the dinner onto two plates. "Thought we would change it up tonight." After he set down the hot pan, he wrapped his arm around my waist and kissed me. "That way you'll have more energy later…"

Energy was never the problem when we were in bed together. "Well, that was nice of you. I have some good news, by the way."

"Yeah?" He backed me up into the corner, what he usually did when he spoke to me. He liked to have me pressed against something at any time of day. He pressed his rock-hard cock against my stomach and stared into my eyes with greed.

"I know this is going to sound strange, but I'm moving in with my brother."

"Really?" He pulled away slightly, giving me some room to breathe. "What brought that on?"

"He got this new apartment, but it's a little too expensive. He needs some help with the rent, and he doesn't want to live with someone he doesn't know. So…he asked me." It was the perfect solution to our problem. "It's in a nice area, so I think you'll be happy."

"I'm very happy." He didn't smile, and his hands still boxed me into the counter. "I'm sad to see you leave, but I'm glad you're going somewhere safe. Looks like everything worked out."

"Yeah."

"But I hope we'll still have our sleepovers." He kissed the corner of my mouth, his tongue gently gliding over the skin.

"Couldn't live without them." I parted my lips to him so I could get access to his tongue.

He pressed his body into mine and tilted my chin so he could have full access to everything he wanted to take. "How about we forget dinner?" He sucked my bottom lip into his mouth and gave it a playful bite.

"You know I hate eating anyway."

Chapter Twenty-Four

Calloway

I drank my scotch in the black booth in the corner. I'd just arrived, but my glass was nearly empty. The bar was a sub-club, a small one a few blocks from ours. Jackson and I liked this place. It was cold, dark, and no one knew who we were.

A few women walked by, and their eyes immediately went to the black ring that circled my finger. The second they spotted it, they dashed off like frightened fish. The ring was a repellent, keeping all interested parties away. In a place like this, it was necessary. I didn't want to deal with the attention, and I didn't have to dish out the hardship of rejection.

Jackson finally arrived, grabbed his drink from the bar, and then joined me in the booth. "This place is sick. I like it. A lot more mellow than our place."

Because ours was a behemoth. With two stories, it had a lot of secrets. "I like it too."

He eyed my black ring. "So, Vanilla is still around?"

"Why wouldn't she be?"

"Thought you would have gotten her out of your system by now."

"No." In fact, I was more obsessed. "So, why did you ask me to meet you?" I had other things to do besides look at my brother's face. Rome just moved out, and now my place was empty. Hopefully, her smell wouldn't fade quickly.

"Can't a guy want to see his brother?"

"Not you."

"Oh, come on." He rolled his eyes. "We're friends, right?"

I saw through his act the moment he started. "Do you want something?"

"No."

Now it was my turn to roll my eyes.

"I really don't."

"Then what's with the meeting?"

He stirred the ice cubes in his glass before he spoke. "It's about Rome."

"What about her?"

"I'm glad you've found a plaything you enjoy, but you really need to think about what you're doing."

Really? A lecture? "Jackson, what the hell are you saying?"

"If you haven't sealed the deal with her by now, then you probably never will."

This conversation still wasn't making sense to me. Why would he want to talk about Rome of all things? Last time I checked, we weren't two boy-crazy chicks. "I haven't asked her yet, Jackson. When I do, it'll happen."

"She's way too vanilla."

"But she's strong and adventurous. She never backs down from a fight, and she never admits weakness. She'll have an open mind about it, and once we get into it, she'll enjoy it." I knew she didn't like being told what to do, but I gave her commands when we fooled around and she didn't mind those. I could push her further than that—make her enjoy lots of things.

He shook his head in disagreement. "I'm serious. Cut her loose."

"Why the fuck do you even care?" My brother was telling me what to do like he had any right to say a goddamn thing. And he was sticking his nose where it didn't belong.

"Because I want you to be happy. Ever since you met this girl, you've abandoned Ruin. And worst of all, you aren't a Dom anymore. She's changing you too much—and not in a good way."

"She's not changing me." I was exactly the same person I'd always been. I didn't come into Ruin as often, but that was because I fucked Vanilla in my bed. If she were a sub, I would come around a lot. "And I think you should shut your mouth before you really tick me off."

"She is changing you, man. And pretty soon, you'll leave Ruin altogether. And I couldn't handle that."

"I admit my relationship with her is different than the others. It's the only relationship that has started off traditional before it became Dom-sub. But that doesn't change anything. I'll teach her the art of the trade. I've done it before. And I'm not leaving Ruin."

"If you stay with her, you will."

"You're making a huge assumption." Ruin was my business, something I took seriously. It was a home to me, a place where I could be myself.

"I know you aren't going to break her, Calloway. She's going to break you."

I narrowed my eyes on his face, offended by the immense insult. "Excuse me?"

"You're pussy-whipped, and you know it. You haven't been to Ruin during working hours for over a month, ever since she moved in. And we both know it's because you aren't man enough to leave the house and tell her where you're going."

I downed the rest of my glass, getting every drop except the ice. I set it down hard enough to vibrate the table. "I'm going to break this glass and shove it in your eye if you keep talking."

"If you can't handle the truth, then that's your problem. But you can't leave Ruin. I need you there."

"Why?"

He didn't give me an answer, and judging by the restraint in his eyes, he wasn't going to. "Because I do. And I know this woman is going to pull you away. She's not the one who's going to submit. You will be the one who breaks."

My eyes narrowed on his face, and I felt rage rush through me like electricity. Jackson and I had our differences, but I'd never truly wanted to hurt him until now. Doubting my domination and assuming Rome had some kind of control over me was one of the biggest insults I'd ever received. I wouldn't break for anyone—not even her. "Get the fuck out."

Jackson slid out of the booth and left his empty glass behind. "I know you're going to be ticked at me. But you'll eventually see that I'm right." He gestured to someone in the bar and beckoned them over to our table.

"Or I'll slit your throat." Whomever it was, I wasn't going to give them the time of day.

Isabella reached our table and slid into the booth across from me. Wearing a skintight dress with her brown hair in loose curls, she was the most beautiful woman in the bar. Every man in the place was eyeing her with obvious lust.

But I didn't feel anything.

Jackson rapped his knuckles against the table. "Enjoy your evening." He walked out and left us alone together in the booth. He felt safe in a public place because I wouldn't throw a punch with so many eyes trained on me. It could ruin one of my reputations—either as the philanthropic charity man or the club owner.

"I'm sorry Jackson brought you into this." She needed time and space to get over me. If my brother kept filling her brain with false hope, she would never move on. It was a sick game he was playing. "Whatever he told you, I can assure you it's false."

She rested her arms on the table, sitting so still she practically looked like a statue. "Actually, I think he has some good points. And I'm worried about you."

"There's nothing to worry about." With Rome, I was happy. Even with the vanilla sex, I was satisfied. When she lived with me, I enjoyed every moment of her presence.

She tilted her head and regarded me with those large almond eyes. "Cal, I know you. I know you better than anyone."

I disagreed with that. Rome knew more about my past than anyone else—even Jackson. But I would never tell her that.

"You might be happy for the time being because she's pretty and new...but that will fade away. The man I know needs control and domination. He needs to give out orders like a commander and expects them to be obeyed. He needs to serve out punishments when necessary. He needs a sub, not a girlfriend. Don't change who you are for one person. As time goes on, your unhappiness will grow. And then you'll be locked into something you can never get out of. You'll be stuck."

I clenched my glass and bit the inside of my jaw. "Neither one of you has your facts straight. She will be my sub. This one just needs more time than the others."

Isabella shook her head slightly, her slender neck flawless. "We both know that's never going to happen. Vanilla women like her never come to the dark side."

"You don't even know her."

"Actually, I do."

My heart dropped into my stomach.

"I did some research. And I can tell she's never going to submit. Women like that are far too proud to get on their knees. You can argue with me all you want, but we both know it's true. Deep inside, you know Jackson and I are right. You won't admit it to yourself because you know you aren't strong enough to walk away. And that's the coldhearted truth."

I squeezed my glass again, wishing it were full. "Even if I agreed with you, I would never be your Dom again. Once a relationship is over, it's over."

She stared at me like she didn't believe a word I said. "You want to know how I know that's bullshit?"

I didn't blink.

"Because I'm the best sub you've ever had, as you've told me dozens of times. I obey every command, and I like it. The longer this continues with Vanilla, the more you're going to miss me. And I just want you to know that I'm here for you—whatever you need." She stretched her arms across the table but didn't touch my resting hand. "Because I'm still your sub. It's still my job to obey you, to understand you. One day, you're going to snap because you aren't getting what you need. But I'll be there—waiting."

I pulled both of my hands under the table so she couldn't touch me. If Rome's ex touched her, I would be livid with jealousy. But I felt the hair on my arms stand on end. I felt my stomach drop. My pulse quickened in my neck, and I could feel the vibration under my skin. Being a Dom was the greatest feeling in the world. There was no high like it. The longer I was with Rome, the more my true colors came out. And sometimes, the self-doubt got to me, deep in my soul, and I worried I wouldn't be able to break her. That she wouldn't give me the chance to be the Dom I was bred to be. She would expect romance, love, and a happily ever after.

But what terrified me even more was what would happen if that moment came. If she refused to submit to me and give me what I needed, would I have the strength to walk away? Because I was obsessed with this woman, had been since the moment I laid eyes on her. I did things with her I never did with anyone else. I took her virginity, I had vanilla sex with her nearly every single night, and I was completely devoted to her.

What if Jackson and Isabella were right?

What if I had changed?

What if I let someone change me?

What's Next

The story continues in
Black Diamond.

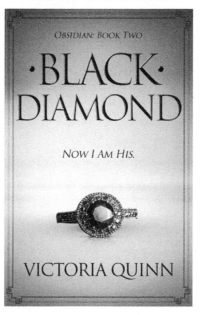

Order a copy now.

Made in the USA
Coppell, TX
05 October 2021